YEARS
of pure reading pleasur

100 Reasons to Celebrate

We invite you to join us in celebrating
Mills & Boon's centenary. Gerald Mills and
Charles Boon founded Mills & Boon Limited
in 1908 and opened offices in London's Covent
Garden. Since then, Mills & Boon has become
a hallmark for romantic fiction, recognised
around the world.

We're proud of our 100 years of publishing
excellence, which wouldn't have been achieved
without the loyalty and enthusiasm of our
authors and readers.

Thank you!

Each month throughout the year there will
be something new and exciting to mark the
centenary, so watch for your favourite authors,
captivating new stories, special limited
edition collections…and more!

The Secretary's Secret
by Michelle Celmer

ᓂᔑᐧᐁ

"This is a bad idea."

"Probably," Nick agreed, easing to meet Zoë halfway. He caressed her cheek with the tips of his fingers, combed them gently through her hair.

"We agreed this wouldn't happen again."

"Did we? We're already here – the damage has been done. Is one more time really going to make that much of a difference?"

It was hard to argue with logic like that, especially when he was nibbling at her ear. What difference could one more time possibly make? "What goes on in this room stays in this room," Zoë said.

His lips brushed her shoulder and her knees went weak. "Agreed."

Then he kissed her and she melted.

One more time, she promised herself. One more time and they would forget this ever happened…

At the Texan's Pleasure
by Mary Lynn Baxter

ට ᴕᴄᴘ ᄋ

"Why did you run out on me?" he asked.

"I have no intention of swimming through the muddy waters of the past," Molly said. "With your cynical judgement of me, I'd just be wasting my time anyway."

No doubt she was on the defensive and probably sounded as cynical as he did, but she didn't care. If she were going to survive this and keep her secret from him, she had to best him at his own game, or at least match him.

"What's wrong?" His eyes consumed her. "You look like something suddenly spooked you."

"I'm fine," she bit out.

"Liar."

"What do you want from me, Worth?"

"What if I said 'you'?"

Molly shook her head, trying to recover from the effect those words spoken in that sexy drawl had on her.

"I wouldn't believe you," she finally whispered.

The Secretary's Secret
MICHELLE CELMER

At the Texan's Pleasure
MARY LYNN BAXTER

MILLS & BOON
Pure reading pleasure

First published in Great Britain 2008
by Harlequin Mills & Boon Limited,
Eton House, 18-24 Paradise Road, Richmond, Surrey TW9 1SR

The publisher acknowledges the copyright holders of the
individual works as follows:

The Secretary's Secret © Michelle Celmer 2007
At the Texan's Pleasure © Mary Lynn Baxter 2006

ISBN: 978 0 263 85893 8

51-0208

Printed and bound in Spain
by Litografía Rosés S.A., Barcelona

THE SECRETARY'S SECRET

by
Michelle Celmer

MICHELLE CELMER

lives in a southeastern Michigan zoo.

Well, okay, it's really a house, but with three kids (two of them teenagers and all three musicians), three dogs ranging from seventy to ninety pounds each, three cats (two long-haired) and a fifty-gallon tank full of various marine life, sometimes it feels like a zoo. It's rarely quiet, seldom clean, and between after-school jobs, various extracurricular activities and band practice, getting everyone home at the same time to share a meal is next to impossible.

You can often find Michelle locked in her office, writing her heart out and loving the fact that she doesn't have to leave the house to go to work, or even change out of her pyjamas.

Michelle loves to hear from her readers. Drop her a line at: PO BOX 300, Clawson, MI 48017, USA, or visit her website at: www.michellecelmer.com.

This book is in honour of the dedicated volunteers
at Regap of Michigan (Retired Greyhounds
as Pets), www.rescuedgreyhound.org.
It has been a pleasure and a privilege to be
a part of something so special.

One

Nick Bateman lay in bed in the honeymoon suite of the hotel, pretending to be asleep, wondering what the hell he'd just done.

Instead of spending his wedding night with the woman who was supposed to be his new wife—the one he'd left at the altar halfway through their vows—he'd slept with Zoë, his office manager.

He would have liked to blame the champagne for what had happened, but two shared bottles wasn't exactly enough to get him rip roaring drunk. He'd been too intoxicated to drive, no question, but sober enough to know it was a really bad idea to sleep with an employee.

And even worse, he considered Zoë one of his best friends.

He rubbed a hand across the opposite side of the mattress and could feel lingering traces of heat. The scent of sex and pheromones and her spicy perfume clung to his skin and the sheets.

He heard a thump and a softly muttered curse from somewhere across the room. She had been slinking through the darkness for several minutes now, probably looking for her clothes.

His only excuse for what he'd let happen, even if it was a lame one, was that on the night of his failed wedding he'd been discouraged and depressed and obviously not thinking straight.

Instead of saying *I do*, he'd said *I don't* and skipped out on his fiancée. His second, in fact. Could he help it if it had only occurred to him just then the terrible mistake he was making? That his desire for a wife and family was clouding his judgment? That after a month of courtship he barely knew the woman standing beside him, and she was in fact—as his friends had tried to warn him—only after his money.

What a nightmare.

He would never forget the look of stunned indignation on Lynn's face when, halfway through their vows, he had turned to her and said, "I'm sorry, I can't do this." He could still feel the sting of her fist where it had connected solidly with his jaw.

He'd deserved it. Despite being a lying, blood-sucking vampire, she didn't deserve to be humiliated that way. Why was it that he couldn't seem to find the right woman? It had been five years since he decided he was ready to settle down. He'd figured by now he would be happily married with at least one baby and another on the way.

Nothing in his life was going the way it was supposed to. The way he'd planned.

After the abrupt end of the service, Zoë had driven him to the hotel where the honeymoon suite awaited and the champagne was already chilling. He'd been in no mood to drink alone, so he'd invited her in. She'd ordered room service—even though he hadn't been particularly hungry—and made him an ice pack for his jaw.

She always took care of him. And damn, had she taken care of him last night.

He wasn't even sure how it started. One minute they were sitting there talking, then she gave him this look, and the next thing he knew his tongue was in her mouth and they were tearing each other's clothes off.

Her mouth had been so hot and sweet, her body soft and warm and responsive. And the sex? It had been freaking fantastic. He'd never been with a woman quite so…*vocal* in bed. He'd never once had to guess what she wanted because she wasn't shy about asking.

God, he'd really slept with Zoë.

It's not that he'd never looked at her in a sexual way. He'd always been attracted to her. She wasn't the kind of woman who hypnotized a man with her dazzling good looks—not that she wasn't pretty—but Zoë's beauty was subtle. It came from the inside, from her quirky personality and strength.

But there were some lines you just didn't cross. The quickest way for a man to ruin a friendship with a woman was to have sex with her.

He knew this from experience.

Thankfully, he hadn't done irrevocable damage. As much as he wanted a family, Zoë wanted to stay single and childless just as badly. Unlike other female employees he'd made the mistake of sleeping with—back when he was still young, arrogant and monumentally stupid—she wouldn't expect or want a commitment.

Which was a *good* thing, right?

There was another thump, and what sounded like a gasp of pain, right beside the bed this time. He had two choices, he could continue to pretend he was asleep and let her stumble around in the dark, or he could face what they had done.

He reached over and switched on the lamp, squinting against the sudden bright light, both surprised and pleased to find a completely bare, shapely rear end not twelve inches from his face.

Zoë Simmons let out a shriek and swung around, blinking against the harsh light, clutching her crumpled dress to her bare breasts. This was like the dream she frequently had where she was walking through the grocery store naked. Only this was worse, because she was awake.

And honestly, right now, she would rather be caught naked in a room full of strangers than with Nick.

"You scared me," she admonished. So much for sneaking out before he woke up. Call her a chicken, but she hadn't been ready to face what they'd done. How many times they had done it.

How many different positions they had done it in…

The bed was in shambles and there were discarded condom wrappers on the bedside table and floor. She winced when she thought of the way they'd touched each other, the places they had touched. How incredibly, shockingly, mind-meltingly *fantastic* it had been.

And how it could never, *ever* happen again.

"Going somewhere?" he asked.

"'Fraid so."

He looked over at the digital clock beside the bed. "It's the middle of the night."

Exactly.

"I thought it would be best if I leave." But God help her, he wasn't making it easy. He sat there naked from the waist up, looking like a Greek god, a picture of bulging muscle and golden skin, and all she wanted to do was climb back into bed with him.

No. *Bad* Zoë.

This had to end, and it had to end *now*.

She edged toward the bathroom, snagging her purse from the floor. "I'm going to go get dressed, then we'll…talk."

She backed into the bathroom, his eyes never

leaving her face. She shut and locked the door, then switched on the light, saw her reflection and let out a sound that ranked somewhere between a horrified gasp and a gurgle of surprise.

Just when she thought this night couldn't get any worse.

Her hair was smashed flat on one side of her head and sticking up on the other, last night's eyeliner was smeared under her red, puffy eyes, and she had pillow indentations all over her left cheek. Unlike Nick who woke up looking like a Playgirl centerfold. It's a miracle he hadn't run screaming from the room when he saw her.

Had there been a window in the bathroom, she would have climbed through it.

She splashed water on her face, used a tissue to wipe away the smudges under her eyes, then dug through her purse for a hair band. Finger combing her hair with damp hands, she pulled it taut and fastened it into a ponytail. She had no clue where her bra and panties had disappeared to, and there was no way in hell she was going to go hunting for them. She would just have to go commando until she got home.

She tugged on her battered dress, smoothing out the wrinkles as best she could. In his haste to undress her, Nick had torn one of the spaghetti straps loose. One side of the bodice hung dangerously low. The form-fitting silk skirt was still a little damp and stained from the glass of champagne she'd spilled on herself.

It was the dress she'd worn to both of Nick's weddings. It looked as if maybe it was time to retire it.

Or incinerate it.

Zoë studied her reflection, hiking the bodice up over her half exposed breast. Not great, but passable. Maybe everyone wouldn't look at her and automatically think, *tramp*, as she traipsed through the five-star hotel lobby. Not that she would run into too many people at three-thirty in the morning.

She heard movement from the other room, and fearing she would catch him as naked and exposed as he had caught her—she cringed at the thought of her big rear end in his face when he turned the light on—she called, "I'm coming out now!"

When he didn't respond, she unlocked the door and edged it open, peeking out. He sat on the bed wearing only the slacks from last night, his chest bare.

And boy what a chest it was. It's not as if she'd never seen it before. But after touching it…and oh my, was that a bite mark on his left shoulder? She also seemed to recall giving him a hickey somewhere south of his belt, not to mention the other things she'd done with her mouth…

Shame seared her inside and out. What had they done?

As she stepped toward him, she noticed the gaping hole in the front of his pants. She was about to point out that the barn door was open, then remembered that in her haste to get his slacks off last night, she'd broken the zipper. They'd torn at each other's clothes, unable to get naked fast enough, as if they'd been working up to that moment for ten long years and couldn't bear to wait a second longer. She would never forget the way he'd plunged inside her, hard and fast and deep. The way she'd wrapped her legs around his hips and ground herself against him, how she'd moaned and begged for more…

Oh God, what had they done?

She clutched her purse to her chest, searching the floor for her shoes. She needed to get out of there pronto, before she did something even stupider, like whip her dress off and jump him.

"I think these belong to you." Nick was holding up her black lace bra and matching thong. "I found them under the covers."

Swell.

"Thanks." She snatched them from him and stuffed both in her tiny purse.

"Should we talk about this?" he asked.

"If it's all the same to you, I'd rather leave and pretend it never happened."

He raked a hand through his short blue-black hair. Thick dark stubble shadowed his jaw, which explained the chafing on her inner thighs.

"That is one way to handle it," he said, sounding almost disappointed.

He had to know as well as she did that this was a fluke. It never should have happened. And it sure as hell would never, *ever* happen again.

Not that he was a bad guy. Nick was rich,

gorgeous and genuinely nice—and okay, a touch stubborn and overbearing at times. And there were occasional moments when she wanted to smack him upside the head. But he was sweet when he wanted to be and generous to a fault.

How he hadn't found the right woman yet, she would never understand. Maybe he was just trying too hard. Either that or he had really bad luck. When it came to finding the wrong woman, he was like a magnet.

Personally, she liked her life just the way it was. No commitments. No accountability to anyone but herself and Dexter, her cat. She'd already done the mommy-caregiver gig back home. While both her parents worked full time jobs she'd been responsible for her eight younger brothers and sisters. All Nick had talked about during the past five years was marrying Susie homemaker and having a brood of children. The closest she was going to get to a diaper was in the grocery store, and that was only because it was across the aisle from the cat food.

The day Zoë turned eighteen she'd run like hell, clear across Michigan, from Petoskey to Detroit. And if it hadn't been for Nick, she wouldn't have lasted a month on her own. Despite having just started his construction company, or maybe because of it, he hadn't fired her when he found out she'd lied on her application about having office experience.

The truth was, she couldn't even type and her phone skills were questionable. Instead of kicking her out the door, which she admittedly deserved, his alpha male gene had gone into overdrive and he'd set out to save her. He'd helped put her through college, trained her in the business—in life. She'd been more than a tad sheltered and naïve.

To this day Zoë didn't know why he'd been so good to her, why he'd taken her under his wing. When they met, something just clicked.

And, in turn, Zoë had been Nick's only family. The only person he could depend on. He never seemed to expect or want more than that.

No way she would throw it all away on one stupid lapse in judgment, because the truth of the matter was, in a relationship, they wouldn't last. They were too different.

They would kill each other the first week.

"We've obviously made a big mistake," she said. She spotted her brand new Jimmy Choo pumps peeking out from under the bed. She used her big toe to drag them out and shoved her feet in. "We've known each other a long time. I'd hate to see our friendship, our working relationship, screwed up because of this."

"That would suck," he agreed. He sure was taking this well. Not that she'd expected him to be upset. But he didn't have to be so…*agreeable*. He could at least pretend he was sorry it wouldn't happen again.

She hooked a thumb over her shoulder. "I'm going to go now."

He pulled himself to his feet. She was wearing three-inch heels and he was still a head taller. "I'll drive you home."

She held up a hand to stop him. "No, no. That's not necessary. I'll call a cab."

He looked down at the clock. "It's after three."

All the more reason not to let him drive her home. In the middle of the night she felt less…accountable. What if, when they got there, she invited him in? She didn't want him getting the wrong idea, and she wasn't sure if she could trust herself.

Astonishing what a night of incredible sex could do to cloud a girl's judgment. "I'd really rather you didn't. I'll be fine, honest."

"Then take my truck," he said, taking her hand and pressing his keys into it. "I'll catch a cab in the morning."

"You're sure?"

"I'm sure."

He gestured toward the bedroom door and followed her into the dark sitting room. When they got to the door she turned to face him. The light from the bedroom illuminated the right side of his face. The side with the dimple.

But he wasn't smiling. He looked almost sad.

Well, duh, he'd just split up with his fiancée. Of course he was sad.

"I'm really sorry about what happened with Lynn. You'll meet someone else, I promise." Someone unlike fiancée number one, who informed him on their wedding day that she'd decided to put off having kids for ten years so she could focus on her career. Or fiancée number two who'd been a real prize. Lynn had obviously been after Nick's money, but he'd been so desperate to satisfy his driving need to procreate, he'd been blind to what he was getting himself into. Thank goodness he'd come to his senses, let himself see her for what she was.

"I know I will," he said.

"This probably goes without saying, but it would be best if we kept what happened to ourselves. Things could get weird around the office if anyone found out."

"Okay," he agreed. "Not a word."

Huh. That was easy.

Almost *too* easy.

"Well, I should go." She hooked her purse over her shoulder and reached for the doorknob. "I guess I'll see you at work Monday."

He leaned forward and propped a hand above her head on the door, so she couldn't pull it open. "Since this isn't going to happen again, how about one last kiss?"

Oh no, *bad* idea. Nick's kiss is what had gotten them into this mess in the first place. The man could work miracles with his mouth. Had he been a lousy kisser, she never would have slept with him. "I don't think that would be a good idea."

He was giving her that look again, that heavy-lidded hungry look he'd had just before they had attacked each other the first time. And suddenly he seemed to be standing a lot closer. And he smelled so good, *looked* so good in the pale light that her head felt a little swimmy.

"Come on," he coaxed, "one little kiss."

Like a magnet she felt drawn to him. She could feel herself leaning forward even as she told him, "That would be a bad idea."

"Probably," he agreed, easing in to meet her halfway. He caressed her cheek with the tips of his fingers, combed them gently through her hair. The hair band pulled loose and a riot of blond curls sprang free, hanging in damp ringlets around her face.

"Nick, don't," she said. But she didn't do anything to stop him. "We agreed this wouldn't happen again."

"Did we?" His hand slipped down to her shoulder. She felt a tug, and heard the snap of her other spaghetti strap being torn. Her dress was now officially strapless. And in another second it would be lying on the floor.

Oh God, here we go again.

Nick pushed the strap of her purse off the opposite shoulder and it landed with a soft thump on the floor at their feet and his truck keys landed beside it. "We're already here, the damage has been done. Is one more time really going to make that much of a difference?"

It was hard to argue with logic like that, especially when he was nibbling her ear. And he was right. The damage had already been done.

What difference could one more time possibly make?

"Just a quick one," she said, reaching for the fastener on his slacks. She tugged it free and shoved them down his hips. "As long as we agree that what goes on in this room stays in this room."

His lips brushed her shoulder and her knees went weak. "Agreed."

Then he kissed her and she melted.

One more time, she promised herself as he bunched the skirt of her dress up around her waist and lifted her off the floor.

"One more time," she murmured as she locked her legs around his hips and he pinned her body to the wall, entered her with one deep, penetrating thrust.

One more time and they would forget this ever happened…

Two

What difference could one more time *possibly* make? Apparently, more than either she or Nick had anticipated.

Zoë glanced up at the clock above her desk, then down to the bottom drawer of the file cabinet where she'd stashed the bag from the pharmacy behind the employment records. The bag that had been sitting there for four days now because she conveniently kept forgetting to bring it home every night after work. Mostly because she'd been trying to convince herself that she was probably overreacting. She was most likely suffering some funky virus that would clear up on its own. A virus that just happened to zap all of her energy, made her queasy every morning when she rolled out of bed and made her breasts swollen and sore.

And, oh yeah, made her period late.

She was sure there had to be a virus like that, because there was no chance in hell this condition was actually something that would require 2 a.m. feedings and diapers.

She would have a much easier time explaining this away if she wasn't ninety-nine percent sure Nick hadn't been wearing a condom that last time up against the hotel room wall.

It's not as if she could come right out and ask him. Not without him freaking out and things getting really complicated. It had taken several weeks to get past the post-coital weirdness. At first, it had been hard to look him in the eye, knowing he'd seen her naked, had touched her intimately.

Every time she looked at his hands, she remembered the way they felt against her skin. Rough and calloused, but oh so tender. And so big they seemed to swallow up every part of her that he touched.

His slim hips reminded her of the way she'd locked her legs around him as he'd pinned her to the wall. The way he'd entered her, swift and deep. How she'd come apart in his arms.

And his mouth. That wonderfully sinful mouth that melted her like butter in a hot skillet…

No. No. *No.*

Bad Zoë.

She shook away the lingering memory of his lean,

muscular body, of his weight sinking her into the mattress, her body shuddering with pleasure. She'd promised herself at least a hundred times a day that she wasn't going to think about that anymore. Finally things seemed to be getting back to normal. She and Nick could have a conversation without that undertone of awkwardness.

Zoë didn't want to risk rocking the boat.

She hadn't even told her sister Faith, and they told each other almost everything. Although, after their last phone conversation Zoë was under the distinct impression Faith knew something was up. It wouldn't be unlike her sister to drop everything and show up unannounced if she thought there was something that Zoë wasn't telling her.

She took a deep, fortifying breath. She was being ridiculous. She should just take the damned test and get it over with. She'd spent the ten bucks, after all. She might as well get her money's worth. Waiting yet another week wouldn't change the final outcome. Either she was or she wasn't. It would be good to know now, so she could decide what to do.

And decide what she would tell Nick.

As she was reaching for the bottom drawer handle, Shannon from accounting appeared in the doorway and Zoë breathed a sigh of relief.

"Hey, hon, you up for lunch with the girls? We're heading over to Shooters."

Despite being a nervous wreck, she was starving. Though she normally ate a salad for lunch, she would sell her soul for a burger and fries and a gigantic milkshake. And for dessert, a double chocolate sundae. Hold the pickles.

"Lunch sounds wonderful."

She grabbed her purse and jacket and gave the file cabinet one last glance before she followed Shannon into the hall.

As soon as she got back from lunch, she promised herself. She would put the test in her purse so she wouldn't forget it, and tonight when she got home she would get to the bottom of this.

Nick walked down the hall to Zoë's office and popped his head inside, finding it empty and feeling a screwy mix of relief and disappointment. He'd come to her office now, knowing she would probably be on her lunch break. Though they'd promised to pretend it hadn't happened, he couldn't seem to make himself forget every erotic detail of their night together. He'd been doing his best to pretend nothing had changed, but something was still a little…*off*.

Something about Zoë—a thing he couldn't quite put his finger on—seemed different.

He couldn't stop himself from wondering, *what if*? What if he'd told her he didn't want to pretend like it hadn't happened?

He just wasn't sure if that's what he really wanted. Were he and Zoë too different for that kind of relationship?

She was a cat person and he had a dog. He was

faded Levi's and worn leather and she was so prim and...*girly*. His music preferences ranged from classic rock to rich, earthy blues with a little jazz piano thrown in for flavor. Zoë seemed to sway toward eighties pop and any female singer, and she had the annoying habit of blaring Christmas music in July.

He was a meat and potatoes man, and as far as he could tell, Zoë existed on salads and bottled mineral water. He watched reality television and ESPN and she preferred crime dramas and chick flicks.

In fact, he couldn't think of a single thing they had in common. Besides the sex, which frankly they did pretty damned well.

Even if they could get past all of their differences, there was the problem of them wanting completely different things from life. In all the years he'd known her, she'd never once expressed a desire to have children. Not that he could blame her given her family history. But he'd grown up an only child raised by an aunt and uncle who'd had no use for the eight-year-old bastard dumped in their care. He'd spent his childhood in boarding schools and camps.

He wanted a family—at least three kids, maybe more. He just had to find a woman who wanted that, too. One who wasn't more interested in climbing the corporate ladder than having a family. And definitely one who wouldn't insist on a two week European honeymoon followed by mansion hunting in one of Detroit's most exclusive communities.

Material things didn't mean much to him. He was

content with his modest condo and modest vehicle. His modest life. All the money in the world didn't buy happiness. Thousands of dollars in gifts from his aunt and uncle had never made up for a lack of love and affection. His children would always know they were loved. They would never be made to feel like an inconvenience. And he sure as hell would never abandon them.

It had taken him years to realize there wasn't anything wrong with him. That he didn't drive people away. With a long history of mental illness, his mother could barely take care of herself much less a child, and his aunt and uncle simply had no interest in being parents. It would have been easy for them to hand him back over to social services when his mom lost custody. At least they'd taken responsibility for him.

If not for the lack of affection, one might even say he'd been spoiled as a kid. If he wanted or needed something all it took was a phone call to his uncle and it was his.

A convertible sports car the day he got his driver's license? No problem.

An all-expenses-paid trip to Cancún for graduation? It's yours.

The best education money can buy at a first-rate East Coast school? Absolutely.

But no one had handed him his education. He'd worked his tail off to make the dean's list every semester, to graduate at the top of his class. To make his aunt and uncle proud, even if they didn't know how to show it. And when he'd asked his uncle to loan him the money to start his company, the entire astronomical sum had been wired to his account within twenty-four hours.

They wouldn't win any awards for parents of the year, but his aunt and uncle had done the best they could.

He would do better.

There had to be a Ms. Right out there just waiting for him to sweep her off her feet. A woman who wanted the same things he did. And hopefully he would find her before he was too old to play ball with his son, to teach his daughter to Rollerblade.

He stepped into Zoë's office, trying to remember where in the file cabinet she kept the personnel files. Seeing as how she wasn't exactly organized, they could be pretty much anywhere.

Despite the disarray, she somehow managed to keep the office running like a finely tuned watch. She'd become indispensable. He would be lost without her.

He started at the top and worked his way down, finding them, of course, in the bottom drawer. He located the file of a new employee, Mark O'Connell, to see if there was some reason why the guy would be missing so much work. Not to mention showing up late. Nick was particular when he hired new employees. He didn't understand how someone with such impeccable references could be so unpredictable on the job.

He grabbed the file and was about to shut the

drawer when he saw the edge of a brown paper bag poking up from the back.

Huh. What could that be? He didn't remember seeing that the last time he looked in here.

He grabbed the bag and pulled it out. He was about to peek inside, when behind him he heard a gasp.

"What are you doing?"

Nick turned, the pharmacy bag in his hand, and Zoë stood in the office doorway, back from lunch, frozen. If he opened that bag, things were going to get really complicated really fast.

"I found this in the file cabinet," he said.

When she finally found her voice, she did her best to keep it calm and rational. Freaking out would only make things worse. "I don't appreciate you going through my things."

He gave her an annoyed look. "How was I supposed to know it's yours? It was in the file cabinet with the personnel files. The files I need to have access to, to run my company."

He was right. She should have kept it in her car, or her purse. Of course, then what excuse would she have had for not using it? She walked toward him and held out a hand. "You're right, I apologize. Can I have it back please?"

He looked at her, then at the bag. "What is it?"

"Something personal."

She took another step toward him, hand outstretched, and he took a step back.

A devious grin curled his lips, showing off the dent in his right cheek. "How much is it worth to you?"

He hadn't teased her in weeks. Now was not the time to start acting like his pain-in-the-behind old self. "That isn't funny, Nick. Give it to me."

He held the bag behind his back. "Make me."

How could a grown man act so damned juvenile? He didn't have kids, so what, he'd act like one?

She stepped toward him, her temper flaring, and held out her hand. "*Please*."

He sidestepped out of her way, around her desk, thoroughly enjoying himself if his goofy grin was any indication.

She felt like punching him.

Couldn't he see that she was fuming mad? Didn't he care that he was upsetting her?

Heat climbed up her throat and into her cheeks. "You're acting like an ass, Nick. Give it back to me *now*."

The angrier she became, the more amused he looked. "Must be something pretty important to get your panties in such a twist," he teased, clasping the bag with two fingers and swinging it just out of her reach. Why did he have to be so darned tall? "If you want it so badly, come and get it."

She slung her hands up in defeat. "Fine, look if you have to. If you find tampons so thoroughly interesting."

Tampons. Didn't she wish.

He raised a brow at her, as if he wasn't sure he should believe her or not. As he lowered the bag, un-

curling the edge to take a peek, she lunged for him.
Her fingers skimmed the bag and he jerked his arm
back, inadvertently flinging the test box out. In slow
motion it spiraled across the room, hit the wall with
a smack and landed label side up on the carpet.

Uh-oh.

For several long seconds time seemed to stand
still, then it surged forward with a force that nearly
gave her whiplash.

Nick looked at the box, then at her, then back at
the box and all the amusement evaporated from his
face. "What the hell is this?"

She closed her eyes. Damn, damn, damn.

"Zoë?"

She opened her eyes and glared at him. "What,
you can't read?"

She grabbed the bag from his slack fingers then
marched over and snatched the box from the floor.

"Zoë, do you think you're—"

"Of course not!" More like, God, she hoped not.

"Are you late?"

She gave him a *duh* look.

"Of course you are, or you wouldn't need the
test." He raked a hand through his hair. "How late
are you exactly?"

"I'm just a little late. I'm sure it's nothing."

"We slept together over a month ago. How late is
a *little* late?"

She shrugged. "Two weeks, maybe three."

"Which is it, two or three?"

Oh, hell. She slumped into her desk chair. "Probably closer to three."

He took a long deep breath and blew it out. She could tell he was fighting to stay calm. "And why am I just hearing about this now?"

"I thought maybe it was a virus or an infection or something," she said, and he gave her an incredulous look. "I was in *denial*, okay?"

"Missed periods can happen for lots of reasons, right? Like stress?"

She flicked her thumbnail nervously back and forth, fraying the edge of the box. Stressed? Who me? "Sure, I guess."

"Besides, we used protection."

"Did we?"

He shot back an indignant, "You know we did."

She felt a glimmer of hope. Condoms could fail, but the odds were slim. Maybe she really wasn't pregnant. Maybe this was all in her head. "Even the last time?"

There was a pause, then he asked, "The last time?"

Suddenly he didn't sound so confident. Suddenly he had an, *Oh-damn-what-have-I-done?* look on his face.

Her stomach began to slither down from her abdomen. "You know, against the wall, by the door. We used a condom then too, right?" she asked hopefully, as if wishing it were true would actually make it true.

He scratched the coarse stubble on his chin. The guy could shave ten times a day but he was so dark he almost always had a five o'clock shadow. "Honestly, I can't remember."

Oh, this was not good. She could feel her control slipping, panic squeezing the air from her lungs. "You can't *remember?*"

He sat on the corner of her desk. "Apparently, you can't either."

He was right. That wasn't fair. This was in no way his fault. "I'm sorry. I'm just…edgy."

"If I had to guess, I would say that since I have no memory of using one, and my wallet was in the other room, we probably didn't."

At least he was being honest. Obviously they had both been too swept away by passion to think about contraceptives. But that had been what, their fourth time? Didn't a man's body take a certain amount of time to…*reinforce the troops*. Were there even any little swimmers left by then?

Leave it to her to have unprotected sex with a guy who had super sperm.

"I guess there's only one way to find out for sure," he said. "Taking the test here would probably be a bad idea, seeing as how anyone could walk into the bathroom. So would you be more comfortable taking it at your place or mine?"

This was really happening. With *Nick* of all people.

When she didn't answer right away he asked, "Or is this something you need to be alone for?"

Being alone was the last thing she wanted. They were in this together. She didn't doubt for an instant that he would be there for her, whatever the outcome. "We'll do it at my house."

He rose to his feet. "Okay, let's go."

Her eyes went wide. "You want to go *now?* It's the middle of the workday."

"It's not like we're going to get fired. I own the company. Besides, you know what they say."

She thought about it for a second then said, "Curiosity killed the cat?"

He grinned. "There's no time like the present."

Three

Nick drove them the ten minutes to Zoë's house in Birmingham. They didn't say much. What could they say? Zoë spent the majority of her time praying, Please, God, let it be negative.

How had she gotten herself into this mess?

Her devout Catholic parents still believed that at the age of twenty-eight she was as pure as the driven snow. If the test was positive, what would she tell them? Well, Mom and Dad, I was snow-white, but I drifted.

They were going to kill her. Or disown her.

Or both.

And this would surely be enough to send her fragile, ailing grandmother hurtling through death's door. She would instantly be labeled the family black sheep.

It didn't matter that her parents had been nagging her to settle down for years.

When are you going to find a nice man? When are you going to have babies?

How about never?

And if the man she settled down with was Nick they would be ecstatic. Despite the fact that he wasn't Catholic, they adored him. Since the first time she'd brought him home for Thanksgiving dinner they'd adopted him into the fold. And Nick had been swept up into the total chaos and craziness that was her family. He loved it almost as much as it drove her nuts.

So, if she were to call home and tell them she and Nick were getting hitched, she'd be daughter of the year. But the premarital sex thing would still be a major issue. In her parents' eyes, what they had done was a sin.

She let her head fall back against the seat and closed her eyes. Maybe this was just a bad dream. Maybe all she needed to do was pinch herself real hard and she would wake up.

She caught a hunk of skin between her thumb and forefinger, the fleshy part under her upper arm that the self-defense people claim is the most sensitive, and gave it a good hard squeeze.

"Ow!"

"What's wrong?"

She opened her eyes and looked around. Still in Nick's monster truck, rumbling down the street, and he was shooting her a concerned look.

She sighed. So much for her dream theory.

"Nothing. I'm just swell," she said, turning to look out the window, barely seeing the houses of her street whizzing past.

"Don't get upset until we know for sure," he said, but she was pretty sure he, like her, already knew what the result would be. They'd had unprotected sex and her period was late. The test was going to be positive.

She was going to have Nick's baby.

When they got to her house, he took her keys from her and opened the door. He'd been inside her house a thousand times, but today it felt so...*surreal*. As if she'd stepped onto the set of film.

A horror film.

She and Nick were the stars, and any second some lunatic was going to pop out of the kitchen wielding a knife and hack them to pieces.

She slipped her jacket off and tossed it over the back of the couch while Nick took in her cluttered living room.

Last night's dinner dishes still sat on the coffee table, the plate covered with little kitty lick marks from Dexter her cat. Newspapers from the past two weeks lay in a messy pile at one end of the couch.

She looked down at the rug, at the tufts of white cat fur poking out from the Berber and realized it had been too long since she'd last vacuumed. Her entire house—entire life—was more than a little chaotic right now. As if acting irresponsibly would somehow prove what a lousy parent she would be.

Nick looked around and made a face. "You really need to hire a maid."

She tossed her purse down on the cluttered coffee table. "I am *so* not in the mood for a lecture on my domestic shortcomings."

He had the decency to look apologetic.

"Sorry." He reached inside his leather bomber jacket and pulled out the test kit. "I guess we should just get this over with, huh?"

"We?" Like he had to go in the bathroom and pee on a stick. Like he had to endure months of torture if it was positive. A guy like him wouldn't last a week on the nest. He may have been tough, may have been able to bench press a compact car, but five minutes of hard labor and he would be toast.

Her mother had done home births for Zoë's three youngest siblings and Zoë had had the misfortune of being stuck in the room with her for the last one. She had witnessed the horror. Going through it once seemed like torture enough, but understandable since most women probably didn't realize what they were getting themselves into. But *nine* times. That was just crazy.

"I'm afraid to go in there," she said.

Nick reached up and dropped one big, work-roughened hand on her shoulder, giving it a gentle squeeze. "We're in this together, Zoë. Whatever the outcome. We'll get through it."

It amazed her at times, how such a big, burly guy who oozed testosterone could be so damned tender and sweet. Not that the stubborn, overbearing alpha male gene had passed him by. He could be a major pain in the behind, too. But he'd never let her down in a time of need and she didn't believe for a second that he would now.

"Okay, here goes." She took the test kit from him and walked to the bathroom, closing and locking the door behind her, her stomach tangled in knots. She opened the box and with a trembling hand spilled the contents out onto the vanity.

"Please, God," she whispered, "let it be negative."

She read the instructions three times, just to be sure she was doing it right, then followed them word for word. It was amazingly quick and simple for such a life-altering procedure. *Too simple.*

Less than five minutes later, after rereading the instructions one more time just to be sure, she had her answer.

Nick paced the living room rug, his eye on the bathroom door, wondering what in the heck was taking Zoë so long. She'd been in there almost twenty minutes now and he hadn't heard a peep out of her. No curdling screams, no thud to indicate she'd hit the floor in a dead faint. And no whoops of joy.

It was ironic that not five minutes before she stepped into her office he'd been thinking about having children. Just not with her, and not quite so soon. Ideally he would like to be married, but life had a way of throwing a curve ball.

At least, his life did.

He let out a thundering sneeze and glanced with disdain at the fluffy white ball of fur sunbathing on the front windowsill. It stared back at him with scornful green eyes.

He was so not a cat person.

He sat on the couch, propped his elbows on his knees and rested his chin on his fisted hands.

So what if she was pregnant?

The truth was, this was all happening so fast, he wasn't sure how he felt about it. What he did know is that if she didn't come out of the damned bathroom soon, he was going to pound the door down. It couldn't possibly take this long. He remembered the box specifically stating something about results in only minutes.

As if conjuring her through sheer will, the bathroom door swung open and Zoë stepped out. Nick shot to his feet. He didn't have to ask what the results were, he could see it in her waxy, pasty-white pallor. Her wide, glassy-eyed disbelief.

"Oh boy," he breathed. Zoë was pregnant.

He was going to be a father. They were going to be parents.

Together.

She looked about two seconds from passing out cold, so he walked over to where she stood and pulled her into his arms. She collapsed against him, her entire body trembling.

She rested her forehead on his chest, wrapped her

arms around him, and he buried his nose in her hair. She smelled spicy and sweet, like cinnamon and apples. He realized, he'd missed this. Since that night in the hotel, he'd been itching to get his arms around her again.

He'd almost forgotten just how good it felt to be close to her, how perfectly she fit in his arms. Something had definitely changed between them that night in the hotel. Something that he doubted would ever change back.

For a while they only held each other, until she'd stopped shaking and she wasn't breathing so hard. Until she had gone from cold and rigid to warm and relaxed in his arms.

He cupped her chin and tilted her face up. "It's going to be okay."

"What are we going to do?" she asked.

"Well, I guess we're going to have a baby," he said, and felt the corners of his mouth begin to tip up.

Zoë gaped at him, her look going from bewilderment to abject horror. She broke from his grasp and took a step back. "Oh my God."

"What?"

"You're smiling. You're *happy* about this."

Was he?

The smile spread to encompass his entire face. He tried to stop it, then realized it was impossible. He really *was* happy. For five years now he'd felt it was time to settle down and start a family. True, this wasn't exactly how he planned it, and he sure as hell hadn't planned on doing it with Zoë, but that didn't mean it wouldn't work. That didn't mean they shouldn't at least give it a shot.

He gave her a shrug. "Yeah, I guess I am. Would you feel better if I was angry?"

"Of course not. But do you have even the slightest clue what we're getting into? What *I'll* have to go through?"

She made it sound as though he was making her remove an appendage. "You're having a baby, Zoë. It's not as if it's never been done before."

"Of course it has, but have you ever actually witnessed a baby being born?"

No, but he definitely wanted to be in the delivery room. He wouldn't miss that for anything. "I'm sure it will be fascinating."

"*Fascinating*? I was there when my mom had Jonah, my youngest brother."

"And?"

"Have you ever seen the movie, *The Thing?*" she asked, and he nodded. "You remember the scene where the alien bursts out of the guy and there is this huge spray of blood and guts? Well, it's kinda' like that. Only it goes on for *hours*. And hurts twice as much.

"And that's only the beginning," she went on, in full rant. "After it's born there are sleepless nights to look forward to and endless dirty diapers. Never having a second to yourself…a *moment's* silence. They cry and whine and demand and smother. Not to mention that they cost a fortune. Then they get older and there's school and homework and rebellion. It never ends. They're yours to worry about and pull your hair out over until the day you *die*."

Wow. He knew she was jaded by her past, but he'd never expected her to be this traumatized.

"Zoë, you were just a kid when you had to take care of your brothers and sisters. It wasn't fair for your parents to burden you with that much responsibility." He rubbed a hand down her arm, trying to get her to relax and see things rationally. "Right now you're still in shock. I know that when you take some time to digest it, you'll be happy."

She closed her eyes and shook her head. "I'm not ready for this. I don't know if I'll *ever* be ready for it."

A startling, disturbing thought occurred to him. What if she didn't want to have the baby? What if she was thinking about terminating the pregnancy? It was her body so, of course, the choice was up to her, but he'd do whatever he could to talk her out of it, to rationalize with her.

"Are you saying you don't want to have the baby?" he asked.

She looked up at him, confused. "It's not like I have a choice."

"Every woman has a choice, Zoë."

She gave him another one of those horrified looks and folded a hand protectively over her stomach. He didn't think she even realized she was doing it. "I'm not going to get rid of it if that's what you mean. What kind of person do you think I am?"

Thankfully, not that kind. "I've never considered raising a baby on my own, but I will if that's what you want."

"Of course that's not what I want! I could never give a baby up. Once you have it, it's yours. My brothers and sisters may have driven me crazy but I love them to death. I wouldn't trade them in for anything."

He rubbed a hand across the stubble on his jaw. "You're confusing the hell out of me."

"I'm keeping the baby," she said firmly. "I'm just…I guess I'm still in shock. This was not a part of my master plan. And you're the last man on earth I saw myself doing it with. No offense."

"None taken." How could he be offended when he'd been thinking the same thing earlier. Although maybe not the *last on earth* part.

She walked over to the couch and crumpled onto the cushions. "My parents are going to kill me. They think I'm still a good Catholic girl. A twenty-eight-year-old, snow-white virgin who goes to church twice a week. What am I going to tell them?"

Nick sat down beside her. He slipped an arm around her shoulder and she leaned into him, soft and warm.

Yeah, this was nice. It felt…right.

And just like that he knew exactly what he needed to do.

"I guess you only have one choice," he said.

"Live the rest of my life in shame?"

Her pessimism made him grin. "No. I think you should marry me."

* * *

Zoë pulled out of Nick's arms and stared up at him. "Marry you? Are you *crazy?*"

Dumb question, Zoë. Of course he was crazy.

Rather than being angry with her, he smiled, as if he'd been expecting her to question his sanity. "What's so crazy about it?"

If he couldn't figure that out himself, he really was nuts.

"If we get married right away, your parents don't have to know you were already pregnant. Problem solved."

And he thought marrying someone he didn't love *wouldn't* be a problem? Not that kind of love anyway. She didn't doubt that he loved her as a friend, and she him, but that wasn't enough.

"We're both feeling emotional and confused," she said. He more than her, obviously. "Maybe we should take a day or two to process this before we make any kind of life altering decisions."

"We're having a baby together, Zoë. You don't get much more life altering than that."

"My point exactly. We have a lot to consider."

"Look, I know you're not crazy about the idea of getting married to anyone—"

"And you're *too* crazy about it. Did you even stop to think that you would be marrying me for all the wrong reasons? You want Susie homemaker. Someone to squeeze out your babies, keep your house clean and have dinner waiting in the oven when you get home from work. Well, take a look around you, Nick. My life is in shambles. My house is a disaster and if I can't microwave myself a meal in five minutes or less, I don't buy it."

He didn't look hurt by her refusal, which made her that much more certain marrying him would be a bad idea. She could never be the cardboard cutout wife he was looking for. She wouldn't be any kind of a wife at all.

And even if they could get past all of that, it still wouldn't work. He was such a good guy. Perfect in so many ways. Except the one that counted the most.

He didn't love her.

She took his hand between her two. It was rough and slightly calloused from years of working construction with his employees. He may have owned the company, may have had more money than God, but he liked getting his hands dirty. He liked to feel the sun on his back and fresh air in his lungs. One day cooped up in the office and he was climbing the walls.

She didn't doubt that he would put just as much of himself into his marriage. He was going to make some lucky woman one hell of a good husband.

Just not her.

"It was a noble gesture. But I think we both need to take some time and decide what it is we really want."

"How much time?" he asked.

"I'm going to have to make a doctor's appointment. Let's get through that first then we'll worry about the other stuff."

Who knows, maybe she got a false positive from the pregnancy test. Maybe she would get a blood test at the doctor's office and find out they had done all this worrying for nothing.

Four

"Congratulations! Your test was positive! If you haven't yet made a follow-up appointment with Doctor Gordon, please dial one. If you need to speak to a nurse, dial two—"

Zoë hung up the phone in her office, cutting short the obnoxiously perky prerecorded message she'd gotten when she phoned the doctor's office for her blood test results.

It was official. Not that it hadn't been official before. The blood test had just been a formality. She was definitely, without a doubt, having Nick's baby.

Oh boy.

Or girl, she supposed.

She would walk down to his office and tell him,

but he'd been in her office every ten minutes wondering if she'd made the call.

She looked down at her watch. Why get up when he was due back in another six minutes?

"Well?"

She looked up to find him standing in her doorway watching her expectantly. "You're early."

"Early?" His brow knit into a frown. "Did you call yet?"

"I called."

He stepped into her office and shut the door. "And?"

She sighed. "As my mother used to say, 'I'm in the family way.'"

"Wow." He took deep breath and blew it out. "Are you okay?"

She nodded. She really was. She'd had a few days to think about it, and she was definitely warming to the idea. Not that it wouldn't complicate things. But it wasn't the end of the world either. She would have one kid. She could handle that. "I'm okay."

He walked over to her desk and sat on the edge, facing her. She could see that he was happy, even though he was trying to hide it. And why should he? What normal woman wouldn't want the father of her baby to be excited?

"It's okay to be happy," she told him. "I promise I won't freak out again."

The corners of his mouth quirked up. "I guess this means we have things to discuss."

She knew exactly what *things* he was referring to. He looked so genuinely excited, so happy, she didn't doubt for one second that he would be a wonderful father. But a husband? She wasn't sure if she was ready for one of those. She didn't know if she would *ever* be ready. The idea of sharing her life with someone, all the compromise and sacrifice it would take…it just seemed like a lot to ask. She was happy with her life the way it was.

That didn't mean she couldn't possibly be happier with Nick there, but what if she wasn't?

As promised, he hadn't said a word about marriage while they waited for the test results. Now he looked as if he was ready for an answer.

"It's nothing personal, Nick. I just…I'm afraid it wouldn't work between us."

"Why wouldn't it? We're friends. We work well together. We understand each other." He leaned in closer, his eyes locked on hers. "Not to mention that in the sexual chemistry department we're off the charts."

God, she wished he wouldn't look at her that way. It scrambled her brain. And she hated that he was right. But good sex—even fantastic sex—wasn't enough to make a marriage work.

He leaned in even closer and she could smell traces of his musky aftershave, see the dots of brown in his hazel eyes. "Can you honestly say you haven't thought about that night at least a dozen times a day since it happened?"

"It wasn't *that* good." She tried to sound cocky, but her voice came out warm and soft instead. It had been more like a hundred times a day.

Nick grinned and leaned forward, resting his hands on the arms of her chair, caging her in. "Yes, it was. It was the best sex you ever had. Admit it."

Heat and testosterone rolled off his body in waves, making her feel light-headed and tingly all over. "Okay, yeah, maybe it was. But that's not the point. I don't want to jump into anything we might regret. What if we get married and find out a month later that we drive each other crazy?"

"Too late for that, sweetheart." He reached up and touched her cheek and her heart shimmied in her chest. "You already do drive me crazy."

Right now, he was doing the same to her. He looked as if any second he might kiss her. And though she knew it would be a bad idea, she wanted him to anyway. She didn't even care that anyone in the office could walk in and catch them. It would take ten minutes tops for the news to travel through the entire building. For the rumors to start. That was exactly what they *didn't* need right now.

She just wished he would make up his mind, wished he would either kiss her or back off. When he sat so close, his eyes locked with hers, it was difficult to think straight.

Which is probably the exact reason he was doing it. To throw her off balance. To make her agree to things she wasn't ready for.

"I mean drive each other crazy in a bad way," she said.

"So what would you like to do? Date?"

"I think we're a bit past the dating stage, don't you? Socially we get along fine. It's the living together part that worries me."

That grin was back on his face, dimple and all, which usually meant trouble. "That sounds like the perfect solution."

Funny, but she didn't remember mentioning one. "Which solution is that?"

"We could live together."

Live together? "Like in the same house?"

"Sure. What better way to see if we're compatible."

She'd never had a roommate. Not since she left home, anyway. Back then she'd had to share a room with three of her sisters. Three people borrowing her clothes and using her makeup without asking. Although, she doubted that would be a problem with Nick. Her clothes were way too small for him even if he wanted to borrow them and when it came to wearing makeup, well…she *hoped* he didn't.

To get any privacy back home she'd had to lock herself in the bathroom, which would last only a minute or two before someone was pounding on the door to get in.

But she had two bathrooms if she needed a place to escape. A full on the main floor and a half down in the finished part of the basement. Granted her house was barely a thousand square feet, but how much room could one guy take up?

Unless he was thinking she was going to move in with him. His condo was twice the size of her house, but it was in a high-rise in Royal Oak, with people living on every side.

No one should ever live that close to their neighbors. It was too creepy, knowing people could hear you through the walls. She dreamed of one day owning an old farmhouse with acres and acres of property. She wondered how Nick, a born and bred city boy, would feel about that. Despite how well they knew each other, there were still so many things they *didn't* know. So much they had never talked about.

Things they could definitely learn if they were living together.

"And if we are compatible?" she asked.

"Then you marry me."

"Just like that?"

He nodded. "Just like that."

She hated to admit it, but this made sense in a weird way.

My God, was she actually considering this? The only thing worse than premarital sex in her parents' eyes was living in sin without the sanctity of marriage. Of course, what they didn't know wouldn't hurt them. Right?

"If we were to do this, and I'm not saying we are, but *if* we did, logically, I think it would be best if you move in with me," she said. "Your condo can get by without you. I have a yard and a garden to take care of."

"Fine with me," he agreed.

"And we should probably keep this to ourselves."

"Zoë." He shot her a very unconvincing hurt look. "Are you ashamed of me?"

Yeah, right, like it mattered. When it came to self-confidence, Nick had it in bucket loads.

"You know how the people in this building can be. I'm just not ready to deal with the gossip. Not until we've made a decision."

"Which will be when?"

"You mean like a time limit," she asked, and he nodded. "How about a month? If by then it's not working out, we give it a rest."

He sat back, folded his arms across his chest and gave her an assessing look. "A month, huh?"

A month should be plenty of time to tell if they were compatible. In areas other than friendship. And the bedroom.

"And if after a month we haven't killed each other, what then? We set a date?"

The mere idea triggered a wave of anxiety. Her heart rate jumped and her palms began to sweat. "If we can make it one month living together, I promise to give your proposal very serious thought."

"And hey," he said with a casual shrug. "If nothing else, we can save money on gas driving to work together, so it won't be a total loss."

"How can you be so calm about this?" The idea of him moving in was making her a nervous wreck.

"Because I'm confident that after a month of living together, you'll be dying to marry me."

She hoped he was right. "What makes you so sure?"

A devilish grin curled his mouth. "This does."

He leaned toward her and she knew exactly what he was going to do. He was going to kiss her. She knew, and she didn't do a thing to stop him. The crazy thing was, she *wanted* him to kiss her. She didn't care that it would only confuse things more, or that anyone could walk in and catch them.

He didn't work into it either. He just took charge and dove in for the kill. He slipped a hand behind her head, threading his fingers through her hair, planted his lips on hers and proceeded to kiss her stockings off. Her body went limp and her toes curled in her pumps.

She'd almost forgotten how good a kisser he was, how exciting and warm he tasted. The memory lapse was purely a self-defense mechanism. Otherwise there would have been a lot of kissing going on these past weeks.

She could feel herself sinking deeper under his spell, melting into a squishy puddle in her chair. Her fingers curled in his hair, nails raked his scalp. His big, warm hand cupped the back of her head with gentle but steady pressure, as if he wasn't going to let her get away.

Yeah, right, like she would even try.

Hearing her office door open barely fazed her, nor

did the, "Zoë, I need—*whoops!*" of whomever had come in. Or the loud click of the door closing behind them as they left. And the very real possibility of the news reaching everyone in the building by day's end.

Nick broke the kiss and backed away, gazing down at her with heavy-lidded eyes. "So much for keeping this to ourselves."

"Yeah, oops." She should care that their secret was out—well, at least one of their secrets—but for some reason she didn't. In fact, she was wondering if maybe he should kiss her again. Her cheeks felt warm and her scalp tingled where his hand had been. She was sure if she tried to get up and walk her legs wouldn't work right.

One kiss and she was a wreck.

"So, when do you want me to move in?" he asked, his dimple winking at her.

How about right now? she thought. But she didn't want to sound too eager. Then again it *was* Friday. That would give him all weekend to settle in.

Oh what the heck?

She looked up at him and smiled. "How about tonight?"

There was a reindeer standing on Zoë's front porch.

Nick stood beside it holding the reins in one hand, a duffle bag in the other.

Okay, it was actually a leash he was holding, and the deer was really a dog. A very large, skinny dog with a shiny coat the color of sable.

"What is that?" she asked through the safety of the screen. Did he really think he was bringing that thing into her house?

"This is my dog, Tucker." At her completely blank look he added, "You knew I had one."

Yeah, she knew, but it never occurred to her that it would be moving in, too. "This is going to be a problem. I have a cat."

"Tucker has a low prey drive, so it shouldn't be an issue."

"Prey drive?" She snapped the lock on the storm door. "Dexter is not prey."

"Tucker is a retired racing greyhound. They use lures to get them to run. Some have higher prey drives than others. Tucker has a low enough drive that he's considered cat safe."

"Cat safe?" She narrowed her eyes at him. "You're sure?"

"He'll probably just ignore the cat." He stood there waiting for her to open the door, but she wasn't convinced yet.

"Will he chew on my shoes?" she asked.

"He's not a chewer. He's a collector."

"What, like stamps?"

Nick grinned. "Cell phones, remote controls, sometimes car keys, but his favorite is slippers. The smellier the better. He's also been known to take the salt and pepper shakers off the table. If anything is missing, his bed is the first place I look."

She looked down at the dog. He looked back up

at her with forlorn brown eyes that begged, "Please love me."

"He won't pee on my rug?"

"He's housebroken. He also doesn't bark, barely sheds and he sleeps twenty-three hours of the day. He's not going to be a problem. In fact, he'll love having a fenced yard to run around."

She looked at the dog, then back at Nick.

"Are you going to let us in? I'm on excessive doses of allergy medication so I can be around your cat. You can at least give Tucker a chance."

He was right. How much trouble could one oversized dog be?

Scratch that. She probably didn't want to know.

She unlocked the door and opened it. "Sorry about the mess. I didn't have time to clean."

Nick and Tucker stepped inside and the room suddenly felt an awful lot smaller. He unsnapped the leash and hung it on the coat tree and Tucker, being a dog, went straight for Zoë's crotch. He gave her a sniff, then looked up, as if he were expecting something. He was even bigger than he looked standing on the porch.

"He's enormous."

"He's an extra large." Nick shrugged out of his leather jacket and hung it over the leash.

"Why is he staring at me?"

"He wants you to pet him."

"Oh." She patted the top of his head gingerly. "Nice doggie."

Satisfied that he'd been adequately welcomed, Tucker trotted off to explore, his nails click-clicking on the hardwood floor. "Will he be okay by himself?"

"Yeah, he won't get into anything."

She gestured to Nick's lone bag. "Is that all you brought?"

"I have a few more things in the truck. I figure as I need stuff I can run over to my place and pick it up."

"I'm giving you the spare bedroom," she told him.

He flashed her a curious look. "I don't remember agreeing to that."

"I think at this point sex will only complicate things." He'd proven that this afternoon when he had kissed her. Her brain had been so overdrenched in pheromones she would have agreed to practically anything. "We should ease into this slowly. We need to get used to living together. We need to be sure this relationship isn't just physical."

That sexy grin curled his mouth. The guy was unbelievably smug. "You really think you can resist me?"

She hoped so, but she could see by the devious glint in his eye he wasn't going to make it easy. "I'll manage."

From the kitchen Zoë heard a hiss, then an ear-splitting canine yip, and Tucker darted into the living room, skidding clumsily across the floor, long gangly legs flailing. Whining like a big baby, he scurried over to Nick and hid behind him. In the kitchen doorway sat Dexter, all whopping eight pounds of him, casually licking one fluffy white paw as though he didn't have a care in the world.

So much for the dog ignoring the cat.

"He's bleeding," Nick said indignantly, examining Tucker's nose. "Your cat attacked my dog."

"I'm sure he was provoked." She found herself feeling very proud of Dexter for protecting his domain. No big dopey dog was going to push him around. "They probably just need time to get used to each other."

Kind of like her and Nick.

"So," she said, suddenly feeling awkward. "I guess we should get you settled in."

Nick followed her down the hall to one of the two downstairs bedrooms. On the left was her office, and on the right her guest room. He stepped inside, taking in the frilly curtains and lacey spread.

"Pink?" He cringed, as though it was painful to look at. "I can feel my testosterone drying up. Maybe I should just sleep on the couch. Or in a tent in the backyard."

"Don't be such a baby," she said and he tossed his bag on the bed. "I was thinking we could just get carryout for dinner."

He shrugged. "Works for me."

"We can order, and while we're waiting for it to be delivered, we can get the rest of your things out of the truck."

He followed her to the kitchen and she pulled open her junk drawer. It held a menu from every local restaurant within delivering distance. "What are you in the mood for," she asked, and he gave her that simmering, sexy look, so she added, "besides *that*."

He grinned. "I'm not picky. You're the pregnant one. You choose."

She chose pizza. A staple item for her these days. The cheesier and gooier the better.

While they waited for it, they brought in the last of his things, most of which were for the dog who lay snoozing on his bed in the living room, occasionally opening one eye to peek around. Probably to make sure the cat was a safe distance away. Dexter lounged on the front windowsill pretending not to notice him.

It wasn't as if Nick had never been to her house, but showing him around, inviting him into her private domain, was just too weird. He would be using her towels to dry himself, washing his clothes in her washing machine and eating food from her dishes. It was so intimate and invasive. The enormity of it all hadn't really hit her until she'd seen him on the porch. She hadn't realized just how used to living alone she'd become in the past ten years. Most of the single women she knew who were her age or younger were looking for a companion. They wanted Mr. Right. She only wanted Mr. Right Now.

Not that she wasn't going to try to make this work.

The tour ended in the kitchen, and when Nick opened the fridge, he frowned. It was pitifully empty. But the freezer was stuffed wall-to-wall with Lean Cuisine dinners.

He gave her a look, and she shrugged. "There was a good sale so I stocked up."

"There's no real food in here," he said. "Don't you *ever* cook?"

Never. It was one of the few things her mother hadn't made her do. She had this nasty habit of burning things. The last time she attempted to cook herself a real meal, she'd wandered out of the room without shutting off the heat under a greasy frying pan and had set her kitchen on fire. Thank God she had a smoke detector and a good fire extinguisher. "Trust me when I say, we're both a lot safer if I don't cook."

For a second she thought he might ask for an explanation, then he just shook his head. He probably figured he was better off not knowing.

"Besides, who needs real food when you have carryout and prenatal vitamins?" she asked cheerfully.

He began opening cupboards, one by one, taking inventory of their lack of contents, shaking his head. Did he think the real food was going to miraculously appear?

"What are you doing?" she asked.

"Making a mental list so I know what to buy. Which at this point is pretty much everything."

"You can buy all the food you want, as long as you don't expect me to cook it."

"It may surprise you to learn that I'm not half bad when it comes to preparing a meal. It's one of the few things I remember doing with my mom."

Though he tried to hide it, she could see a dash of

wistful sadness flash across his face. The way it always did when he mentioned his mom.

"How old were you?"

"Five or six I guess."

"She was okay then?"

He shrugged. "I don't know if you could ever say she was completely okay. But life would be almost normal for months at a time, then the meds would stop working, or the side effects would be so bad she would stop taking them. Gradually she got so bad, nothing seemed to work. I was eight when social services removed me."

"And you haven't seen her since?"

He shook his head. "Nope."

She couldn't imagine going all those years without seeing her parents. Not knowing where they were or what they were doing.

"I used to get an occasional letter, but not for about six years now. She moved around a lot, going from shelter to shelter. I haven't been able to find her."

"What would you do if you did find her?"

"I'd try to get her in an institution or a group home. Her mental illness is degenerative. She won't ever get better, or even be able to function in society. But the truth is, she's probably dead by now."

He sounded almost cold. If she hadn't known Nick so well, she might have missed the hint of sadness in his tone. It made her want to pull him in her arms and give him a big hug. How could he stand it, not knowing if she was dead or alive? Not knowing if she was out there somewhere suffering. Cold and lonely and hungry.

"Are you worried about the baby?" he asked.

"What do you mean?"

"About the fact that mental illness can be genetic."

Honestly, she'd never even considered that. She didn't know all that much about mental illness, and even less about genetics. "Should I be worried?"

"My mom's illness stems from brain damage she sustained in a car wreck when she was a kid. So no, the baby won't be predisposed to it. Unless it runs on your side."

"My parents had nine kids, which if you ask me is completely nuts. But as far as I know, neither of them are technically mentally ill. Unless it was some big secret, I don't recall *anyone* in my family ever being mentally ill. And it's a big family."

"Speaking of big families, that's something we've never talked about," he said. "If this does work out, and we decide to get married, how will you feel about having more kids?"

Did the phrase, *over my dead body* mean anything to him? And how would he react if she was adamant about not having any more children.

That was something they would worry about later, when it became clear how far they planned to take this.

"I'm not sure," she told him, which wasn't completely untrue. There was a chance, however slim, that she would agree on one more baby.

"It's something I feel strongly about," he added.

She could see that, and she couldn't help feeling they were starting with one strike already against them.

Five

Zoë woke at eleven-thirty Saturday morning with a painfully full bladder and a warm weight resting on her feet. She pried her lids open and looked to the foot of the bed to find a pair of hopeful brown eyes gazing back at her.

"What are you doing in my bed?" Just her luck, Tucker was one of those dogs attracted to humans who didn't like them. She gave him a nudge with her foot. "Shoo. Get lost."

Tucker exhaled a long-suffering sigh and dropped his head down on the comforter, eyes sad. Up on the dresser beside the bed, Dexter watched over them, giving Tucker the evil eye.

"Go sleep in your own bed." She gave him another

gentle shove. He tried one more forlorn look, and she pointed to the door. "Out."

With a sigh he unfolded his lanky body and jumped down from the bed, landing with a thud on the rug, the tags on his collar jingling as he trotted out the door and down the stairs.

She sat up and her stomach did a quick pitch and roll. So far she'd gotten away with negligible morning sickness. A bit of queasiness first thing in the morning that usually settled after she choked down a bagel or muffin.

She eased herself out of bed and shoved her arms into her robe, but when she looked down for her slippers they were no longer on the side of the bed where she was sure she'd left them.

Darn dog.

She shuffled half-asleep across the ice-cold bare floor and down the stairs to the bathroom. She smelled something that resembled food and her stomach gave an empty moan followed by a slightly questionable grumble. She used the facilities and brushed her teeth. She tried to brush her hair into submission and wound up with a head full of blond frizz.

Oh well. If he was going to stay here, he would have to learn to live with the fact that she woke up looking like a beast. It also hadn't escaped her attention that the bathroom smelled decidedly more male than it had the previous morning, and when she opened the medicine chest, she found a shelf full of *guy* things there. Aftershave, cologne, shaving gel and a razor. Along with several other tubes and bottles of various male things.

She shook her head. Weird.

She found her way to the kitchen, doing a double take as she passed through the living room. She blinked and rubbed her eyes, sure that it was an illusion. But no, the clutter was gone. The newspapers and old magazines and dirty dishes. The random tufts of cat fluff had been vacuumed away. He'd even dusted.

A man who did housework? Had she died and gone to heaven, or had she woken up in the twilight zone?

Tucker lay on his bed beside the couch, the tips of two furry pink slippers sticking out from under his belly. *Her* slippers.

"Give my slippers back you mangy thief." Tucker just gazed back at her with innocent brown eyes that said, *Slippers? What slippers?*

Since he didn't seem inclined to move any time soon, she reached down and tugged them out from under him. Lucky for the dog they weren't chewed up and covered with slobber. Regardless, she would have to start keeping them on the top shelf of her closet.

She found Nick in the kitchen standing at the stove, cooking something that looked like an omelet. He wore a red flannel shirt with the sleeves rolled to his elbows, one that accentuated the wide breadth of his shoulders. His perfect behind was tucked into a pair of faded blue jeans that weren't quite tight, but not exactly loose either. On his feet he wore steel-toed leather work boots.

"That smells good."

Nick turned and smiled. "'Morning."

He was showered and shaved and way too cheerful. He looked her up and down and asked, "Rough night?"

"You know those women who wake up looking well-rested and radiant? I'm not one of them."

He only grinned. He probably figured silence was his best defense. To say she didn't look like a troll would be a lie, and to admit it would hurt her feelings.

Smart man.

"Thanks for cleaning up," she said. "You didn't have to do that."

"If I'm going to live here, I'm going to pitch in." He turned back to the stove. "The eggs will be done in a minute and there's juice in the fridge."

Juice?

She had no juice. Just a half gallon of skim milk that went chunky three days ago. Come to think of it, she didn't have eggs, either. Or the bacon that was frying in the skillet beside the nonexistent eggs. Or the hash brown patties sitting in the toaster. "Where did all this food come from?"

"I went shopping."

He shopped, too? She *was* in the twilight zone.

"If you're trying to impress me, it's working." She opened the refrigerator and found it packed with food. Milk, juice and eggs and bags of fresh fruit and vegetables. She wondered if he did windows, too. "What else have you done this morning?"

He grabbed two plates from the cupboard. It sure hadn't taken him long to familiarize himself with her kitchen. "I jogged, showered, cleaned and shopped, and I stopped by my place to pick up a few more things."

"Jeez, when did you get up?"

"Fiveish."

"It's Saturday."

He shrugged. "What can I say—I'm a morning person."

"I'm sorry, but that is just sick and wrong." Not that it wasn't kind of nice waking up and having breakfast ready. She poured herself a glass of organic apple juice—organic?—and sat at the table in the nook. Nick set a plate of food in front of her. Eggs, bacon, hash browns and buttered toast. She wondered if it was real butter. "Looks good. Thanks."

Nick slid into the seat across from her, dwarfing the small table, his booted feet bumping her toes. Invading her space. The man took up so much darned room.

She closed her eyes and said a short, silent, guilt induced blessing. A holdover from her strict Catholic upbringing. Some traditions were just impossible to break.

Nick dug right into his breakfast and, like everything else, ate with enthusiasm and gusto. No doubt about it, the guy enjoyed life to the fullest.

She picked at her food, nibbling tiny bites and chasing it down with sips of juice.

"Not hungry?" he asked.

"Not really." She bit off a wedge of toast. "Mild morning sickness."

"Anything I can do?"

"You could have the baby for me."

He gave her a "yeah, you wish" look.

After a few minutes of nibbling, her stomach gradually began to settle, and she began to feel her appetite returning. Though she didn't typically eat a big breakfast, she stopped just short of picking up her plate and licking it clean. She even reached across the table to nab the last slice of bacon off Nick's plate.

"Not hungry, huh?"

"I guess I was hungrier than I thought."

Nick got up and cleared the dishes from the table. "I was thinking about heading into the office for a few hours. Want to tag along?"

She had enough of the office Monday through Friday. Her weekends were hers. "I don't think so."

Normally she would wait until after dinner to do the day's dishes—sometimes three days later—but out of guilt she took the dirty plates and juice glasses from the sink and stacked them in the dishwasher. "It's supposed to get up in the high fifties today. I was planning on working in the garden. I need to get my gladiola bulbs planted."

"Then I'll stay and help."

She closed the dishwasher and wiped her hands on a towel. "Nick, your living here doesn't mean we'll be attached at the hip. We don't have to spend every second of the day together."

"I'm not asking for every second of your time. But I'm also not looking for a roommate I'll only see in passing." He folded a work-roughened hand over her shoulder. Its warm weight began to do funny things to her insides. "If we're going to do this, we're going to do it right. We're going to be a couple."

A couple of *what,* that was the question.

A couple of idiots for thinking this might actually work? Or a couple of fools for not realizing they were too different for this kind of relationship?

Having a big, strapping man around definitely had its advantages.

It might have taken Zoë two or three weekends to turn over the dirt to create a new flower garden and prepare it for planting. That meant two or three weeks of sore arms, an aching back and dirty fingernails. Nick, macho guy that he was, had nearly the entire area turned over and de-sodded in three hours.

She'd offered to help, but he said he would never let a woman in her condition do a man's job. Normally a comment like that would have gotten him a whack over the head with a shovel, but then he started driving the pitchfork into the soil and she became distracted watching the powerful flex of his thighs against worn denim. The way they cupped his behind just right.

As the temperature climbed up close to sixty, Nick shed first his jacket, then he peeled off his tattered Yale sweatshirt. She found herself increasingly distracted from her chore of picking weeds from the turned soil and dumping them in a bucket to go in the compost pile. She was much more interested in watching the play of muscles under the thin, white, sweat-soaked T-shirt.

What would it feel like to touch him again? What would he do if she got up right now and ran her hand up his back…

She shook away the thought. No. *Bad Zoë*. No touching allowed. Not yet anyway. Not until it was clear this relationship wasn't based solely on sex.

He was just so…*male*. And she was suffering from a serious excess of estrogen or pheromones, or whichever hormone it was that made a woman feel like molesting every man in sight.

One would never guess from the look of him that Nick had been raised among the rich and sophisticated. Not that he gave the impression of being a thug, either. He wore jeans and a flannel shirt the way most other men wore a three piece suit. When Nick entered a room, no matter the size, he filled it. He drew attention with his strength and character. With his unwavering confidence and larger-than-life presence. But he was so easygoing, he could impress without intimidating.

He was also a loyal friend and a fair employer. The kind of man a person could count on.

That didn't mean he was a pushover, though. People didn't mess with Nick. He may have had the patience of a saint, but cross him and watch out. His wick was long, but the impending explosion was catastrophic.

Something bumped Zoë's shoulder and she turned

from watching Nick to find a long snout in her face. Before she could react, Tucker gave her a big sloppy kiss right on the mouth.

"Aaaagh!" She frantically wiped dog slobber off her face with the sleeve of her sweater. "Go away, you disgusting animal!"

Nick turned to see what the problem was. "What's wrong?"

"Your dog just slobbered on my face."

Nick grinned. He probably trained the dog to do that just to annoy her. "That's his way of saying he likes you."

"Couldn't he find a less disgusting way to show affection? One that doesn't involve his spit."

He drove the pitchfork into the ground and leaned on the handle, a bead of sweat running down the side of his face. "I've been thinking about this arrangement we have and it occurred to me that we've been out together lots of times, but never as a couple."

"Like a date?"

"Right. So I was wondering if maybe you would like to go out with me tonight."

"As a couple?"

"I was thinking something along the lines of dinner and a movie."

Interesting. "Like a *real* date?"

"Yep."

She hadn't been on *any* kind of date—real or pretend—in longer that she wanted to admit. Her social life had been less than exciting lately. Most men seemed to want one thing, and they expected it on the first date no less. She obviously had no objections to sex before marriage, but even she thought two people should get to know each other before they hopped in the sack together.

"I get pregnant, you move in, *then* you ask me out on a date. Amazing how backward we're doing all of this, isn't it?"

"Is that a yes?"

"Yes. I'd love to go on a date with you."

He surveyed the ground he had yet to turn over. "This should only take me another fifteen or twenty minutes. Then I'll need to shower."

"Me, too. Why don't I hop in first while you finish up."

She hiked herself up, brushing dirt from her gardening gloves and the knees of her jeans. She knew it was something she would have to get used to, but the idea of showering while he was in her house was a little weird. Maybe if she hurried, she could get in and out while he was still outside.

Unless he wanted to conserve water and shower together…

No. *Bad* Zoë.

She gave herself a mental slap. There would be no shower sharing. At least not yet. But that *was* something couples did, right?

"One more thing," Nick called after her as she dashed to the house. She turned and found him flashing her that simmering, sexy smile.

Uh-oh, what was he up to?

"Since this is a real date, I'll be expecting a good-night kiss."

Nick glanced through the darkness at Zoë. She sat beside him in the truck, her head resting against the window, a damp tissue crumpled in her hand. Since they left the theater, her sobs had calmed to an occasional hiccup and sniffle.

On a first date disaster scale of one to ten, they had ranked a solid eleven. But technically the date wouldn't be over until they got home, so he wasn't going to count his chickens. It could get a lot better—or a lot worse.

Agreeing on a movie had been the first hitch. She had wanted to go to some artsy foreign film playing in Birmingham, and he wanted to see the latest martial arts action flick.

After a long debate-argument, they finally compromised—he being the one to do most of the compromising—and agreed on a romantic comedy.

As a trade-off, she'd let him pick the restaurant this time. He chose a four-star Middle Eastern place in Southfield he'd heard fantastic things about. He'd also learned a valuable lesson. Never try to feed a pregnant woman new, exotic food. When the server had set their plates in front of them, the unfamiliar textures and scents had turned her skin a peculiar shade of green. One bite had her bolting to the bathroom.

She'd had to wait outside while he paid the bill and the waitress packed up their uneaten dinner in carryout containers.

Since they were both still hungry, they had stopped at a fast food drive-thru and ate burgers and fries on the way to the theater.

He didn't normally get into chick flicks, but the film hadn't been as boring as he had anticipated, and their experience at the movie theater had been blessedly uneventful. Until the end, that is, when Zoë dissolved into uncontrollable sobs. Which was a little strange considering the movie had a happy ending. She'd been crying so hard he'd practically had to carry her out of the theater.

He'd gotten more than a few evil looks from female moviegoers—as if her emotional breakdown was somehow his fault—and several sympathetic head shakes from their male counterparts.

He wasn't going to pretend he had even the slightest clue what had happened. Or how to fix it. What he did know was that good night kiss he was hoping for seemed unlikely at this point. As did any possibility of seducing his way into her bed.

Beside him, Zoë sniffed and dabbed at her eyes with a tissue.

"You okay?" he asked, giving her shoulder a reassuring pat.

She wiped her nose and said in a wobbly voice, "I ruined our first date."

Ruined was such a strong word. There had been

good points. Given time, he could probably think up a few. "You didn't ruin anything."

"I got sick at dinner then had a breakdown in the movie theater."

He was going to say that it could have been worse, but they were still a few minutes from home. No point tempting fate.

"What if it's a sign?" she hiccupped. "What if this is God's way of telling us our relationship is going to be a disaster? Maybe this is our punishment for the premarital sex."

He'd never spent much time with a pregnant woman, but he was almost one hundred percent sure this was one of those mood swings he'd heard expectant fathers talk about. "Zoë, I think this has more to do with hormones than divine intervention."

"It was our first date. It was supposed to be special."

It was completely off the wall, but despite the fact that her face was all swollen and blotchy and her nose was running, he didn't think he'd ever seen her look more beautiful.

It wasn't often he got the opportunity to take care of Zoë. She was so damned capable and independent. He liked that she needed him. That she had a vulnerable side.

He took her free hand, linking his fingers through hers. "Just being with you made it special."

She looked up at him through the dark, tears welling in her red, puffy eyes and leaking down her cheeks. "That's s-so s-sweet."

But not so sweet that she would be willing to spend the rest of her life with him.

The words sat on the tip of his tongue but he bit them back. He had no interest in trying to guilt her into marriage. If and when they exchanged vows, he wanted her to mean every word she said.

And if that never happened? If she decided she didn't want to marry him?

Well, they would burn that bridge when they came to it.

Six

Sunday—thank goodness—proved to be a quiet and uneventful day. Zoë woke once again to a hot breakfast, and after the kitchen was cleaned, she and Nick had lounged around, chatting and reading the newspaper. Nick had adopted the recliner and Zoë shared the couch with the dog—who in two days had become her shadow. Later Nick watched football and drank beer while she retaught herself to knit, in the hopes of making the baby a blanket.

It felt so…domestic. And though she had never been a big fan of football—or any sport for that matter—it was nice just being in the same room with him, each doing their own thing. It had been…comfortable.

Isn't that how her parents had done it? When they

weren't working that is, which wasn't very often. Her father would park himself in the La-Z-Boy and her mom would grade papers or do needlepoint.

Maybe that was what all real couples did.

Nick fixed authentic, spicy enchiladas for dinner, which as he promised were delicious. And were probably the reason she woke Monday morning feeling as if someone had siphoned battery acid into her stomach.

She didn't manage to drag herself to work until after ten. She knew there was a problem the instant she stepped into her office and saw Shannon sitting at her desk, a determined look on her face.

The kiss.

She'd been so wrapped up in the living together thing, she had completely forgotten someone saw her and Nick kissing on Friday. Obviously, it had gotten around and Shannon was expecting an explanation.

Zoë shrugged out of her jacket and collapsed into her visitor's chair, since her own chair was occupied. "Go ahead, get it over with."

"It isn't bad enough that you don't tell me you're playing hide the salami with the boss—"

"Charming," Zoë interjected.

"—but this morning I take a call from your doctor's office and I'm told your prescription has been called into the pharmacy. Your prescription for *prenatal vitamins*."

Oh crud. Zoë felt all the blood drain from her face.

Shannon smiled smugly. "Is there by any chance something you neglected to tell me?"

Zoë winced. The kiss getting out was bad enough. She really wasn't ready for everyone to find out about her pregnancy.

"I admit I was deeply hurt."

She didn't look hurt. She looked as if she was preparing to give Zoë a thorough razzing. That was definitely more her style. Zoë and everyone else in the office had learned not to take it personally. Shannon leaned forward, elbows on the desk, fingers steepled under her chin. "But considering you probably just made me five-hundred and thirty-eight dollars richer, I might have to forgive you."

Five-hundred and thirty-eight dollars? "How did I manage that?"

"I won the pool."

"*Pool?*" Why did she get the feeling she didn't want to know what Shannon was talking about?

"Every time Nick skips out on a fiancée there's a betting pool to guess how long it will take him to find a replacement. I said within a week."

"The office has been *betting* on Nick's dating habits?" How is it that she had never heard about this?

"There's been some obvious tension between you guys since the wedding. Lots of long lingering looks when the other isn't watching. I put two and two together." She flashed Zoë a smug smile. "Looks like I was right, huh?"

She so did not need this hassle. There would be

questions that required explanations she just wasn't ready to give.

Zoë blew out a breath. "Who knows?"

"About you and Nick sucking face? Pretty much the whole office. It was Tiffany that walked in on you."

"I should have known, she never knocks." She also had a big mouth, and Zoë was pretty sure she had a crush on Nick.

"What about the baby? How many people know about that?"

Shannon sat back in the chair. "You see, that's tricky. Without telling everyone, I'll have a hard time proving the entire timeline, and the fact that I actually won. I had to ask myself, what's more important to me? Our friendship or being able to buy that forty inch flat screen television I've had my eye on. And as a result, reap the reward of many weeks of fantastic sex from my very grateful spouse."

"So it all boils down to our friendship or good sex?"

"You may not believe this, but after three kids and ten years of marriage, good sex can be pretty hard to come by."

Which probably meant that her secret didn't have a chance of hell in staying that way. "So what did you decide?"

She grinned. "That our friendship means more to me. But, honey, you're going to owe me big time for this one."

"Thank-you," Zoë said softly, close to tears again. Which was so not her. She never cried.

Would this emotional roller-coaster ride never end?

"That doesn't mean I don't want details. So spill."

"We didn't plan this," she told Shannon. "It was supposed to be a one time thing. A drunken mistake."

"But you got a little surprise instead?"

Zoë nodded. "The whole thing is a fluke."

"This was no fluke, Zoë."

She wished she could believe that. "He asked me to marry him."

Shannon didn't look surprised. "That sounds about right for Nick. What did you tell him?"

"That I'm not ready for that. We've decided to try living together for a while first."

"Which sounds about right for you."

Zoë frowned. "What's that supposed to mean?"

"No offense, but you *always* play it safe. You keep everyone at arm's length."

"I do not!" Zoë said, feeling instantly defensive. "You and I have been friends for a long time."

"And you know pretty much everything about me, right?"

"I guess so."

"And what do I know about you? What have you told me about your family?"

She bit her lip, trying to remember what she might have told Shannon, a sinking feeling in her chest. "You, um, know I have a big family."

"I know there are nine of you, but I have no idea how many brothers or sisters you have. I don't know their names. I know you grew up in Petoskey but you never talk about what it was like there. How it was for you growing up. You never talk about school or friends. *Nothing* personal. To get you to open up at all I have to practically drag it out of you. You have a lot of friends here, but besides Nick, I don't think *anyone* really knows you."

She hated to admit it, but Shannon was right. Zoë didn't get personal with too many people. Just her sister and Nick, and Nick hadn't been by choice. He had just sort of insinuated himself into her life, settling in like a pesky houseguest who never left. And there had always been a bit of resistance on her part. There still was. She always held a tiny piece of herself back.

Was Shannon right? Had Zoë been keeping everyone at arm's length?

An uneasy feeling settled in her stomach. Maybe her aversion to marriage had less to do with her family and was instead just a strange quirk in her personality. Maybe she'd never learned how to let herself open up to people. And if she didn't change, what kind of future could she and Nick possibly have? If they had one at all. If she refused to marry him, would it ruin their friendship? Would they wind up resenting each other?

The thought made her heart shudder with fear.

Nick was such a huge part of her life. What would she do without him?

If they were going to make this work, she would have to learn to open up and let him in.

All the way in.

"I'm not saying this to hurt your feelings," Shannon said, looking apologetic. "I think you're a wonderful, kind person. I consider you a good friend. Which is why I'd like to see this thing with Nick work out. You may not realize it now, but you two are perfect for each other."

"I told him no sex," Zoë blurted out, then turned twenty different shades of red. Why had she said that?

Shannon's eyes rounded. "No sex? Ever?"

"Not ever. Just until we're sure our relationship isn't just physical."

"One night of sex in what, ten years of friendship, and you're worried the relationship is only physical?"

Zoë hadn't realized until just now how ridiculous that sounded. And how equally ridiculous it must have sounded to Nick. What he must think of her.

"Do you think denying him sex is my way of keeping him at arm's length?"

"Honey, it doesn't matter what I think. The question is, what do *you* think?"

She was thinking that insisting they live together first had been her roundabout way of putting off making a difficult decision. One that shouldn't have been difficult in the first place. After ten years of friendship, she should know what she was feeling. Either she loved him or she didn't.

And if she didn't, maybe it was only because she hadn't let herself.

Nick had been incredibly patient with her so far, but

at some point he was going to grow tired of chasing her. How could she risk losing the one man she might have been destined to spend the rest of her life with?

She had to make a decision, and she had to make it soon.

"I don't care what his excuse is," Nick barked into the phone. His foreman, John Miglione, had just delivered the news that one of his employees had left for lunch and failed to return—for the fourth time in two weeks. On top of that the man called in sick at least once a week. There was nothing Nick hated more than firing people, but he needed reliable employees. A smart man knew that to survive in business he should surround himself with competent people. The weak links had to go. "Tell him one more time and he's out of a job."

"Will do, Nick. And there's one more thing."

He was silent for a second, as if he were working up to something, and Nick knew exactly what that something was.

"I know you want to ask, so just go ahead and get it over with."

"Is it true about you and Zoë?"

"That depends on what you heard."

"That Tiffany walked in on you two getting down and dirty."

"Tiffany exaggerates. It was just a kiss."

"Does that mean you two are…"

"Possibly. We're giving it a trial run."

"Well, it's about time."

Nick shook his head. "Do you know that you're the third person who said that to me today."

Zoë appeared in his office doorway—speak of the devil. He held up a finger to let her know he would only be a minute.

John laughed. "Then that should tell you something, genius. Give her a big wet one for me. I'll talk to you later."

He shook his head and hung up the phone, turning to Zoë. "What's up?"

"Is this a bad time?" she asked.

"No. John just called about O'Connell. He didn't come back after lunch—again. He seemed like a decent guy when we hired him. Overqualified even, but he can't seem to get his act together."

"That's too bad." She closed and locked the office door.

Did they have a meeting he'd forgotten? And if so, why lock the door?

Without a word she crossed the room and walked around his desk looking very…*determined*.

Determined to do what, he wasn't sure.

There was definitely something up.

"What's going on?" he asked.

With her eyes pinned on his face, she began unbuttoning her blouse.

Huh?

He watched as she slipped the garment off her shoulders and let it drop to the floor. He was too stunned to do anything but sit there as she climbed in his lap. She straddled his legs, her skirt bunching at her upper thighs, wrapped her arms around his neck and kissed him.

No, this wasn't just a kiss. This was a sexual attack. A wet, deep, oral assault. And he was completely defenseless.

He knew she was passionate, but man, he'd never expected this.

She feasted on his mouth, clawing her fingers through his hair, arching her body against him. She rode him like he was her own personal amusement park attraction.

It was hot as hell, the way she was throwing herself at him, still, something wasn't right. Something he couldn't quite put his finger on.

Something was…*missing*.

He felt her tugging his shirt from the waist of his jeans, fumbling with the buckle on his belt.

What the heck was going on?

He wasn't one to turn down sex, even if it was in the middle of the afternoon in his office. In fact, the idea of sex *anywhere* with Zoë was enough to get his engine primed, but something about this just wasn't right. She was kissing him, rubbing her satin and lace-covered breasts against his chest, yet he wasn't feeling a damn thing. He didn't even have a hard-on.

He grabbed Zoë's shoulders, held her at arm's length and asked, "What are you doing?"

"Seducing you," she said, like that should have

been completely obvious, sounding more exasperated than turned on.

"I see that. But why?"

She looked at him as though he was speaking an alien language. "Why?"

"You said you wanted to wait," he reminded her.

"I'm not allowed to change my mind?"

"Of course you are." But he had a strong feeling she hadn't changed her mind, or something had changed it without her consent. It was as if she was going through the motions, but her heart wasn't really in it. "Just tell me why."

She blew out an exasperated breath. "Do I need a reason? Jeez! I thought you would be jumping at the chance. I thought you would have me naked by now."

"Normally, I would. It just feels like…I don't know. Like you're doing this because you have to. Or I'm forcing you or something."

"You're *not* forcing me."

"I'm sorry, but something about this just doesn't feel right."

A delicate little wrinkle formed between her brows. "Are you turning me down?"

It was hard for him to believe, too. In fact, he couldn't think of a single time when he'd turned a woman down. "At least until you tell me what's up. Why the sudden change of heart?"

She slid out of his lap, snatched her shirt up from the floor and covered herself with it. "I thought this was what you wanted."

He could see that he'd hurt her feelings, but he needed to know what was going on. They had to be honest with each other or this relationship would never have a chance.

"Of course it's what I want. But is it what you want?"

She gave him that confused look again. "I don't understand. I'm here, aren't I?"

"Zoë, why did you come in here?"

She tugged her shirt on and buttoned it. "You know why."

"What I mean is, what *motivated* you?"

Her frown deepened. "I wanted to have sex with you."

He sighed. This was going nowhere. "Let's try this. Let me give you a scenario, and you tell me if I'm right. Okay?"

She nodded and smoothed the creases from her wrinkled skirt.

"You were sitting at your desk thinking about me, remembering that night in the hotel. You became so overcome with lust and passion that you couldn't wait another minute to have me, so you raced down to my office."

She just stared at him, so he asked, "Was it something like that?"

She bit her lip. "Um…"

He was a little disappointed, but not surprised. "Talk to me Zoë. Tell me what's going on."

"I thought that if I didn't have sex with you soon, maybe you were going to get sick of waiting.

Maybe you would find someone else. Someone… better."

That had to be the dumbest thing he had ever heard. "Contrary to what you might believe, a man can go three days living with a woman and not have sex." He leaned back in the chair and folded his arms over his chest. "Hell, there have been times I've lasted a whole week. And if it becomes a problem, there's no reason why I can't…take matters into my own hands, so to speak."

Her cheeks flushed pink and she lowered her eyes to the floor. It amazed him that a woman who so excelled at talking dirty could possibly be embarrassed by this conversation.

He patted his legs. "Come'ere. Have a seat."

She hesitated—the woman who had just thrown herself at him with guns blazing—then sat primly on his knee, tucking her skirt around her legs.

This was definitely not going to cut it.

He wrapped his hands around her waist. She gasped as he pulled her snug against his chest, her behind tucked firmly into his lap.

That was much better.

"Okay, now what made you think I would dump you if you didn't sleep with me?"

She looked up at him, so much conflict and confusion in her eyes. "I keep everyone at arm's length."

"Arm's length?" What was she talking about?

"I'm too private. I don't let people in. You're

going to get sick of me shutting you out and find someone else."

Where was she getting this garbage? How could a woman so intelligent act so dumb? "And sex is supposed to fix that?"

She shrugged. "It's a start."

"Do you honestly think I'm that shallow?"

She shook her head, looking guilty for even thinking it.

"If I thought you were shutting me out emotionally, sex ten times a day wouldn't make a damned bit of difference."

She gnawed at the skin on her lower lip. "I guess I never thought of it like that."

"I guess not." He brushed a few wayward blond curls back and tucked them behind her ear. "You must have had a good reason for wanting to wait, and I respect that. If you're not ready, that's okay. I understand."

The crinkle in her brow grew deeper. "That's just it. I'm not sure if the reason I had was a good one. We've been friends for years and managed not to have sex. So why would I think our relationship would only be physical? And it's not like I don't want to have sex. It's all I think about lately. When I'm not sick, or sobbing my eyes out, that is."

A grin curled his mouth.

"I have this really annoying habit of looking at your butt. I never even used to notice it, and now I can't peel my eyes off of it. And I want to touch it. I want to touch you *everywhere*. So why am I still telling you no?"

He shrugged. She was adorable when she was confused and frustrated.

"I'm afraid I'm doing it because I don't let people close to me."

"Maybe it's just that you're dealing with an awful lot right now and a sexual relationship is more than you're ready for."

"You think?" she asked, a hopeful look in her eyes.

"When I make love to you, Zoë, I want it to be like that night in the hotel. I want you to want me as much as I want you."

Her lips curved in a dreamy smile. "It really was good, wasn't it?"

He couldn't help grinning himself. "Oh, yeah."

She cupped his face in her hands. Her skin was warm and soft and smelled like soap. "You know what? You're a great guy."

Then she kissed him. A sweet, tender kiss packed with so much simple, genuine affection it nearly knocked him out of his chair.

Now, this was definitely more like it. He would rather hold and kiss her this way for five minutes than have an entire night of meaningless sex.

That night in the hotel he knew that there was something more between them. Something they had both buried away. Maybe she just wasn't ready to take that last step. But she would be eventually.

He was certain of it.

Seven

When Zoë pulled into her driveway later that evening there was a car parked there.

"Oh, fudge."

That's what she got for dodging her sister's calls. And giving her a key. She should have known that if she didn't come clean, Faith would pop in for a surprise visit.

Maybe she subconsciously wanted her here. Maybe she needed someone to tell her what to do.

She parked her conservative Volvo beside her sister's flashy little crimson Miata. They had always been polar opposites. Zoë the practical, responsible sister and Faith the wild child.

When they were kids, Faith had always wanted to

loosen Zoë up and teach her to have fun, while Zoë ran herself ragged trying to keep Faith out of trouble. If their parents knew how many times Zoë had covered for her when she'd snuck out after midnight to meet a boyfriend or go to a wild party, they would have strokes.

She gathered her things and headed for the front door. She stepped inside and called, "I'm home."

Faith appeared from the kitchen, her flame-red hair cut stylishly short and gelled into spiky points, a drastic change from the waist-length curls she'd had last time. She was dressed in body-hugging black jeans and a stretchy chenille sweater the exact same green as her eyes.

She clicked across the room in spiked high heels and hugged Zoë fiercely. "Surprise!"

"What are you doing here?" she asked, wrapped up in a scented cloud of perfume and hairspray.

"Don't even pretend you don't know why I'm here. You haven't been returning my calls and that always means something is wrong."

"Nothing is wrong, I promise." She stepped back and looked her sister up and down. She looked perfect, as usual. She wore just enough makeup to look attractive, without being overdone. Her acrylic nails were just the right length and painted a warm shade of pink. Attractive, but not overly flashy. Faith has always been the pretty one. "You look gorgeous! I love the new haircut."

"And you look exhausted. But don't even change the

subject. Why was there an enormous dog in your house and what's with all the guy stuff in the spare bedroom?"

"Those are Nick's things. So is the dog." She looked around, wondering why Tucker hadn't met her at the door. She was kind of getting used to the crotch sniff greetings and sloppy dog kisses. "Where is the dog?"

"I let him out. And why is Nick staying here? Is he getting his place sprayed for bugs or something?"

Before Zoë could explain, the front door opened and Nick walked though, his regular old big gorgeous self. She saw him through different eyes now and couldn't help wondering if it would be obvious to the world what she was feeling. Not that she thought there was a snowball's chance in hell of keeping this from her sister now.

"Pork chop!" Nick said, giving Faith a big hug, lifting her right off her feet.

"Sugar lump!" Faith squealed, hugging him back.

Zoë felt the tiniest twinge of jealousy. Faith had always been so outgoing and friendly. So full of warmth and affection. Why couldn't Zoë be more like that?

Nick set her down and took a good look at her. "Wow. You look great."

"Right back attcha, stud. Zoë was just about to explain why you're staying here. Is something wrong? Did you lose your condo?"

"Um, no," Nick said, looking to Zoë for guidance, like she had the slightest clue how to explain this.

Maybe it would be best to just come right out and say it. "The thing is, I'm pregnant."

Faith's mouth fell open and for about ten seconds she looked too stunned to speak. Maybe just saying it hadn't been the best way to go after all. "You're *what?*"

"Pregnant."

"*Pregnant?* And you didn't *tell* me?"

"Sorry. I was going to call you. I only found out for sure a couple of days ago. I've been a bit… confused."

"Which still doesn't explain what Nick is doing here."

Zoë and Nick looked at each other, then back at Faith. Did they really need to spell it out? Were they so unlikely a couple that Faith would never guess it?

Faith looked from Zoë to Nick, then back to Zoë again. Then she gasped. "It's *Nick's?*"

"You have to swear not to say anything to Mom and Dad," Zoë pleaded. "I haven't decided what to tell them yet."

"How did this happen?" Faith demanded.

"The usual way," Nick said, and Zoë felt her cheeks begin to burn with embarrassment.

"When did you two start seeing each other? And why didn't anyone tell me?"

"Why don't I start dinner while you two talk," Nick said. He beat a path to the kitchen like his pants were in flames and he needed a fire extinguisher.

Coward.

"You and Nick?" Faith said, shaking her head, like she just couldn't believe it.

Zoë felt a jab of annoyance. It's not as if she and

Nick were a different species for God's sake! "Is it really so hard to imagine that Nick would be attracted to someone like me?"

"Of course not. I've always thought you and Nick would be a great couple. I just didn't know you thought so, too."

"I didn't," she admitted. At least not consciously. Maybe all this time the idea had been there, lurking in the back of her mind.

"I want the whole story," Faith said, giving her a pointed look. "And I expect *details*."

Zoë knew exactly what kind of details her sister was referring to.

"Then you had better sit down and get comfortable. This is going to take a while."

Nick, Zoë and Faith sat up until well after midnight chatting. They probably would have stayed up all night if Nick and Zoë hadn't had to go to work the next morning.

Since Nick had the guest room, Faith bunked with Zoë. They took turns in the bathroom, changed into their jammies, then climbed under the covers together, giggling in the dark like they had when they were kids. Back then they'd shared bunk beds. Faith on top and Zoë below.

"Are you sure you can't stay for a few days?" Zoë asked. She didn't see her sister nearly as much as she would have liked to. She wished she lived closer. Especially now that Faith was going to be an aunt.

"I really have to get back. I just had to make sure you were okay. I promised I wouldn't be gone long."

"Promised who?"

Zoë could see the flash of Faith's teeth as she smiled. "I'm seeing someone new. No one really knows about it yet."

"And you accuse me of keeping secrets," Zoë admonished.

"Yeah, well, Mom and Dad aren't exactly going to approve of this, either."

"Let me guess, he's Lutheran."

"Nope."

"Jewish?"

"Atheist."

Zoë cringed. "Ooooh, yikes."

"And he's not a he, he's a she."

For a second Zoë was too surprised to reply. A *she?* "You're dating a *woman?*"

"Are you totally grossed out?" she asked, her voice lacking its usual confidence.

"Of course not! I just…I'm surprised, that's all."

"It kind of surprised me, too."

"What happened? Did you just one day decide, hey, maybe I'll try something new?"

"You know me, I'll try anything once. Her name is Mia. Are you sure it doesn't gross you out?"

She wouldn't lie to herself and not admit it wasn't a little weird to think of her sister in a new way, but all that mattered was that Faith was happy. "I promise, I'm not grossed out."

"That's good, because as strange as it probably sounds, I think I might be in love with her."

It must have been serious, because like Zoë, Faith didn't do love. She didn't let herself get tied down. Didn't talk about having a family. Ever. She just wanted to have fun.

The truth was, Zoë felt jealous. Not about the same sex part. She was firmly rooted in her heterosexuality. She liked men, plain and simple.

What she envied was that Faith had clicked with someone and she went for it, no question. Even though she knew it could potentially get complicated, she wasn't afraid to take a chance.

Why couldn't Zoë be like that? Why couldn't she just open up and let this thing with Nick happen? Why was he sleeping in the guest room when he should have been in bed with her?

"I'm thinking of telling Mom and Dad," Faith said.

"Wow, it must be serious."

"I swear, I've never felt like this about anyone. I know they're going to freak, and possibly disown me. I guess it's a risk I'm willing to take. I feel I owe it to Mia not to try and hide it. I don't want her to think I'm ashamed of our relationship. I'd like you to meet her, too. Maybe we could come down and stay for a couple days."

"I'd like that," Zoë said, and realized she really meant it. She wanted to meet the person that had captured her sister's heart. "Maybe next weekend."

They talked for a while longer, until Faith drifted

off to sleep. Zoë lay there awake until after one, her mind unable to rest. She couldn't stop thinking about all the things that had changed over the past few weeks. She felt as if her entire life had been flipped upside down, spun around and set back down slightly askew.

But not in a bad way. Things would never be the same, but she was beginning to realize that wasn't necessarily a bad thing.

She tossed and turned for another few minutes, then decided to try a glass of warm milk to help her sleep. Which was kind of weird since she'd never in her life had warm milk and the idea sounded pretty gross. She climbed out of bed and tripped over Tucker who lay sleeping on her rug. She couldn't find her slippers in the dark, and she didn't want to disturb her sister by switching on the light, so she padded across the cold floor in bare feet. She headed down the dark stairway but instead of her feet taking her to the kitchen, she found herself standing in the partially open door of the guest room. Maybe that had been her intention all along, and the warm milk was just her way of convincing herself to walk down the stairs in the first place.

She could tell by his slow and deep breathing that Nick was asleep.

Instead of turning around and going to the kitchen, she tiptoed into the room. She had no idea what she was doing, or even why she was doing it. But it wasn't enough to stop her.

Maybe everything wasn't supposed to make

sense. Maybe it was okay to do things simply because it felt good.

Nick was turned away from her, on his right side, his wide shoulders bare. She felt a deep ache in her heart, a pull of longing that propelled her closer to the bed. Closer to him. She wasn't here for sex, she knew that much. She just wanted to be near him.

Without thinking, or considering the consequences, she pulled back the covers and very quietly slipped in beside him. The sheets were cool and soft and smelled of his aftershave.

She rolled onto her side, facing away from him, carefully tucking the covers around her shoulders. Beside her, Nick stirred.

"Zoë?" he said in a voice rough from sleep and rolled toward her.

"Sorry. I didn't mean to wake you."

"S'okay," he mumbled and curled up behind her, enfolding her in the warmth of his body, wrapping a thick arm around her. He spread one large hand over her belly, easing her closer, burying his nose in her hair.

Oh, this was nice.

She held her breath, waiting to see what he would do next, what he would touch, if he would kiss her. And to her surprise, he didn't do a thing. He just snuggled up to her and fell back to sleep. It was as if he knew exactly what she wanted without her even having to ask.

She sighed and placed her hand over his, twining their fingers together. This was definitely more effective than warm milk. Already her lids were beginning to feel heavy. The heat of his body soothed her, his slow, steady breathing warmed the back of her neck and the deep thud of his beating heart lulled her to sleep.

It was a good thing she was having the boss's baby. In any other situation Zoë's erratic work schedule would surely get her fired. And so much for them saving gas driving together.

It was past eleven when she finally strolled into work. Her sister had already been gone by the time she got out of bed, but Faith left a note saying she would call so they could talk about her and Mia visiting next weekend. Nick, she added, had made her breakfast before he left for work.

Zoë hadn't heard or felt him get out of bed. Typically sharing a mattress meant a restless night's sleep for her. Last night, curled up in Nick's arms, she'd slept like the dead and woke feeling well-rested for the first time in weeks.

One very good reason to invite him upstairs to sleep tonight. In fact, maybe it would be better if he moved *all* of his things up there. Maybe it was time to begin treating this exactly the way they should, as an intimate, monogamous relationship between two people who cared deeply for each other. Maybe even loved each other. And if she wasn't actually in love with him yet, she was darned close.

She dropped her purse and jacket in her office

then took the hall down to Nick's office, getting more than a few curious looks and several knowing smiles along the way. News of the kiss had definitely made the rounds. And instead of feeling ashamed or self-conscious, she found herself holding her head a little higher, her back straighter. She found herself answering their looks with a smile that said she was proud to be with a man of Nick's integrity, a man who was so admired by his peers.

If they only knew the *whole* story.

She *wanted* people to know. She was proud to be having Nick's baby.

The thought nearly blew her away.

The only logical explanation was that for years there had been feelings between them that they had either been denying or stowing away. And now that those feelings had been acknowledged and set free, they were multiplying at an exponential rate.

Nick's office was empty, and she remembered belatedly that he had planned to work on-site today—an inspection had been scheduled that he wanted to be there for. She felt a dash of disappointment that she would have to wait all afternoon to see him.

She turned to leave and plowed into a brick wall of a man coming from the opposite direction.

"Whoa!" He grabbed her arms to keep her from toppling over on her butt. She recognized him as O'Connell, the man they had hired only a few weeks ago. The one who'd been giving Nick so much trouble. "Sorry," he said gruffly.

"No, it was my fault." She backed away from him. "I wasn't looking where I was going."

He was *enormous,* with long sandy brown hair, a bushy beard and craggy, almost harsh features. He wore the typical construction worker's uniform—work-faded, dusty jeans, a quilted flannel shirt and steel toed work boots.

"He's not in?" he asked in a deep rumble of a voice.

"No. He's on-site. He should be back sometime later this afternoon."

He gave her a solemn nod and started to walk away, his heavy footsteps vibrating the floor under her feet.

"Can I give you a bit of advice?"

He stopped and turned back to her.

"Nick is a patient man and a fair employer, but you're pushing him over the line."

He narrowed his eyes at her, looking downright fierce. She might have been intimidated, but she'd spent the last ten years around men like him. They looked big and tough, but deep down most were just big teddy bears.

"Is that supposed to scare me?" he asked.

"Your references from your last job were impeccable. Your work is quality. So what's the problem? Why do you keep screwing up?"

"You wouldn't understand," he said gruffly, a distinct hint of sadness lurking behind a pair of piercing blue deep-set eyes. She couldn't help thinking there was more to this situation than he was letting show. And a damned good reason why he was missing work.

She could read people that way.

She propped her hands on her hips and gave him one of her stubborn looks. "Oh yeah, tough guy? Why don't you try me?"

Eight

It was nearly three by the time Nick got back to the office and the only thing on his mind, the only thing that had been on his mind all day, was stopping in to see Zoë. He barely remembered her climbing into bed with him last night, so waking to find her curled in his arms had been a pleasant surprise. And if he hadn't had an appointment with an inspector, he might not have gotten out of bed.

He wasn't going to pretend to know what had motivated her to do it. She was the one calling the shots, setting the pace. But he felt as if they had taken a giant step forward last night.

They had made progress.

He headed into his office to drop off his briefcase

and jacket, and found Zoë sitting at his desk. O'Connell, his problem employee, was standing by the door, as if he'd just been on his way out.

"Nice of you to show up," Nick told him, feeling his good mood fizzle away.

"Boss." O'Connell nodded Nick's way then shot Zoë a half smile. "Thanks."

Nick felt his hackles go up. What the hell was that all about? Why was he smiling at Nick's woman? And why were her eyes red and puffy? Had she been crying?

She sniffled and returned the smile, which pissed off Nick even more. "No problem. You just have to promise you won't make a move until I talk to Nick."

"I won't." He gave her a nod, and ignoring Nick, walked out.

"What was that all about?" Nick demanded. "Why are you crying? Did he hurt you?"

She chuckled and waved away his concerns. "I'm fine. This is nothing. Just the usual overactive hormones."

"What did you need to talk to me about?"

"Come in and shut the door."

He did as she asked and walked over to his desk. "What's going on? I don't like you being alone in here with him. I don't trust him."

A grin split her face. "Nick, are you *jealous*?"

"Of course not," he said automatically, then frowned. Damn, he *was* jealous. He was behaving like a suspicious spouse. "I'm sorry."

"He came in to quit," Zoë told him.

"That's convenient. It'll save me the trouble of firing him."

"I told him I wouldn't let him. And you're not firing him, either."

Maybe she was forgetting who owned the company. "Why the hell not?" he snapped.

"This guy came highly recommended from his last employer. They couldn't say enough good things about him. I knew something had to be up."

"And?"

"So I asked. Like we should have a week ago."

"*And?*" he repeated impatiently.

"And it took some prying, but I finally got him to admit why he's been missing so much work."

No doubt O'Connell had tried to con his way into keeping the job, pulling on Zoë's heartstrings. She was emotionally unstable enough these days to fall for just about anything.

He folded his arms across his chest. "This should be good."

"He has a sick daughter."

Nick frowned. That he hadn't expected. A drug or alcohol problem maybe, but not a sick kid. He didn't even know O'Connell was married. "How sick?"

"She has a rare form of leukemia."

And what if it was all bull? "You're sure he's not just saying that to—"

"He showed me pictures," she interjected, her voice going wobbly and her eyes welling with tears again. "Taken in the children's ward of the hospital. She looks like such a sweet little girl. Only seven years old." She sniffled and wiped away the tears spilling down her cheeks. "Sorry. It was just so sad. He got misty-eyed when he talked about her. I could see how much he loves her, and how hard it's been for him."

Nick cursed and shook his head. "Why the hell didn't he say anything?"

"Because he's a big burly macho guy who thinks he can carry the weight of the world on his shoulders. He lost his wife three years ago, so it's just the two of them. They moved here from up north to be close to Children's Hospital in Detroit. There's a specialist there who thinks he can help her. Only problem is, she has to go in for treatment several times a week and sometimes he can't find anyone to help him. Some days she's so sick from the chemo and radiation he can't leave her."

"I would have given him the days off."

"It gets worse. Even with insurance, medical bills are eating up all his money and they're about to get evicted from the apartment they're staying in. Although from what he says, it sounds like the place is a dump and it's in a terrible neighborhood. He said they have no choice but to go back up north so he can move in with his parents."

"And what about his daughter?"

"This treatment is her last option. Without it she'll probably die."

Nick leaned forward in his seat. "What can we do to help him?"

A grin split Zoë's face. "I talked to him about the company possibly loaning him some money."

"And?"

"He says he's already too far in debt." She plucked a tissue from the box on his desk and wiped the last of her tears away. "I think he's too proud to take a handout."

"We have to do something." There had to be a way to help this guy. A way that wouldn't bruise his pride.

He looked over at Zoë and saw that she was still smiling at him, her eyes full of warmth and affection. "What?"

"You're a good man, Nick."

He shrugged. "Anyone would want to help him."

"No, they wouldn't. But I knew you wouldn't question helping him. You would do it without a second thought."

She got up from his chair and walked to the door. He thought she was going to leave, instead she snapped the lock.

What was she up to?

She turned and started walking toward him, the weeping gone. Instead she gazed down at him a heavy-lidded, almost sleepy look in her eyes. This was awfully familiar. Where had he seen this before…?

Oh yeah, she'd been wearing an identical expression that night in the hotel, seconds before they pounced on each other.

Oh man, here we go again.

Her cheeks were rosy, her lips damp and full, like

plump, dew covered strawberries. He didn't doubt they would be just as sweet and juicy.

She exhaled a breathy sigh and fanned her face. "Phew, it's getting awfully warm in here, isn't it?"

It didn't feel particularly warm to him, although, if she was going to do what he thought she was going to do, it would be a lot warmer in a minute or two. "If you say so."

She reached up, her eyes pinned on his face, and began unfastening the buttons on her shirt. Very slowly, one by one, inch by luscious inch, exposing a narrow strip of pale, creamy skin.

He could see in her eyes, she wanted him. She wasn't doing it because she knew it was what *he* wanted. And she sure wasn't in a hurry.

Well, hell, it *was* getting hot in here.

"I don't want to wait any longer," she said in a husky voice.

"What if someone needs me for something?" he asked, figuring it would be irresponsible to not object at least a little. They were, after all, at work.

"They'll just have to wait their turn."

Well then. He leaned back in his chair to enjoy the show, felt his heart rate skyrocket when she slipped the blouse from her shoulders and let it drop to the floor. Underneath she wore a siren-red transparent lace bra that barely covered the essentials. Her skin looked pale and creamy soft, her nipples taut and nearly as rosy as the fabric that did little to cover them. She wasn't what he would call well-endowed, but what she did have was firm and perfectly shaped. Just enough to fit in his cupped hand with barely any overflow.

And he was so hard that any second he was going to bust out his zipper.

Zoë unfastened her slacks and pushed them down. And when he saw the thong she wore underneath he stopped breathing. In the same vibrant shade as her bra, it was so scandalously brief and transparent it left *nothing* to the imagination.

Had she dressed this way for him or did she always wear sexy underwear to work?

She flashed him a mischievous smile. "See anything you like?"

He lowered his eyes to his crotch, to his very obvious erection. "What do you think?"

He followed the movements of her hand as she stroked a path between the swell of her breasts, trailed it down her taut stomach, stopping briefly to circle her navel, then lower still, brushing her fingers over the itsy bitsy patch of lace.

She leaned forward, resting her hands on the arms of his chair, giving him a beautiful view of her cleavage. "Thinking about stopping me again?"

Oh, hell no. He reached up and hooked a hand behind her neck, pulling her face to his, his fingers tangling through the softness of her pale curls. "Kiss me."

Her lips were soft and warm and so sweet as she brushed them against his own. She slipped into his lap, straddling his thighs, pulling at his clothes—

The knob on his office door rattled, then there was a loud pounding. "Nick! Open up!" John called.

Damn it.

"I'm busy," he shouted in the direction of the door. He had a nearly naked, aroused woman in his lap who seemed intent on getting him naked, too. No way in hell he wasn't going to make love to her.

"It's an emergency."

He closed his eyes, let his head fall back, and cursed.

Zoë let go of the hem of his shirt and called, "What happened?"

There was a brief pause, as Nick was sure his foreman was putting two and two together, then he said, "Sorry to interrupt, but I just got a call that there was an accident at the Troy site."

Zoë sighed and Nick cursed again.

"How bad?" he called.

"I'm not sure. I only know they took one of our guys to the hospital."

He scrubbed his hands across his face and mumbled, "I don't believe this."

"Give us a minute," Zoë said, and he looked up at her apologetically. "I know, you have to go."

She climbed out of his lap and grabbed her clothes from the floor. He stood up and tucked his shirt back in.

He watched her dress, knowing his own face mirrored her look of disappointment. "We have piss-poor timing, don't we?"

She buttoned her blouse and tucked it into her slacks. "No kidding."

As she headed for the door, Nick grabbed her arm and tugged her to him. "Tonight," he said, "you're all mine."

Unfortunately *tonight* never transpired.

Zoë ran home to let the dog out at five, then went back to the office and stayed until eight to make up for some of the time she'd been missing and work she'd been neglecting the past couple of days. She expected Nick to be back home when she pulled in at eight-fifteen, but the driveway was empty and the house dark.

The intense tug of disappointment she felt took her by surprise. Coming home to an empty house had never bothered her before. Well, not usually. Sometimes it sucked being alone, but she always had Dexter to keep her company.

In only a couple of days she'd grown used to having Nick around.

She raided the frozen dinners in the freezer, unable to choose between her two favorites.

"What do you think?" she asked the dog, holding them both up. "Chicken Alfredo or lasagna?"

He looked up at her with a goofy dog smile, his long skinny tail wagging like mad and whacking the table leg.

"You want me to make both?"

He barked, which he almost *never* did, so she took that as a yes. She'd never been much of a dog person, but Tucker wasn't half-bad. She couldn't help growing attached to him, especially when he shadowed her every step, gazing up at her with lovesick puppy eyes.

She nuked both dinners and ate in front of the television, tossing bites to Tucker who gobbled them up enthusiastically. When they were finished eating, Zoë stretched out on the couch with the cat curled up on her feet and the dog sacked out on the rug beside her. She channel surfed, running across a show about babies on the Discovery Channel. She settled in to watch it and the next thing she knew, someone was nudging her awake.

Nine

Zoë pried her eyes open, feeling drugged from sleep. The television was off and Nick stood over her grinning, illuminated only by the light in the hallway.

"What time is it?" she mumbled.

"After midnight."

"I guess I fell asleep." She yawned and stretched. "How did it go at the hospital?"

"Nothing fatal. A couple of cracked ribs and a broken collarbone. He'll be off work for a while, but he'll make a full recovery." He extended a hand toward her. "C'mon, let's get you into bed." At her curious look he added, "To sleep. I think we're both too tired for any fooling around."

He was right. It had been a long eventful day for them both.

He took her hand and hoisted her off the couch.

"Are you coming to bed, too?"

"With you?" he asked, and she nodded. "Do you want me to?"

She really, truly did. "I want you to."

He flashed her that dimpled grin. "Then I will."

"I have to brush my teeth first."

"Me, too. You mind sharing the sink, or do you prefer to take turns?"

It's not as if she had never shared a sink before, and often with three or four other people all rushing to get ready before the school bus honked out front. Besides, that was what couples did, right? "I don't mind."

It was a little weird watching Nick brush his teeth. It was one of those normal everyday things that a person did that she never really thought about, but doing it together felt very personal and intimate. Like learning a secret.

She drew the line at staying in the bathroom while he used the facilities—some secrets should stay secret—and went upstairs to change into her pajamas. In her bedroom she found Tucker and Dexter curled up together on her bed.

She propped her hands on her hips and told Dexter firmly, "You little traitor."

Dexter looked up guiltily.

"Get down," she said, tugging on the covers. Like

new best buddies, both animals jumped off the bed and headed down the stairs together.

It would seem that even Dexter had already adjusted to having them here. That had to be some sort of sign, didn't it?

She stripped down and slipped into an oversized, extra long T-shirt with a Happy Bunny logo on the front. She was already under the covers by the time Nick came upstairs. She curled up on her side and watched as he sat on the edge of the bed and first pulled off his work boots and then his socks. Next he unbuttoned his shirt, tugged it off, and draped it across the footboard.

She sighed with pleasure at the sight of all that beautiful bare skin over ropes of lean muscle. Despite his dark coloring and coarse beard, he wasn't all that hairy. Just a sprinkling on his pecs that trailed down into a narrow path, bisecting his abs and disappearing under the waistband of his jeans.

Looking completely at ease in her bedroom, he rose to his feet and unfastened his jeans. He shoved them down and kicked them off, revealing long powerful legs. Men's legs didn't typically do much for her, but as far as she was concerned Nick's were perfect.

Wearing only his boxers, he slipped into bed beside her. He rolled on his side facing her, leaned close and gave her a brief, but incredibly sweet kiss. His chin felt rough against her skin. He smelled of toothpaste and soap and just a hint of aftershave. "Good night."

"Good night." She reached behind her and

switched off the lamp. As her eyes adjusted to the dark, she could see that Nick had closed his eyes. He must have been pretty tired considering he was typically out of bed before 6 a.m.

Yep, she was tired, too. Absolutely exhausted. Much too tired to finish what they had started in his office this afternoon.

So why couldn't she seem to close her eyes? Why was the urge to touch Nick nagging at her?

She didn't want to wait. She wanted sex now, damn it!

She laid a hand on Nick's arm, rubbing from wrist to shoulder. "Nick, you awake?"

He didn't respond so she gave him a gentle shake. "Nick, wake up."

He answered with a half mumble, half snore.

He was sound asleep.

Swell.

She sighed and rolled onto her back. Two days ago she hadn't been ready for sex, now it was all she could seem to think about. If only they could get their schedules coordinated.

Tomorrow, she decided. Tomorrow they were going to get down and dirty and *nothing* was going to stop them.

"I think I figured out a way to help O'Connell," Nick said the next morning at the breakfast table. He'd fixed them pancakes, sausage patties and freshly squeezed juice from organically grown oranges.

The way she'd been eating lately, she was going to gain a hundred pounds before this baby was done cooking.

"How?" she asked, stabbing her third sausage patty.

"Well, his immediate problem is finding a place to live that he can afford, right? Well, I have a two bedroom condo sitting empty in Royal Oak. They can stay there rent free."

"You're a genius! That's absolutely *perfect*. Do you think he'd go for it?"

"Since it's paid off, and I'm not getting any rent for it now, it's technically not a handout."

"I can't believe we didn't think of it before. And it's even closer to the hospital than the place he's staying in now."

"There's only one possible drawback. Unless I want to kick him and his daughter out at some point, you're going to be stuck with me for God only knows how long."

"And that's okay with you?" she asked.

He nodded. "It really is. How about you?"

She smiled. "It's really okay with me, too."

"You're sure? This is a pretty big step."

A step she honestly felt ready to take. She knew exactly what she wanted, and she was going for it, damn it. "I'm absolutely, and completely sure."

He flashed her that dimpled grin. "Should I talk to O'Connell or do you want to?"

"Since it's your place it would probably be better if you talked to him. It might be easier to accept coming from a guy than me." Then she added, "And you should do it right away."

"Just give me a minute to load the dishwasher," he said, carrying their plates to the sink. "Then we'll get out of here."

Suddenly she couldn't wait to get this settled. After hedging all this time, she was so ready to get Nick moved permanently into her home—into her life—she didn't want to wait another minute.

She followed him to the sink and said, "Nick, look at me."

When he turned to face her, she curled her fingers into the front of his shirt, pulled him down to her level, and gave him a long, deep, wet kiss. One designed to let him know exactly how much she wanted him.

His strong arms circled her, pressing her closer. One big hand plunged through her hair to cup the back of her head while the other traveled downward to fit itself comfortably over her backside.

Zoë pressed her body against him, feeling as if she couldn't get close enough. As if she would *never* be close enough to him.

She knew in that second, without a doubt, she was in love with this man. She was going to marry him, and they were going to have a family. She suddenly understood the appeal of marriage and babies.

Because the babies she had would be Nick's. And it would be his arms she would wake in every morning.

Nick pulled away and flashed her a hungry grin. "Wow, what was that for?"

"It was just a sample of what you have to look forward to later."

He stroked the side of her throat with his thumb, his eyes dark with desire. "I can't wait."

"Me, neither. And the sooner we get to work, the sooner we get to come home."

After only a minimal amount of coercion on Nick's part, and a bit of hedging from O'Connell, he accepted Nick's offer and agreed to move in right away. When O'Connell thanked him, his eyes were filled with such deep gratitude and utter relief, it nearly choked Nick up.

No doubt the guy really loved his little girl. Nick couldn't imagine being in his shoes, the life of his child hanging in the balance. Living with the fear that he couldn't afford the medical treatment needed to save her. Especially after having lost his wife to cancer.

After O'Connell left to pack, Nick sat at his desk thinking about how precious life really was. He tried to imagine it without Zoë. The idea made him sick inside. She was indelibly etched into his life. He had a bond with her that he'd never felt with another woman. That he'd never felt with *anyone*.

"I guess things went well."

Nick looked up to see Zoë standing in his doorway, a big grin on her face. Damn she was pretty. She had that ethereal glow of good health that pregnant women were supposed to have.

She looked…happy.

"What makes you say that?" he asked.

"O'Connell just came up to me in the break room and gave me a bear of a hug and a big kiss." She laughed. "You should have seen the jaws drop. Everyone is going to think I'm cheating on you."

Nick's brow furrowed. "He kissed you?"

"Relax," she said, her grin widening. "It was only on my cheek. And he *smiled*, Nick. Up until that moment I didn't even know he had teeth!"

He didn't like the idea of anyone but him kissing her, but she looked so happy, he felt a grin of his own tugging at the corners of his mouth.

"We really helped him," she said.

He nodded. "We really did."

She crossed the room and slid into his lap, weaving her arms around his neck. "It feels good."

"It certainly does," he growled, tugging her more firmly against him.

She kissed him, drawing his lower lip between her teeth and nibbling. Damn did he love when she did that. She tasted like sweet tea and raspberry-filled donuts.

"Maybe we should lock the door and celebrate," she said, rubbing herself against him. Driving him crazy was more like it. And God it was tempting. After so many near misses, all he had to do lately was look at her and he was instantly hard. He really needed to get this woman into bed. But he wasn't interested in a quickie at the office, when he made love to Zoë, he planned to take his time.

Meaning it would have to wait. *Again*.

"No time," he told her. "We have to get over to my condo and pack up my things. I told him he could move in right away."

She gave him an adorable little pout, then sighed and said, "Well then, I guess we had better hurry. And I don't care if we don't get home until 2 a.m., we are getting naked tonight."

Sounded like a good plan to him.

It was after eight when they finally got Nick's things loaded in the back of his truck and headed home.

Home. The word had a totally different meaning to her now.

While helping him pack, Zoë made a startling and somewhat disturbing discovery. Nick had no pictures from his childhood, no family mementos. Nothing to indicate he even had a family. It was as if he had no past at all, or at least not one he had any desire to look back on.

She had boxes and boxes of photos and old birthday cards, pictures her younger siblings had drawn for her, and even a couple of their baby teeth. She had at least one or two items from each member of her family.

Only then did it truly sink in, did she realize what it must have been like for him growing up. How lonely he must have been, and why having a family was so important to him now.

He'd never truly experienced a *real* family and now she wanted to be the one who gave him that. She wanted to be the one who finally made him feel complete. She planned to spend the rest of her life making up for every lonely day, every isolated minute he had ever spent. Even if that meant having another baby. Or even a third.

Which, of course, would necessitate them getting a bigger house. She wondered if he would mind moving into a more rural setting. Maybe Romeo or Armada. They could have a huge yard for Tucker and the kids to play in. She could have an enormous flower garden, and maybe start growing vegetables. She could can pickles and jam, the way her grandmother used to. Maybe she could even take an extended leave from work and try the stay-at-home-mom thing for a while. Or at the very least work part time from home.

A world of opportunities she'd never even considered had opened up to her and she couldn't wait to see just where life would lead her.

"You're awfully quiet," Nick said, as he backed his truck into the driveway and parked beside her car. "Everything okay?"

She turned to him and smiled. "I'm just conserving my energy for other things."

He put the truck in park and killed the engine. "I want to say to hell with the unloading, but everything I own is sitting back there. I could probably just toss it all into the garage."

"The lock on the door is broken." It wasn't as if she lived in a bad neighborhood. Birmingham was considered upscale by most accounts, but there was no point taking chances. "If we move fast, we can get the boxes unloaded in no time. Consider it foreplay."

"You don't pick up anything heavier than a phone book," he said firmly and she rolled her eyes. He was such a guy.

They climbed out and he opened the tailgate while she unlocked the front door. She could hear Tucker inside, hopping around excitedly like an overgrown rabbit. They had stopped by home only a couple of hours ago to feed him and let him out, but he greeted her as if she'd been gone for days.

"I know, I know," she said, patting his head as she pushed her way through the door. "We missed you, too, you big oaf."

She grabbed Tucker's collar so he wouldn't bolt and held the door open for Nick. He brushed past her with two boxes marked Bedroom. He carried them down the hall and past the stairs.

"Where are you going with those?" she asked.

He turned to her, a puzzled look on his face. "To the bedroom."

"But our bedroom is upstairs."

A slow grin curled his mouth. "*Our* bedroom."

"Our bedroom," she repeated. And because she knew what was coming next, she added, "And yes, I'm sure."

Savoring the mildly stunned, incredibly happy expression on his face, she headed out the door to grab more boxes. If he thought he was happy now, he should just wait until she'd gotten her hands on him.

After she was through with him, a bulldozer couldn't pry the smile from his face.

"That's it," Nick said, closing and locking the front door.

They had hauled everything inside in under twenty minutes and the anticipation was killing her.

Now it was time to get to the good stuff.

"You know what that means," Zoë said, looking up at him from under lids that were already heavy with pent-up lust. Her legs and arms felt warm and weak and her head felt dizzy. She couldn't recall a time in her life when she'd been more turned on by the idea of making love to someone.

She took off her jacket and tossed it over the back of the couch. With a look to match her own, Nick did the same.

As she pulled her shirt up over her head, every inch of her skin buzzed with sexual awareness. The brush of lace from her bra teased her already sensitive nipples. The vee of skin between her thighs ached to be caressed. Even her hair felt alive and tingly.

Nick yanked his shirt over his head and dropped it on the floor. His skin looked deep golden tan in the dim lamplight. Her heart tapped out a wild beat as he walked toward her, unfastening his jeans. She couldn't wait to get her hands on him, touch and taste every inch. How could she have denied herself this? Why hadn't she realized how good it would be?

He stopped in front of her and she felt dizzy with

anticipation, every cell screaming to be touched. He lowered his head to kiss her and she rose up on her toes to meet him halfway. Their lips touched and she went hot all over, as if someone had replaced the blood in her veins with liquid fire.

He unfastened her jeans, shoving them down and she stopped kissing him just long enough to wiggle out of them and kick them into the dark corner beside the couch.

Her heart beat harder, in perfect time with the sudden loud pounding on the front door.

Nick groaned and pressed his forehead to hers, his breath coming hard and fast. "I don't *believe* this."

She didn't have a clue who it could be this time of night, but whatever they wanted couldn't possibly be as important as her getting into Nick's pants this very second.

"They'll go away." She slipped her hand inside his open fly and stroked the firm ridge of his erection through his boxers. He closed his eyes and groaned. He lifted her right off her feet and backed her against the wall separating the kitchen from the living room. She hooked her legs over his hips and gasped as the length of his erection rocked against her, her breasts crushed into his chest.

She kissed him and his mouth tasted hot and tangy. She felt as if she couldn't get enough, as though she could eat him alive and crawl all over him. She clawed at his jeans, shoving them and his boxers down, then cupped his bare behind, digging her nails into his flesh, feeling wild and sexy and completely out of control. No man had ever made her want to let go this way, to give so much of herself.

The pounding on the door persisted for a minute or two, then through a haze of arousal Zoë heard the jingle of keys, and the rattle of the doorknob being turned. Nick must have heard it too because he stopped kissing her and went stone still.

It happened so fast, neither had time to react. One minute they were alone, the next her sister was standing in the open doorway staring at them, mouth agape. Thank goodness there weren't many lights on, but there was no mistaking exactly what was happening.

For several seconds time stood still. No one moved or said a word. Faith looked down at Zoë's hands, still clutching Nick's behind. She said, "Nice ass," then burst into tears and walked back out the door.

Ten

"I'm so sorry," Faith hiccupped for the umpteenth time since Nick and Zoë had yanked their clothes on and tugged her back inside the house. Zoë sat on the couch by Faith. Nick stood across the room wearing a typical male slightly confused, mildly alarmed expression, looking as though any second he might bolt.

Faith was not the crying type, not even when she was a kid, which led Zoë to believe something really awful had happened. At first Faith had been crying too hard to string together a coherent sentence. They were only able to assess that she wasn't in need of medical attention and no one had died.

Faith sniffled and tugged another tissue from the box in her lap. "I can't believe I fell apart like that, and I really can't believe I walked in on you right in the middle of…well, you know."

"Stop apologizing," Zoë told her. "Tell us what happened."

Faith wiped away the mascara smudges under her eyes. "I am such an idiot."

Nick pushed off the wall where he'd been leaning. "Why don't I leave you two alone to talk."

Before Zoë or Faith could answer, he was on his way up the stairs.

"Wow," Faith said. "I sure scared him off."

Zoë shrugged. "What can I say, he's a guy. He's been getting more than his share of emotional stuff from me these days. I think he's suffering from an overload."

Faith sat there for a second, quietly toying with the tissue, then she looked up at Zoë and said, "I got dumped."

"Oh, Faith." Zoë rubbed her sister's shoulder.

As if Tucker could sense her unhappiness and wanted to help, he walked over to the couch and laid his head in Faith's lap, gazing up at her with what Zoë could swear was a look of sympathy.

Faith sniffled and scratched him behind the ears. "I told her I loved her, and I wanted us to move in together. I told her I was going to tell my parents the truth, no matter the consequences, and she told me I probably didn't want to do that. Then she said she decided to go back to her husband."

"I didn't know that she was married."

"Neither did I. Long story short, Mia said she had

just been experimenting, and basically trying to make her husband jealous. And I guess it worked. He wants her back." Faith sniffled and wiped away fresh tears. "She was so…*cold*. Like she never cared about me at all. Like I was some high school science experiment."

"Oh, sweetie, I'm so sorry. I know how much you cared about her."

"I feel so stupid. But I can't help thinking I deserved this."

That was just crazy. "How could you possibly deserve to be treated this way?"

"Do you know how many men I've dumped who claimed to 'love' me?"

"Honey, you deserve to be happy just as much as anyone else."

"Speaking of being happy," Faith said, brightening. "It looks like things with you and Nick are going pretty well, huh?"

Zoë felt guilty admitting how happy she was in light of her sister's heartache, but she couldn't contain her joy. "I'm going to tell him yes. I'm going to marry him."

"Oh my gosh!" Faith squealed excitedly and gave her a big hug. "I can't think of a more perfect man for you." She held Zoë at arm's length and grinned. "Not to mention that he has a mighty find rear end."

Zoë grinned. "No kidding."

"Speaking of that, I should go and let you guys get back to business. I can stay in a hotel."

"You're not staying in a hotel. The spare bedroom is free now. Stay as long as you like."

"I don't have to be to work until Monday, so maybe I will hide out here for a couple of days, if you don't mind."

"We would love to have you," Zoë said, rising from the couch, anxious to get upstairs and finish what she and Nick had started. "Maybe we can go shopping tomorrow. Spending money always helps me chase away a bad mood."

"Just so you know, I'll be sleeping with these on." She held up a pair of headphones and an MP3 player, and grinned mischievously. "So be as loud as you like. I won't hear a thing."

When Zoë finally made it upstairs, Tucker on her heel, Nick was sitting in bed, bare-chested and gorgeous, reading a hardcover novel.

"Everything all right?" he asked.

"She got dumped."

"That's kind of what I figured." He closed the book and set it on the nightstand. "Is she okay?"

"Bruised but not broken." She peeled her shirt off and tossed it in the general direction of the hamper, missing her target by several feet. "I hope you don't mind, but she's going to stick around for a couple days. I don't think she wants to be alone."

"Of course I don't mind. But I guess that nixes tonight's scheduled activities, huh?"

She peeled off her jeans and dropped them

where she stood. "I don't care if the house burns down, nothing is going to stop me from getting you naked tonight."

"That's convenient." He flashed her a sexy, dimpled grin, and tossed back the covers. "Because I'm already naked."

Holy moly! Naked and *very* aroused. She raised a brow at him. "Did you start without me?"

"It won't go away. I need you to put me out of my misery."

"It would be my pleasure." She walked around to his side of the bed, dropping her bra and panties along the way. The way his eyes raked over her—she felt as if she were the sexiest, most desirable woman on the planet.

He patted his thighs. "Come'ere."

She climbed in his lap, straddling him. His crisp leg hair tickled her skin as she lowered herself onto his thighs. His body felt warm and solid as he looped an arm around her waist and drew her closer.

"Here we are," he said, tucking her hair back behind her ears.

Finally. "Just you and me."

He stroked her cheek, his eyes searching her face. "I want you to know that there is no one else on earth that I would rather be with right now. That I would *ever* want to be with."

His words warmed her from the inside out. There was no one she would rather be with, either. "Me, too."

She still wanted him, couldn't wait to feel him

inside her again, but that sense of urgency was gone. Now she wanted to take her time, savor every minute. He must have felt the same way, because for the longest time they only played with each other, kissing and stroking and tasting. Exploring each other as if it was the first time, yet she felt as if they had learned each other a hundred years ago.

How could something be exciting and new, yet this comfortable and familiar?

"I love the way this feels," he said, using his thumbs to gently caress the smooth skin at the junction of her thighs. He watched his movements, as if he found the sight of it fascinating. His featherlight strokes made her hot and cold at the same time and her head started getting that dizzy, detached feeling.

She rose up on her knees to give him a better look, gripping the headboard on either side of him and he groaned his appreciation.

He leaned forward, his hair brushing against her stomach and touched her with his tongue. Just one quick flick, but his mouth was so hot, the sensation so shockingly intense, she gasped with surprise and jerked away.

He looked up, a grin on his face, and said, "Delicious."

She might have been embarrassed, but she was too turned on. He cupped her behind in his big, warm hands and pulled her back to his mouth, lapping and tasting while she balanced precariously between torture and bliss. Every slow, deep stroke of his tongue took her higher, until she could hardly stand it. She wanted to grab his head and push him deeper.

She wanted more, and at the same time she was on total sensory overload.

She was aware of the sound of her own voice, but the words were jumbled and incoherent. The wet heat of his tongue, the rasp of his beard stubble on her bare skin—it was too much.

The pleasure started somewhere deep inside, in her soul maybe, and radiated outward. It gripped her with such momentum, time seemed to grind to an abrupt halt. Every muscle in her body clenched tight and her eyes clamped shut. Her hands tangled in his hair, trapping him close as she rode the waves of pleasure. Her body shook and quaked for what felt like forever.

Her heart throbbed in time with the steady pulse between her thighs. She didn't know if it was Nick's incredible skills or the pregnancy hormones, or maybe even a combination of both, but she had never come so hard in her entire life.

She sank down into his lap and rested her forehead against his shoulder, wanting to tell him how out-of-this-world, amazingly and unbelievably sensational he'd just made her feel, how she was pretty sure she'd just had her first out-of-body experience, but she was barely able to breathe much less use her mouth to form words.

So instead, she kissed him, tasting herself on his

lips and finding it unbelievably erotic. She reached down between them and wrapped her fingers around the impressive girth of his erection. He groaned low in his chest and kissed her harder.

She stroked him slowly, felt him pulse in her hand. He was hot to the touch and velvet smooth. She wanted to take him into her mouth, but when she made a move to bend forward he caught her head in his hands, tangling his fingers through her hair. "Don't."

"I want to."

"I want to make love to you."

"Can't we do both."

He shook his head. "I'm so hot for you right now, it's going to have to be one or the other, and I need to be inside of you."

Well, if he put it that way. Besides, what was the rush? They had the rest of their lives to try anything they wanted. And though she had never been particularly creative or adventurous in bed, she wanted to try it all with Nick.

"You know the best thing about pregnant sex?" he asked wrapping his hands around her hips.

"Huh?"

He fed her a mischievous grin. "No need for a condom."

Nick guided her and she lowered herself on top of him. He sank inside her slow and smooth and oh so deep.

He hissed out a breath, his grip on her tightening. For a moment they sat that way, not moving, barely even breathing. It was almost scary what a perfect fit they were, how connected she felt to him. There was no doubt in her mind that Nick was the man she was supposed to spend the rest of her life with. She wanted to have babies with him and grow old with him.

And she wanted him to know exactly how she was feeling. "Nick, I love you."

He smiled, caught her face between his hands and kissed her, tender and sweet. And she couldn't stop her body from moving, from rising and sinking in a slow, steady rhythm. She watched with fascination as a look of pure ecstasy washed over his face. He let her set the pace, let her do most of the work while he kissed and touched her and whispered sexy, exciting things to her. She found herself answering him, using words she never would have expected to come out of a good Catholic girl's mouth. Dirty things he seemed to love hearing.

He reached between them, caressing the sensitive bud he had so skillfully manipulated with his tongue, and the reaction was instantaneous. Pleasure slammed her from all sides, hard, deep and intense. Forget an out-of-body experience. She wasn't even on the same planet. Only when she heard Nick groan her name, when his body rocked up to meet hers, did she realize she'd taken him along for the ride.

They sat there for several minutes afterward, catching their breath. She kept telling herself she should move, but he was still hard and he felt so good inside her. She waited, watching the minutes tick by on the alarm clock, two, then three, then five, but it still didn't go away. In fact, instead of getting soft, she was pretty sure he was getting harder.

Just for fun, she wiggled her hips and he answered her with a rumble of pleasure.

"You weren't kidding about it not going away." She sat up and smiled. "I'm impressed."

"You know what that means," he said, returning her smile. "We'll just have to do it again."

"Do you remember when we first met?" Nick asked. Zoë lay in his arms her head resting against his chest. She smelled so warm and sweet and girly. It was getting late, and they both had to get up and go to work, but his mind was moving a million miles an hour.

"Of course. I came for an interview, and did a pretty fair job of lying through my teeth."

He played with her hair, looping a curl around his index finger then letting it spring free. There were so many places on her body to play with, so many things to touch. He was pretty sure that tonight he'd managed to play with or touch just about every single one. As far as sex went, Zoë didn't seem to have a single reservation or hang-up. He could do or try pretty much anything and she was always ready for more. Things so forbidden and intimate he'd never had the guts to try them so early in a relationship. Of course, they'd had ten years to develop a deep sense of trust.

It had just taken them a while to get to the good stuff.

"I knew an eighteen-year-old couldn't possibly

have the experience you listed on your application, but you looked so young and vulnerable. I couldn't turn you away."

She looked up at him. "Are you saying you took pity on me?"

He grinned. "Pretty much, yeah."

She propped her chin on his chest. "As much as I wanted to get away from my family, those first few months were hard. I never anticipated how lonely I would be. You were incredibly patient with me considering how bad I stunk as a secretary."

He chuckled. "But you tried so hard, I didn't have the heart to fire you. I knew deep down that you were special. And you were cute."

"I never told you this, but I had a major crush on you for the first year."

"I could kind of tell."

She looked surprised. "Really?"

"Yeah, and I was tempted, believe me. But at the time I wasn't looking for a relationship, and I didn't want to risk killing our friendship with a one-night stand. I liked you too much."

"Want to hear something weird. Almost every boyfriend I've had over the years has felt threatened by my relationship with you."

"Want to hear something even weirder? I've had the same problem with *every* one of my girlfriends. It was as if they couldn't believe a guy like me could have a woman as a good friend."

"Maybe they were seeing something we didn't."

"Maybe." He stroked the wispy curls back from her face. "I never told you what Lynn said right before our wedding, the real reason she decked me."

"What did she say?"

"As we were getting out of the car in the court-house parking lot, she told me that she would only marry me if I fired you."

Zoë's eyes widened. "You're kidding!"

"She didn't want me seeing you anymore, either. I had to break all ties with you."

"That's crazy. What did you say?"

"At first I thought she was joking, and when I realized she was serious, I was too stunned to say anything. It's not as if I wasn't already having major doubts, but up until that moment I had really planned to go through with it."

"Yet, you waited until the last minute to dump her."

"She was so…manipulative. I guess I wanted to punish her, or knock her down a few pegs at least. You should have seen the smug look on her face when we were standing there. When I backed out, I was more or less saying that I was choosing you over her."

"That had to sting." She sounded sympathetic, but he could tell she was getting a lot of satisfaction from this. She liked hearing that he'd picked her over the woman he'd asked to marry him.

"I'm ashamed to admit it, but I actually enjoyed dumping her."

"That makes two of us, because I enjoyed it, too."

"Now I'm exactly where I'm supposed to be." He

spread his hand over her flat belly, where their child was growing. "Here with you and the baby."

Zoë sighed and rested her head on Nick's chest, cupping her hand over his. So was she, exactly where she belonged. And she wanted to tell him so, right now. But after making him wait for an answer to his marriage proposal, somehow just saying yes didn't seem good enough.

Nick," she said, stroking the tops of his fingers.

"Huh?"

"Would you marry me?"

He was silent, so she looked up and saw that he was grinning. A great big dimpled grin full of love and affection. He had gotten the message loud and clear. He leaned forward, caught her face in his hands and kissed her. *"Absolutely."*

A part of her sighed with relief. Not that she thought he was going to say no. Maybe it was because things were finally settled, it felt as though her life was back on track.

Yet there was something else. A niggling in the back of her mind. A tiny seed of doubt. "I think we should do it soon," She said, feeling a sudden urgency to get this settled. To get on with their life together. Like maybe deep down she thought he might change her mind. "You know, because of the baby."

"How soon?"

"How does next Friday work for you?"

His smile got even bigger. "Friday would be perfect."

"Something really small, like the justice of the peace?"

"Whatever you want."

She settled into his arms and snuggled against him, knowing deep down to her soul that she was doing the right thing, and hoping he felt the same way.

He was quiet for several minutes then asked, "Can I tell you a secret?"

"You can tell me anything."

"I've never once told anyone I love them."

She propped herself up on her elbow to look at him. His eyes were so…*sad*. "How is that possible? You were engaged two times."

"Weird huh?"

"You didn't love them?" A part of her wanted him to say he hadn't. The selfish part that wanted him to love only her.

"I don't know. Maybe I did in my own way. Maybe I'm not physically capable."

Maybe growing up the way he had, had damaged him somehow. How terribly sad that a person could go through their entire life never feeling real love.

"I'm a different person with you, Zoë. We're going to be a family."

She let her head drop back down, breathed in the scent of him, felt his heart thump against her ear.

A family. Her and Nick.

Did that mean he loved her? And if he did, why didn't he say the words? Was he really not capable? Or was admitting that to her just the first step? And if it had been, at least it was a step in the right direction.

He was quiet for a while, then his breathing became slow and steady and she knew he had fallen asleep.

He did love her. And it wasn't just wishful thinking. She knew it in her heart. She sensed it when he looked at her, could feel it when he touched her. When he was ready, he would tell her.

She would just have to be patient.

Eleven

Zoë felt like death warmed over the next morning at seven when Nick nudged her awake. She managed to pry one eye open far enough to see that he was already showered and dressed and far too awake considering how late they had fallen asleep. And it must have been pretty obvious that she was in no shape to go to work, because he just kissed her, tucked the covers up over her shoulders and said he would see her later.

She fell back to sleep and had strange, disturbing dreams. She dreamed it was her wedding day, and she was walking down the aisle, her arm looped in her father's. Instead of a white gown, she wore the dress she'd worn to both of Nick's weddings, complete with broken straps and stains, and it had been dyed crimson—the same shade as her sister's car.

Not that anyone seemed to think that was out of the ordinary. Row upon row of people dressed in white sat on either side smiling and nodding. Bunches of blood-red roses decorated the aisle, giving everyone a pale, ethereal look.

Her mind kept telling her that everything was normal, but something didn't feel right.

She could see Nick waiting for her by the altar, wearing the same suit he'd worn at his last wedding. He was smiling, but it looked unnatural and plastic, as if he was being forced to stand there against his will. She kept walking toward him, telling herself everything was going to be okay, but instead of getting closer, the longer she walked, the farther away he was getting. The cloying scent of roses crowded the air. But instead of smelling like flowers, it smelled metallic, like blood. It burned her nose and made her stomach ache.

Something definitely wasn't right.

She started walking faster, trying desperately to reach him, but Nick was fading from her vision. Disappearing. She called out to him, but he didn't seem to hear her.

She broke into a run but her legs felt heavy and weak and cramps knotted her insides, doubling her over. The fog grew thicker, closing in around her like wet paper. She clawed her way through it, felt it filling her lungs, constricting her air. She couldn't see, couldn't breathe, could hear nothing but the frantic pounding of her heart.

She called for him again but it was no use. Nick and her father, the smiling people, they were all gone. She was all alone with the sick feeling that she'd just become number three. Nick had left her at the altar, just like the others.

She felt a firm hand on her shoulder and someone called her name.

Zoë shot up in bed, disoriented and out of breath.

"Hey, you okay?" Faith stood beside the bed, a look of concern on her face.

"Bad dream." Her voice sounded weak and scratchy.

"You called for Nick. He already left for work." She touched Zoë's forehead. "You're all sweaty."

Faith was right. The sheet was clinging to her damp skin and her hair felt wet. She felt hot and cold at the same time and everything was fuzzy and surreal.

Zoë blinked several times and fought to pull herself awake, but couldn't shake the sensation of being caught somewhere between sleep and consciousness. It took a minute to realize that the cramps in her stomach hadn't faded with the dream.

It wasn't real, she told herself. She was fine. But the pain was very real and too intense.

Fear skittered across her spine, and her heart gave a violent jolt in her chest.

Faith looked downright scared now. "Zoë, what's wrong? You're white as a sheet."

Everything was fine. The baby was fine, she assured herself, but the tips of her fingers had begun to go numb with fear. She felt as if she couldn't pull in a full breath.

That was when Zoë felt it. The warm gush between her legs.

No, this was not happening.

She and Nick were going to get married. They were going to have a baby together.

"Zoë?" Faith's hand was on her shoulder again and there was real fear in her voice. "Talk to me."

The pain intensified, cramps gripped deeper.

No, no, no, this couldn't be happening. She had to find a way to stop it. She had to *do* something.

She looked up at her sister, tears welling in her eyes. "I think I'm losing the baby."

Nick stood impatiently waiting for the hospital elevator to reach the third floor. He didn't have a clue what was going on, only a message from Faith telling him to get to Royal Oak Beaumont Hospital.

He'd been out of the office all morning, and because he had forgotten to charge it last night, his cell phone was dead. He was unaware of any problem until twenty minutes ago when Shannon accosted him on his way to his office.

He'd tried both Faith's and Zoë's cell phones before he left but neither was answering.

There had to be some rational explanation, he kept telling himself. Nothing was wrong. He was sure that she was fine.

And still a knot of fear had lodged itself in his gut. What if she wasn't fine? What would he do then?

The elevator dinged and the doors slid open. He

crossed the hall to the nurses' station and gave the nurse, an older woman with a fatigued face, Zoë's name.

"Room thirteen-forty," she said in a voice that mirrored her tired expression. She motioned with a jerk of her thumb. "That way, around the corner."

He started down the hall, his heart beating faster and harder with every step.

She was fine. Everything would be okay.

He rounded the corner and saw Faith standing outside one of the rooms. When she turned and saw him coming, he could see by the expression on her face that everything was *not* okay.

His heart took a sudden dive and landed with a plop in the pit of his stomach.

"What happened," he demanded. "Is Zoë okay?"

"She's fine," Faith said. "They're going to keep her overnight just to be safe."

Relief hit his so hard and swift his knees nearly buckled. He braced a hand against the door frame to steady himself. He hadn't realized until just then how scared he'd been. He didn't know what he would have done if she'd been hurt or sick.

So why was she here?

Then it hit him. He'd been so worried about Zoë, he'd completely forgotten about the pregnancy.

"The baby?" he asked.

Faith paused and bit her lip, looking exactly like Zoë did when something was wrong.

Damn it.

They had lost the baby.

What was this going to do to Zoë? Lately she had really warmed to the idea of becoming a mother. He knew this was going to be tough for her to handle. She would feel so guilty. And what if it had something to do with last night? He would never forgive himself if this was his fault.

Right now, he just needed to see for himself that Zoë was okay. "Can I go in?"

"Of course. She's been waiting for you."

Taking a deep breath, he walked past Faith into the room. Zoë sat in the bed wearing a hospital gown looking so small and vulnerable. So alone and numb.

"Hey," he said, walking over to the bed. As he got closer, he could see that she was holding back tears, fighting to keep it together.

It was just like her to think she had to be strong for everyone else.

She looked up at him, her eyes so full of hurt. "We lost the baby."

He had known, but hearing the words felt like a stab in his gut.

"She told me. I'm so sorry I didn't get here sooner." He sat on the edge of the bed and she sat stiffly beside him. She was so tense, one good poke would probably snap her in half. Did she think he was going to make her go through this alone?

"I'm so sorry," she whispered, her voice trembling.

"Zoë, it's okay. It's not your fault." He put an arm around her and nudged her toward him, and everything in her seemed to let go. A soft sob racked through her and she dissolved into his arms. She cried quietly for several minutes and he just held her. He had no idea what to say, what to do. He didn't even know what had happened.

"I-I thought you might be mad," she finally said, her voice quiet and miserable.

He grabbed a tissue and handed it to her. "Why would I be mad?"

She shrugged and wiped away the tears. "I know how much you wanted this."

"But your being okay means a lot more to me."

"It's so weird. I was so freaked out about being pregnant, now I feel so…empty. I really wanted this baby, Nick."

"I know you did." He stroked back a stray curl that clung to her damp cheek. He didn't even want to know, but he had to ask. "Do they know what caused it? I mean, last night…"

"It wasn't that. They did an ultrasound and I could tell by the look on her face that the technician saw something wrong, but she wouldn't say what. She said the doctor would be in soon to see me. That was like an hour ago."

"I'm so sorry I wasn't here for you." Nick rubbed her back soothingly. Sometimes he forgot how petite she was. How vulnerable. His first instinct was to protect her. To say anything to make her hurt less. "I'm sure everything is fine."

"What if it isn't?" she said, sounding genuinely frightened. "What if something is really wrong? I thought I never wanted kids, but the idea of never being able to—" Her voice hitched.

"There's no point in worrying until we know what's going on."

But that got Nick thinking, what if she couldn't have kids? What if they could *never* have a child together? After all these years of longing for a family, waiting for just the right time, could he marry a woman who was infertile?

The answer surprised him.

The truth was, it didn't make a damned bit of difference, if the woman he was marrying was Zoë. Maybe at first his desire to marry her was partially due to the pregnancy, but not any longer. He wanted her.

Baby or no baby.

Before he could tell her that, Doctor Gordon walked in, Faith on his heels. Zoë wrapped her hand around his and squeezed. He could feel her trembling.

"First, I just went over the results of the ultrasound. I want to assure you that neither of you is in any way at fault. There is a thin membrane that has separated Zoë's uterus into two sections. This constricted the baby's growth, causing the miscarriage."

He went on to explain that she was actually lucky that the egg had implanted itself on the smaller side. Had it been on the other side it's quite possible she could have progressed well into the fourth or even fifth month before miscarrying, which would have been a much more devastating loss.

Nick found it tough to think of losing a baby as a good thing, but what the doctor said made sense.

Zoë didn't say anything, just kept a death grip on his hand, so Nick asked what he knew she was probably afraid to. "Is this something you can fix?"

"I can perform a simple outpatient procedure to remove the membrane," he said. "With no complications, recovery time is usually only a week or two."

"And then she'll be okay? She'll be able to get pregnant?" He wanted to know more for Zoë's sake than his own. He didn't want any question in her mind.

"Did you have any difficulty conceiving?"

"Nope," Zoë and Nick said in unison and the doctor cracked a smile. Getting pregnant had been the easy part.

"Then I see no reason why, with the surgery, she wouldn't be able to conceive and carry a baby to term." He flashed Zoë a reassuring smile. "I think you're going to be just fine."

The grip on Nick's hand eased. He could almost feel the relief pouring through her. He knew how doctors worked. In this litigious society they didn't give false hope. Zoë would be okay. They would get past this. She would have the surgery and they could try again.

"I'd like to see you in the office in two weeks," Doctor Gordon told Zoë. "If everything looks good we can schedule the procedure."

Zoë and Nick each asked a few more questions, then thanked him. When he was gone, Faith walked around the bed and gave Zoë a big hug and a kiss on the cheek. "I'm glad everything is okay."

"Thanks," Zoë said, and some unspoken understanding seemed to pass between them.

She had no idea how lucky she was to have that kind of bond with someone. To have family. Now he would know, too. When they got married, her family would be his.

"I'm going to run down to the cafeteria and give you guys some time alone," Faith told them. "I'll see you in a bit."

After she left, Zoë said, "So, I guess you're off the hook, huh?"

She couldn't possibly mean what he thought she meant. Nick took her hand and held it. "Which hook would that be?"

"There's no baby. You don't have to marry me now."

"I'm going to pretend you didn't say that."

"What if I can't have another baby, Nick?"

"That's too bad, sweetheart. You're stuck with me." A tear rolled down her cheek and he brushed it away with his thumb. "You heard what the doctor said. There's no reason to worry about that now. You'll have the surgery and everything will be fine."

She nodded, but didn't look completely convinced.

"There is something missing, though," he said.

She frowned. "Missing?"

"We still have to make it official." Enjoying her puzzled look, he reached into his jacket pocket and pulled out the small velvet box. He lifted the lid and watched her jaw drop when she saw the two carat marquee cut platinum diamond engagement ring that had taken him three hours at six different jewelers to choose.

"Oh my God," she breathed, looking genuinely stunned. "You got me a ring?"

"Yeah, and it took me all morning to find the perfect one." He took the ring from its satin bed. She held her breath as he slipped it on the ring finger of her right hand. It was a perfect fit. Feminine but not too flashy.

She held up her hand and the stone shimmered in the fluorescent lights. "How did you know what size?"

"I borrowed a ring from your jewelry box before I left this morning. Do you like it?"

"It's exactly what I would have chosen." Tears welled in her eyes. Happy ones, he hoped. Then she looked up at him with a watery smile. "It's perfect, Nick."

"So now it's official. And since there's no rush, we can wait and plan something nice if you want. Something bigger. I hear most women spend their lives planning their wedding day."

She shook her head. "Not me. I don't need a big wedding. And I don't want to wait. I want to do it next Friday, like we planned."

"Are you sure you'll be feeling up to it? You've been through a lot today—"

"I feel better already knowing everything is going to okay. I want to try again as soon as the doctor says it's safe. I want us to have a baby."

He squeezed her hand. "Whatever you want."

"And I want more than one. At least two, maybe even three."

Wow. When she changed her mind, she really did a complete one-eighty. "We'll never fit a family of five into your house or my condo. I'll have to build us something bigger."

"With a yard big enough for Tucker and the kids to play in? And a huge garden?"

"Whatever you want."

"That's what I want," she said, wrapping her arms around him and hugging him tight. "That's exactly what I want."

She looked happy, and sounded happy, so why did Nick get the feeling something wasn't right?

Twelve

Zoë took the rest of the week off and though Nick thought she needed more time, she was tired of sitting around feeling sorry for herself and went back to work Monday morning.

It had been the right thing to do. Four days later she felt as though she had begun to heal both physically and mentally. She felt ready to move on.

She kept reminding herself what the doctor said, how much worse it would have been if she'd been four or five months along. The baby would have been almost fully developed. A little person. They would have known if it was a boy or a girl.

And they would have spent the days following

the miscarriage not recovering, but
funeral. The idea gave her a cold chill.

So really, losing the baby so early, when it
a speck of life she hadn't even felt move, w
blessing in disguise.

As badly as Nick wanted children, she had
expected him to be really upset, but he had seemed
more concerned about her health than the fact that
they had lost a child. Not that he hadn't made it clear
he was concerned about future fertility issues, and he
seemed so relieved when the doctor said the surgery
would probably fix the problem.

She couldn't help wondering, what if it didn't?
Nick hadn't even been willing to discuss it. What if
something went wrong and she could never have
kids? How would Nick feel about marrying her then?

Of course, by then they would already be married.

Maybe that was why he'd suggested putting the
wedding off for a while. Maybe he wanted to be sure
she was okay before he tied himself down to her.
Maybe he didn't want to marry a woman who
couldn't give him children.

She closed her eyes and shook her head.

That was ridiculous. He'd gotten her a beautiful ring
and he'd been unbelievably sweet the past few days.

At the hospital, all she had wanted was to come
home, but when she got home, it felt as though everything had changed. Getting back to her regular
routine had been so difficult. He had stayed beside
her the entire first day after it happened. He'd brought

her tea and held her when she cried, which was almost constantly.

Why would he do any of that if he didn't want to marry her? If he didn't love her?

And if he did love her, why didn't he say it?

"Hey Zoë, how ya feeling?"

Zoë looked up to find Shannon standing in her office doorway. Again. It was her third time today checking up on Zoë and it was barely three o'clock. She'd been doing this all week, watching over Zoë like a mother hen. "You can stop hovering. I'm fine."

She flashed Zoë a squinty-eyed assessing look. After a few seconds, her face softened, as if she was satisfied that Zoë was being honest. "You know where I am if you need me," she said, then disappeared down the hall.

Word of what happened had traveled through the entire office in record time. She'd received several flower arrangements and sympathy cards over the weekend. They had been addressed to both her and Nick, so that cat was definitely out of the bag. Not that she cared. Everyone would have found out soon enough. They also knew that she and Nick were getting married.

Several men in his crew had wanted to throw him a bachelor party tonight, but he said that in light of what they had just been through, he didn't think it was appropriate. Zoë had said the same thing when the girls in the office had approached her about a trip across the Ambassador Bridge to the male strip club in Windsor.

She just wanted to get this wedding over and done with. Every day she waited she was more anxious, more worried that she would make it all the way to the altar only to have him say he couldn't go through with it.

Or what if he didn't show up at all? They were taking the traditional route and spending the night before their wedding apart. Nick's idea. She was staying home and he was bunking with O'Connell in his condo. Maybe she should have insisted they drive together, so she could at least be sure he would make an appearance.

She nearly groaned out loud.

This was ridiculous. She was being silly and paranoid. Of course he was going to show up. Not only was he going to show up, but he was going to marry her. Even if he hadn't actually said that he loved her.

In less than twenty-four hours she would be Mrs. Nick Bateman. Someone's *wife*. A month ago that fact would have given her hives, but for some reason the idea of getting married didn't seem all that weird to her anymore. She'd changed over the past few weeks. Being with Nick had made her realize that sharing her life with someone didn't mean sacrificing her freedom. It didn't mean compromising herself as a person.

She didn't even mind having his big dumb dog around. In fact, they felt a lot like a family. And someday their little family would grow to include children. A little boy with Nick's dimples and hazel eyes, or maybe a little girl with Zoë's curly hair and stubborn streak.

The possibilities were endless.

Tiffany from accounting barged into her office without knocking—the way she always did—and dropped an invoice on Zoë's desk.

"I need this approved," she snapped.

Nice, Zoë thought. It was common knowledge that Tiffany had been after Nick for the better part of her first six months working here. According to Shannon, Tiffany had been convinced she was next in line after the Lynn relationship had tanked, but Nick had completely blown off her very obvious advances. When she reduced herself to bluntly asking him out, he'd told her very politely—because that was his way—to give it a rest.

She was young, big-breasted and beautiful, and probably not used to men telling her no. Since she had caught Zoë and Nick playing tonsil hockey in the office that day, her panties had been in a serious twist and Zoë had been on the receiving end of a whole lotta attitude.

What Tiffany didn't seem to realize is that Zoë had the authority to fire her jealous little behind—and probably would have if the girl wasn't such a hard worker.

"I'll get this back to you by Monday," Zoë said, hoping Tiffany would take the hint and leave.

She didn't.

"So, tomorrow's the big day, huh?"

"Yup," Zoë replied, pretending to be engrossed by the open file on her computer screen. If you ignored a pest, it was supposed to go away, right?

"Considering Nick's reputation, aren't you nervous?"

Just ignore her, she told herself. She's only trying to get a rise out of you. She looked up, forcing what she hoped passed for a patient smile, but probably looked more like a grimace. "Tiffany, I'm a little busy here."

Tiffany went on as if Zoë hadn't already, in a round about way, told her to get lost. "I'm just worried about you. I'm sure you're feeling vulnerable right now."

Oh please! Now she was going to pretend to be concerned for Zoë's welfare? What an absolute crock.

"I appreciate your concern." *Not*. "But I feel a little uncomfortable discussing personal matters with you."

"You have to be at least a little worried," she persisted. "I mean, before he had a reason to marry you. And now, well…" She trailed off and let the statement hang in the air for Zoë to absorb.

And it did. Zoë had to struggle against the urge to vault over the desk and claw Tiffany's eyes out.

What Tiffany was really saying, was that Zoë was no longer pregnant, so Nick would have no reason to marry her. She couldn't deny the trickle of icy fear that slid through her veins. Because nothing Tiffany said was untrue. Bitchy and rude, yes, but not necessarily inconceivable.

"It would be bad enough being left at the altar, but what if he didn't even show up?"

Zoë's fists clenched tightly in her lap. *Don't kill her. Don't kill her,* she chanted to herself. But oh how good it would feel to blacken one of her pretty blue eyes. Or hell, maybe both of them. Tiffany may have been eight years younger and a head taller, but Zoë was pretty sure she could take her.

"Shut up, Tiffany," Shannon snapped from the doorway, appearing like an angel of mercy. "You're just jealous because you asked Nick out and he turned you down flat."

Tiffany's cheeks blushed a bright crimson and she shot Shannon a nasty look. "My money is on Nick dumping her. I guess we'll just see, won't we?"

She stomped from the room and Shannon mumbled, "What a bitch."

Zoë leaned back in her seat and exhaled deeply. "If you hadn't come in just now, I could see a possible assault charge in my very near future."

"Don't listen to her, Zoë. She has no idea what she's talking about."

"What did she mean by her money?" Zoë asked, even though she already had a pretty good idea.

"Just ignore her."

"What did she mean, Shannon?"

Shannon bit her lip, looking very uncomfortable. "I wasn't going to tell you…"

"It's another pool, isn't it?" Just what she needed, the employees betting on her getting her heart sliced and diced.

Shannon nodded, and Zoë's heart plummeted. She felt like going home, crawling into bed, covering her head and staying there forever.

"What are they betting on exactly this time?" she asked, trying to keep her voice light. Pretending that she didn't feel hurt and betrayed by people she considered her friends.

"They're betting on whether or not Nick will marry you, dump you at the altar, or not show up at all."

Zoë felt physically ill. Her voice shook when she asked, "Where did you put your money? Do you think he's going to dump me?"

"I didn't bet on this one, but if I had, I would have put my money on Nick marrying you. No question. In my life I've never known two people more perfect for each other."

"You don't think he was marrying me because of the baby?"

"As far as I'm concerned, the pregnancy just sped things up a bit. I don't doubt that he wants kids, and maybe that had been a motivating factor before when he asked those other women to marry him, but this is different. I know it is."

Zoë wanted to believe that, but she had to admit, she had doubts. Maybe if he would just tell her he loved her.

If by some miracle he didn't leave her at the altar, if they actually got married, did she want to spend her life with a man who just liked her a lot? Didn't she deserve better than that?

"It's all going to work out," Shannon assured her.

She used to think so, now she wasn't so sure. The question was, what did she plan to do about it?

"Are you sure you don't want me to be there?" Faith asked for the billionth time. "I could hop in the car and if I do ninety all the way I can be there just in time for the wedding."

Three hours, Zoë thought. She was marrying Nick in three hours. It seemed so unreal.

She'd slept in fits and bursts last night and crawled out of bed before the crack of dawn. She was too nervous to eat. Too distracted to do much more than sit at the kitchen table sipping her tea and skimming the newspaper.

According to the *Oakland Press,* the temperature would reach the midsixties with sunny skies all day. She couldn't ask for better weather.

It was her wedding day for heaven's sake! She should be happy. So why couldn't she work up a bit of enthusiasm? She hadn't even managed to drag herself into the shower yet and the dress she and Shannon had spent all day Wednesday shopping for still hung wrapped in plastic in the backseat of her car.

"Zoë?" Faith asked.

"I'm not even sure if I'm going," she admitted.

"Don't even talk like that. I've never seen you so happy. I know you've been through a lot in the past week. Maybe Nick is right, maybe you should wait a while and plan a real wedding. One your family and friends can attend."

And risk being dumped at the altar in front of the entire Simmons clan? Don't think so.

"I've just got prewedding jitters," she told her sister, so she wouldn't actually jump in the car and come down. "Everything will be great."

"Nick loves you."

"I know he does."

But therein lay the problem. She really *didn't* know. Nick hadn't said so, and she'd been too much of a chicken to come right out and ask him.

What if he said no?

Sorry, Zoë, I'm not capable of love, but I sure do like you a lot.

"I have to let you go so I can get ready," Zoë said.

"You're sure you're okay?"

"I'm fine." Lie, lie lie. She was *so* not fine.

"You'll call me later and let me know how it went?"

"I promise."

She hung up the phone and sighed, still not ready to drag herself to the bathroom for a shower. Instead she made herself another cup of tea and sat back down at the table.

Two hours later she was still sitting there, and only then did it sink in that she couldn't do it. She couldn't marry him.

The question now was, what would she tell Nick?

Thirteen

Nick stood in the lobby of the courthouse, alternating between watching the door, checking the time on his watch and pulling his phone from his pocket to make sure it was still on. His starched shirt was stiff and uncomfortable under his suit coat and his new tie was beginning to feel like a noose around his neck.

He'd tried Zoë's house phone and cell but she hadn't answered. He'd even called Faith, then spoke to Shannon in the office, but no one had heard from her for hours.

A smart man, a *realistic* man, would have left a long time ago. Right after he realized his fiancée was, in fact, not going to show up for their wedding.

He should have been at least a little angry at Zoë

for leaving him high and dry, but the truth was, he had it coming.

He deserved this.

In fact, he was glad she'd done it. It was the push he'd needed to realize just how much of an ass he'd been.

What reason had he given Zoë for believing he would marry her? Hell, as far as she knew, he might not have even shown up. Sure he'd said he wanted to marry her, but he'd fed the same line to two other women.

What he had failed to do was prove to Zoë that she was different. That she was the *one*.

He loved her, and he should have told her so.

And it's not as if he hadn't had chances. That night when they had made love and she had told him she loved him, he could have said he loved her, too. And later, when he'd admitted to her that he'd never said the words. He could have told her then.

He could have said it in the hospital, or any time the entire next day they had spent side-by-side, mourning their loss. So many times the words had been balanced on the tip of his tongue, ready to be spoken, but something always stopped him. He had always held back.

Maybe that was simply what he had taught himself to do. His mother had been the only one who loved him and she'd left. By no fault of her own, but that hadn't made it hurt any less.

His aunt and uncle might have loved him, but if they had, they never said so. As he grew up, it was just easier not letting anyone get too close. Not letting himself fall in love.

Talk about a cliché. But clichés were born for a reason, weren't they? Maybe deep down he was still that little boy who was afraid to get his heart broken again.

But it was too late, he was in love with Zoë. The only thing he'd accomplished by keeping that to himself was hurting her.

"I love her," he said to himself, surprised to find that it wasn't that hard to say at all. In fact, he liked the sound of it, the feel of the words forming in his mouth.

It felt…natural.

He pushed off the wall and headed for the stairs, knowing exactly what he needed to do.

It was time he said goodbye to the little boy and started acting like a man.

Zoë wasn't sure how long after their scheduled wedding Nick finally showed up. She sat alone on the swing in the backyard, still in her pajamas, with her legs pulled up and her knees tucked under her chin, wondering if he actually *would* show up. Maybe he was so angry he would never speak to her again.

But then the backdoor had opened and Nick walked through, still dressed in his suit. He crossed the lawn to the swing, hands tucked in the pockets of his slacks, looking more tired than angry.

And boy did he look good in a suit. Almost as good as he looked out of it.

What was wrong with her? She just stood the guy up and now she's picturing him naked?

"You seem to have forgotten that we had a date this afternoon."

She cringed and looked up at him apologetically. "I am so sorry, Nick."

"No." He sat beside her on the swing, loosening his tie. "I'm the one who's sorry."

He didn't hate her after all, not that she ever really believed he would. Maybe she thought she deserved it. "This is completely my fault. I guess I just…got scared."

"Scared that I would back out at the last minute. Or possibly not show up at all?"

She nodded, thankful that he said it for her. And even more thankful that he understood.

"I gave you no reason to believe otherwise." He took her hand and held it, lacing his fingers through hers. "Which makes this entire mess very much my fault."

"I should have trusted you."

He laughed, but there wasn't a trace of humor in the sound. "What did I ever do to earn your trust? Ask you to marry me? Stick a ring on your finger? Well, so what? I did the same thing with two other women and I'm not married to either of them, am I?"

Jeez, twist the knife a little deeper why don't you? Was he *trying* to make her feel worse?

"Um, I'm not quite sure what your point is, but for the record, this isn't helping."

"My point is, I knew exactly what you needed

from me, but I was too much of a coward to give it to you. That line I fed you about the ring making it official was bull. The only way to make this relationship official is for me to stop acting like an ass and tell you how I feel."

"I could have asked," she said.

He shot her a look. "You shouldn't have to."

No, she shouldn't, which is probably why she hadn't. Call her stubborn and a little old-fashioned, but she believed that when you felt a certain way about someone, you told them so.

He cupped her chin in his hand and lifted her face to his. "I never thought it was possible to love someone as much as I love you. Maybe that's why I didn't let myself trust it."

She could feel tears welling in her eyes and burning her nose, and she didn't even have those pesky hormones as an excuse this time.

He kissed her gently. "I love you, Zoë. With all my heart."

She closed her eyes and sighed. No words had ever sounded sweeter or meant so much. Because she knew they came directly from his heart. "I love you too, Nick."

"I have a favor to ask. This is going to sound a little strange, but I'm asking you to trust me."

"Okay."

"Could I possibly have that ring back for a minute?"

It was a little strange, but she trusted him. She slipped it off her finger and set it in his hand.

"I figured it was about time I do this right." He slid off the swing and got down on one knee in front of her. Zoë held her breath and the tears that had been hovering inside her lids began to spill over. "Zoë Simmons, would you do me the honor of becoming my wife?"

"Absolutely," she said. He slipped the ring back on her finger and she threw her arms around his neck and hugged him.

"I know you didn't want a big wedding, but I don't think you have much choice now."

She pulled back and looked at him. He had a very sly, devious grin on that gorgeous face. "Why?"

"Because when I hung up the phone after asking your parents' permission to marry you, they were already working on the guest list."

Her mouth fell open. "You called and asked their *permission?*"

He grinned. "I told you, I wanted to do it right this time."

Oh my gosh, she was now officially daughter of the year. And only a couple of weeks ago she'd been worried about excommunication. "So what did you say?"

"I told them I was in love with you, and I wanted their permission to marry you."

She couldn't believe he'd actually asked permission. "What did they say?"

He grinned. "They both said, it's about time."

Epilogue

Nick trudged down the stairs to the first floor, side-stepping to avoid the half-naked Barbie doll lying in the hallway and kicking aside a handful of Matchbox cars in the den doorway. This all should have been picked up by now.

When he saw the video game on the television screen, he knew why it wasn't.

He crossed the room and shut the television off and received a collective, *"Daaaaaaad!"* from their oldest children, nine-year-old Steven and eight-year-old Lila.

"Don't dad me. You're supposed to be cleaning up your toys. It's almost bedtime."

Six-year-old Nathan, who had inherited not only his father's dark hair and hazel eyes, but also his clean gene, was already working diligently to get all the LEGOS put back in their bin.

"Jenny burped," he said, pointing to the six-month-old tucked under Nick's left arm. The one struggling and squirming to get down and practice the new crawling thing she'd mastered just yesterday.

He didn't have a burp cloth handy, so he wiped away the spit-up with the hem of his shirt, wondering if a day had passed in the last nine years when he hadn't walked around with the remains of someone else's dinner on his clothes.

"Daddy!" four-year-old Olivia, the outspoken one of the bunch, screeched from the doorway, not three feet away. She had two volumes. Loud, and *really* loud. "Mommy is in the kitchen eating cookies again."

He crouched down in front of her, and being closer to the floor and freedom, Jenny let out an earsplitting squeal and struggled to get loose. "Liv' honey, what did Mommy and Daddy tell you about tattling?"

Olivia's lower lip curled into her signature pout. "I want cookies, too."

"Not before bed."

"Then why does Mommy get to eat cookies before bed?" Nathan asked.

"Because she's a grown-up," Lila said, giving him a shove as she walked past him. "She can eat cookies whenever she wants."

"You can have cookies tomorrow," Nick told her.

"She ate like the whole box," Steven mumbled. "There won't be any left tomorrow."

"Hey, mister, I heard that." Zoë stood in the den doorway, hands on her hips. Her hair hung in damp tendrils from a recent bath and her pink robe was conspicuously dotted with cookie crumbs. "Lila, can you please watch your sister for a minute? Daddy and I need to have a quick meeting."

"Sure, Mom!" she said, brightly, taking her baby sister from Nick's arms. Watching Jenny meant she didn't have to clean.

Zoë motioned him out of the room, mumbling, "Five kids. Whose bright idea was that?"

It hadn't actually been anyone's *idea*. After Steven and Lila, who were both carefully planned, they figured they had their boy and girl, so they were all set. But then Lila had started getting a little bit older and Zoë started having those baby cravings again.

They were a little lax with the contraceptives thinking that if it was meant to be, it was meant to be, and along came Nathan nine months later. Olivia was their first real oops baby, and the result of a bit too much champagne on New Year's Eve.

Jenny, oops baby number two, had been conceived when they thought they were being careful. Obviously not careful enough, her doctor had said when the test came back positive.

After Jenny was born, to avoid any further oopses, her doctor had finally put her on the pill. It was wreaking havoc on her menstrual cycle, and she'd been awfully weepy lately, but thank God it appeared to be working. Their only other option had been a vasectomy. Either that or he would have to move into an apartment down the street since after almost eleven years of marriage he still couldn't seem to keep his hands off her.

She led him to the first floor meeting room—the half bath next to the kitchen. One of the few places besides their bedroom that they could truly be alone.

She turned to him, her cheeks rosy from her bath, her eyes bright. It amazed him sometimes how much he loved her. It was as if, once he opened up his heart to her, it went a little crazy making up for lost time.

Each time he thought he couldn't possibly love her more than he already did, he would hear her reading Olivia a bedtime story, changing her voice for all the different characters, or he would catch her blowing raspberries on Jenny's belly while she changed her diaper. There were a million little things she did that made him love her more every day.

He might have been worried that he loved her too much, but she felt the exact same way about him.

"What's up?" he asked.

She blew out a big breath and said, "We have a problem."

He frowned. "What kind of problem?"

"Well, not a problem exactly, more like a slight inconvenience."

He folded his arms across his chest and sighed. "What did they break this time?"

"Nothing was broken. You know how my periods have been screwy since Jenny was born."

"Yeah?"

She bit her lip. "And, um, how I've been feeling a little yucky lately? Really tired and kinda nauseous."

Uh-oh, he had a feeling he knew where this was going. "I thought that was from the birth control."

"So did I. At first."

"But?"

"But then I noticed that it had been a while since I had my period."

"So what you're saying is, you're late."

She nodded. "I'm late."

He took a big breath and blew it out. Here we go again. "How late?"

"Two weeks, maybe three."

He raised an eyebrow at her. "Which is it, two or three?"

She bit her lip again. "Um, probably closer to three."

"Does this mean I need to make a trip to the pharmacy and get a test?"

"I went four days ago before I picked the kids up from school."

"*Four* days?"

She shrugged. "Denial. I finally worked up the courage to take it tonight after my bath."

Asking was merely a formality at this point. "And?"

She sighed. "Oops."

He tried not to smile, but he could feel a grin tugging at the corners of his mouth.

She rolled her eyes. "I know you're happy about this so you might as well just go ahead and smile."

He gripped the lapels of her robe and tugged her to him, brushing a kiss across her lips. "I love you."

"Six kids," she said, shaking her head. She looked a little shell-shocked, but he could tell she was happy, too.

The truth was, they could have six more and she wouldn't hear a complaint from him. He had plenty of love in his heart to go around.

"Not bad for a woman who once said she never wanted kids."

"Steven will be barely ten when the baby's born meaning we will have six kids under the age of eleven." She ran her fingers through the hair at his temples that had just begun to turn gray. "We must be completely nuts."

"Probably," he agreed, but insanity was highly underrated.

"I guess this is what I get for marrying a man who wanted a big family, huh?"

"Yeah, because you know what they say."

She thought about it for a second then said, "Fools rush in where angels fear to tread?"

He grinned. "Be careful what you wish for, you just might get it."

* * * * *

AT THE TEXAN'S
PLEASURE

by
Mary Lynn Baxter

Dear Reader,

What a pleasure to write the kind of books I love to read. What a pleasure to write. My career has evolved from teaching books, to selling books and now to writing books. I can't think of a career more rewarding or fun.

At the Texan's Pleasure is another tale in a list of many where there are secrets to hide. In this particular story the heroine is the one with the big secret. I love secrets. As I plot, it's so challenging and intriguing to figure out what my characters are hiding from each other – and often times from themselves – then capitalise on those secrets.

I hope you, as my faithful reader, will feel the same way when you read *At the Texan's Pleasure*. Thank you for being so loyal and enjoying the written word, which, by the way, is one of my greatest passions.

Many happy endings!

Mary Lynn Baxter

MARY LYNN BAXTER

A native Texan, Mary Lynn Baxter knew instinctively that books would occupy an important part of her life. Always an avid reader, she became a school librarian, then a bookstore owner, before writing her first novel. Now Mary Lynn Baxter is an award-winning author, who has written more than thirty novels, many of which have appeared on the *USA TODAY* list.

One

What was she doing?

Molly Stewart Bailey couldn't ignore her queasy stomach a moment longer, so she pulled off the highway onto the side of the road. Quickly she turned to see if her unexpected action had awakened her son Trent who was sound asleep in his car seat, his head lobbed to one side. For a second Molly considered jumping out of the car and propping his head back upright.

She squelched that idea as traffic was swishing by her at a rapid rate and in her present state of despair, she was liable to get run over. Still, she paused and continued to look at her son, who favored her, with dark brown hair, smoky blue eyes and clearly defined features.

A friend once told Molly she had the most uncluttered face ever. When she recalled that, it made her smile.

Not today.

Her mind was in too much turmoil; maybe that was why she kept her eyes on her child.

The only feature he had of his father was…

Suddenly Molly slammed the door shut on that thought. Now was the worst possible time to travel down memory lane. As it was, it would take every ounce of fortitude and courage she could muster to do what she was about to do. But she had no choice, even though choices had consequences. In this case, the consequences could change her life forever, and not for the better either.

That was why she had to guard her heart and its secret with every bit of fight she had in her.

Shaking her head to clear it, Molly pulled back onto the highway, soon to realize she was closer to the Cavanaugh Ranch than suspected. Once again she felt a wave of nausea wash through her. So much for her vow never to return to east Texas, much less to this precise location.

But then who could've known her mother would fall and injure her back to such an extent she was now bedridden? Molly stifled a sigh and tried to concentrate on something mundane like her surroundings, the tall oaks decorated in their fall colors of reds, browns and golds, the pines whose limbs seem to reach to the heavens—the ponds whose waters glistened like diamonds, and the meadowlands dotted with fenced-in cattle.

Only she found she couldn't fix her mind on anything other than gaining ground on her destination.

Nothing could usurp the fact that after almost five years she was about to see Worth Cavanaugh again. In the flesh. Cold chills darted through Molly, and she shivered. Stop it! she told herself. She had to get control of her splattered emotions and never let go of them. Otherwise, she was in for a world of hurt for the next couple of weeks, if not longer.

Gripping the steering wheel harder, Molly made the last turn before entering the long strip of graveled road which led to the ranch house atop the hill. Once there, she stopped the car and took several deep breaths, which helped settle her nerves. She'd known this endeavor wouldn't be easy, but she hadn't envisioned it being this difficult. It seemed that every nerve in her body was riding on the surface of her skin.

Not a good thing, she told herself, and not at all like her. As a registered nurse, she prided herself on having nerves of steel. Her job actually demanded it. But the *who* she was about to encounter didn't have anything to do with her job. It was personal. She would soon come face-to-face with the one man she had hoped never to see again, the man who had not only broken her heart but had jerked it out and stomped on it.

"Don't, Molly!" she chastised herself out loud, then quickly glanced in the rearview mirror at Trent. Her self-imposed rebuke hadn't impacted him at all. He was still sleeping soundly. She frowned, realizing that in a few moments, she'd have to awaken him, which would not be to his liking, or hers. When he didn't get his full nap, he tended to be grumpy and oftentimes hard to manage.

Waking up in a ranch setting would most likely right his world quickly, as she'd been telling him about the horses and cattle he'd see every day. She had even bought him a new pair of cowboy boots and hat in honor of this visit to see his grandmother.

Trent had insisted on wearing his new attire today, which brought a smile to Molly's face, recalling how he'd paraded around the house, peering at himself in the mirror every chance he got, a big grin on his face.

Another sigh filtered through her at the same time the smile disappeared. Worth's house stood in front of her, and for a second she was tempted to jerk the gearshift in Reverse and back down the drive. Out of sight; out of mind. That thought was only fleeting as the needy edge in her mother's voice rose up to haunt her, recalling this visit wasn't about her, Molly, but rather her mother.

As long as she kept that uppermost in her mind, she would do just fine. Molly owed Maxine Stewart more than she could ever hope to repay, and not because she was her mother, either. Maxine had stood by her, though she had been kept in the dark about much of what had gone on in her daughter's life these last few years. If for no other reason, Molly would always love her for that.

"Mommy."

Glad for the interruption, Molly flung her head around and smiled at her son who was now wide-eyed and kicking his booted feet. "Hey, it's about time you woke up."

"When can I see the horses and cows?" Trent asked right off the bat.

Molly grinned. "First things first, okay? We'll see Granna, then the animals."

"Granna'll take me."

Molly heard that comment just as she exited the Toyota Camry and came around to release Trent from his car seat. Then helping him out, she said, "Remember Granna can't do anything. She's in bed with a hurt back."

Trent frowned as he jumped to the ground, his eyes scanning the surroundings. Molly followed suit, taking in the lovely manicured lawn close to the modern ranch house. Then her gaze dipped beyond to the sloping grounds where animals grazed in the distance near a blue pond.

"Mommy, look, I see lots of cows."

"Me, too," Molly said absently, turning Trent by the shoulders and steering him in the direction of the side door to her mother's small living quarters. Although Maxine's bedroom and sitting room were part of the main house, Worth had been thoughtful enough to add a private entrance, for which Molly was especially grateful today.

As splintered as she was, she didn't need to run into Worth, not until she'd at least seen her mother and found out for herself how seriously she was injured. Beyond that, Molly intended to take the moments as they came and deal with them no matter how painful or unsettling.

"Mom, we're here," Molly called out, knocking on the door, then opening it.

Maxine Stewart lay propped up on a pillow in her bed, a broad smile on her still-attractive face, her arms reaching out to Trent, who seemed hesitant to move.

"It's okay, honey, go give Granna a hug."

"I'm expecting a big hug, you cutie tootie. Granna's been waiting a long time for this day."

Though Trent still appeared reluctant, he made his way toward his grandmother and let her put her arms around him, giving him a bear hug. Finally pushing Trent to arm's length, Maxine's eyes glistened with tears. "My, what a big boy you are."

"I'll be five my next birthday," Trent said with pride.

Maxine winked at him. "Granna hasn't forgotten. I already have your birthday present."

"Wow!" Trent said with awe.

"Don't get too excited," Molly cautioned. "Next month you'll only be four and a half, which means your birthday's a while off yet."

"Can I have it now?"

Molly grinned, tousling his hair. "Not a chance, boy." Then it was her turn to hug her mother, though through it all, her heart took yet another beating, but for an entirely different reason.

Maxine's once unlined face had wrinkles that were unavoidably noticeable and dark circles under her eyes where none used to be. Her mother appeared frail, so much frailer than she had ever been.

Though Maxine wasn't a robust woman, she'd always been the picture of health and beauty. Friends and strangers who saw the two of them together knew they were mother and daughter because they favored each other so much. Some even told them they could pass for sisters.

Pain. That was the culprit that had so changed and aged her mother. Peering at Maxine closely through trained eyes, Molly didn't see any signs of that pain turning Maxine loose any time soon, not if the X-rays her doctor had sent Molly to peruse were correct. At this point, Molly saw no reason to question the diagnosis.

"Mom, how are you really doing?" Molly asked into the short silence.

"Good."

Molly rolled her eyes. "Hey, remember who you're talking to."

Maxine made a face. "A nurse, I know."

"All the more reason you need to be honest and 'fess up."

"Okay, my back hurts like you-know-what," Maxine admitted down in the mouth, casting a glance at Trent who was busy wandering around the room, fingering this and that.

"That's why I'm here."

"Only not for long, surely." Maxine made a face. "You just can't leave your job. I'd feel even worse if you lost it because of me."

"Hey, calm down," Molly said, leaning down and kissing Maxine on the cheek. "I have a great doctor for a boss. Besides, I have sick days, as well as vacation days, I haven't used. Four weeks' worth, actually."

"Still…"

"It's all right, I promise. I'm not going to do anything that puts my career in jeopardy."

Maxine gave a visible sigh of relief. "I'm glad to hear that." She smiled. "It's so good to see you and Trent. You're a sight for my sore eyes." Maxine faced her grandson and her smile widened. "He's grown so much since I last saw him."

"He's growing much too fast," Molly said with a crack in her voice. "He's no longer my baby."

"That's not so." Maxine looked back at Molly. "He'll always be your baby just like you'll always be mine."

Tears welled up in Molly's eyes, but she blinked them away, hopefully before her mother could see them. "So tell me what's going on here."

"Are you referring to my job?"

Molly was taken aback. "No. I wouldn't think there's a problem with that."

"I hope you're right," Maxine said, her brows drawing together. "Worth let me hire a part-time helper several months ago, which is good. She's more or less running the house now, with me telling her what to do, of course."

"So is that working out?"

"Yes, but this home needs a full-time housekeeper, especially with Worth thinking about entering politics."

The last person Molly wanted to talk about was Worth. Actually, she'd rather not know anything about him *period*. Under the circumstances, she knew that wasn't possible.

"I just can't help but be a little fearful of eventually losing my job," Maxine said, "especially if I don't start improving."

"Oh, come on, Mom, Worth's not going to let you go. You know better than that."

"Maybe I do, but you know how your mind plays tricks on you and convinces you otherwise." Maxine paused. "I guess what I'm saying is that my mind is my own worst enemy."

"That comes from lying in bed with nothing to keep you occupied." Molly smiled with a wink. "But now that Trent and I are here, that's going to change." Speaking of Trent made her turn to check on him, only to find he was no longer in the room.

"Did you see Trent leave?" Molly asked, trying to temper her building panic.

"No, but he can't go far."

That was when she noticed the door leading to the main house was open. "I'll be right back," Molly flung over her shoulder as she dashed out of the room, soon finding herself in the house's main living area. "Trent Bailey, where are you?"

"Who is Trent?"

Molly stopped in her tracks, and stared into the face of Worth Cavanaugh. For what seemed the longest time, not only did her body shut down, but their eyes also met and locked, though neither said a word. But that didn't matter. The tension was such that they might as well have been screaming at one another.

"Hello, Worth." Somehow Molly managed to get those words through cotton-dry lips.

"What are you doing here?" he demanded in a curt tone, choosing to ignore her greeting.

"I would think that's obvious."

"Maxine failed to tell me you were coming." Instead of curt, his tone was now in the freezer, showing no chance of thawing.

"That's also obvious."

Another silence.

"Again, who's Trent?"

"My son."

Worth's black eyes flickered and his mouth stretched into a

pencil-thin line. "Lucky you," he finally said in a caustic his eyes filled with scorn as they traveled up and down her body.

The word *bastard* was about to fly out of her mouth when Trent rounded the corner, racing to her side. "Mommy, I went to see the moo cows."

Molly pulled him against her, clamping her hand on his shoulder. When he started to squirm, her hold tightened. As if sensing he was in trouble, Trent stopped wiggling and stared up at Worth with open curiosity.

"Trent," Molly said in a tight voice, "this is Mr. Cavanaugh."

Worth merely nodded at the boy, then looking up at Molly said, "I'd like to talk to you alone."

Biting back another choice word, Molly peered down at Trent. "Go back to Granna's room, honey. And don't leave. I'll be there shortly."

"Okay," Trent said, whirling and running back down the hall.

Don't run, Molly wanted to shout, but she knew it wouldn't do any good. Trent was already out of hearing range.

"So how old is he?"

Molly shook her head as though to clear it, Worth's question taking her by surprise. "Almost four," she said, lying with such ease that it shocked her.

"Good-looking kid."

"Thanks."

Instead of receding, the tension between them continued to rise until Molly felt either she or the room would explode. Or maybe both. She sensed Worth felt the same way, as his features seemed to darken by the second.

"How long are you planning to stay?" he asked, the muscle in one jaw moving up and down, something that always happened when he was angry or disturbed.

"I'm not sure." She paused. "Maybe a week. Maybe longer. I'm not sure. Do you have a problem with my being here?"

"Not in the least," he countered in a harsh tone.

"Is there an addendum to that?"

"Yeah," he said in a parting shot, "just stay out of *my* way."

Two

He'd been blindsided and he hated it.

This was *his* domain, dammit, and he had control over what went on here. Or at least he thought he did. Worth muttered a curse, rubbing the five o'clock shadow that covered a good portion of his face as he continued to stand on the porch outside his room. In the distance, he could see the last remnants of a sun fast sinking into oblivion.

Worth peered at his watch and noted that it was not quite five. He loved the fall of the year, especially October because the leaves changed colors. There was one exception, however. The time change. He didn't like anything about falling backward, robbing him of an hour of light at the end of day. As a hands-on rancher, light was a precious commodity.

At this particular moment, whether it was daylight or not wasn't what his frustration was all about. Time had nothing to do with the gnawing deep in his gut. But he sure as hell knew what did.

Molly.

Back in his life.

No way.

Not possible.

Not happening.

Only it had.

She was in his house.

And there wasn't one thing he could do about it short of pitching her and the kid out the door. He muttered another colorful expletive, but again that did nothing to untie the growing knot in his stomach.

Granted, he'd known he would eventually see her again. To think not would've been ludicrous and unrealistic. After all, her mother worked for him. But since he hadn't seen Molly in nearly five years, he'd begun to think that maybe fate was smiling on him.

Heretofore, during her vacation, Maxine had always gone to visit Molly. He'd assumed that would continue to be the case.

Of course, that was before Maxine had fallen and injured her back to the extent she'd been confined to bed. Molly returning to the ranch seemed to fit the logical order of events, which wouldn't have been as much of a problem, if only he'd known about it.

He didn't like surprises, especially not surprises of this nature. Almost walking head-on into her had definitely been a blow—a blow from which he hadn't yet recovered.

The kid hadn't helped, either.

Worth rubbed the back of his neck, feeling the hard coiled muscles under his fingers. Nothing short of asking them to leave would give him any relief. That wasn't about to happen, at least not for several days anyway.

Meanwhile, he'd just have to put up with the situation. If Molly did like she was told and stayed out of his way, then he could manage. If not… Hell, he wasn't about to go down that treacherous road. It would only make him madder and more frustrated.

He just wished she still didn't look so damn good. Lovelier than even he remembered. And his memory was excellent. Never a day went by that some little something didn't remind him of her. While that never failed to shoot his blood pressure up, he'd learned to shove thoughts of her aside and move on.

Now though, that wasn't doable. He'd most likely see her every day whether he wanted to or not, regardless of what he'd told her. Having gotten over the initial shock somewhat and his head screwed back on straight had brought that reality home. As long as she was on his property, he couldn't avoid her altogether. He couldn't avoid the kid, either.

No doubt about it, she couldn't deny the kid. Looked just like her, which wasn't a bad thing. Molly's dark hair that reminded him of soot, was short and stylish, a perfect backdrop for those smoky colored eyes. And that sultry voice—God, it had always been a turn-on and still was.

Even though he knew she was twenty-seven, seven years younger than he, she didn't look it. With her unmarked skin that reminded him of porcelain at its finest, she could pass for less than twenty.

However, if one were to look closer, her figure bore testimony to her actual age. While remaining thin, with a to-die-for body, he noticed that it was more rounded, even slightly voluptuous in certain places, particularly her breasts and stomach.

Having borne a child was responsible for those added factors. Instead of detracting from her beauty, they merely enhanced it, making her body sexier than ever. Though he was loathe to admit it, he'd have to be dead not to notice. He might be many things, but dead wasn't one of them.

There had been times, however, when he'd wished he were dead. All because of her.

After Molly had run off, leaving him high and dry, she'd killed something vital inside him, which had never been revived. Part of his heart and soul were dead and Molly was to blame.

He despised her for that.

At least that was what he'd always told himself. But seeing her for that few minutes had turned his perfect world upside down—socked him in the gut, actually. Only not for long, he vowed. Already he was remembering her for the liar she really was.

And with that recall, his confidence rebounded. Even though she was staying in a small suite not far from his didn't mean one damn thing, although at first he'd questioned his placement of her and Trent.

Then he'd told himself, what the hell. Where she stayed didn't mean a thing to him. Hence, he'd had Maxine's part-time helper, Kathy, show them to that particular suite, mainly because it was close to Molly's mother.

In addition, he'd reminded himself, she wouldn't be at the ranch long enough to matter where she slept. He knew she was a nurse with some large doctors' group in Houston. Hell, he'd heard Maxine brag about that until she'd finally gotten the message that he wasn't interested in hearing about her daughter.

He often wondered what Molly had told her mother about their past relationship. He suspected it had been nowhere near the truth, which reinforced his anger. A good thing, he told himself. As long as he held onto that anger and hatred, he'd come out the winner.

And to hell with her.

Suddenly Worth heard a phone ring. It was only after the third ring he realized it was his cell. Without checking who was calling, he barked, "Cavanaugh."

"My, you sound like you're in a sour mood."

"Hello, Olivia."

He didn't miss the aggravated sigh that filtered through the line. "Is that all you have to say?"

"What do you want me to say?"

"Hello, sweetheart, would do for starters."

He didn't answer. First, he'd never called her sweetheart and didn't intend to start now. Second, but most important, she'd hit the nail on the head. He was in a sour mood, but now was not the time to tell her why. He simply wasn't up to fighting the war that would occur if he told her Molly was back in town, staying at the ranch.

More to the point, it wasn't any of Olivia's business.

"Okay, you win," Olivia replied in an offhanded manner. "I'll let you pout, or whatever the hell you're doing."

"Did you want anything in particular?" Worth asked in a cold tone, knowing he was being a first-class jerk. Yet he felt no need to apologize.

"What time are you picking me up?"

Worth's mind went blank. "Picking you up?"

"Yes," she said, not bothering to hide her growing irrita-tion. "Remember you promised to take me to dinner tonight."

"Oh, right."

"You'd forgotten all about that, hadn't you?"

He had, but again he wasn't going to admit it. "I'll be there around sevenish."

Another sigh. "You know, Worth, I think you take great pride in being an ass."

Silence.

"And while we're on the subject of dinner," Olivia added,

"don't forget about the party at my house tomorrow night concerning your political future."

"I haven't, Olivia." His tone was weary. "I know my parents are invited along with a possible potential backer."

"At least you remembered something."

With that, she hung up.

That was two women he'd ruffled today. He wondered if his mother was next in line. Probably so, he told himself. On a normal day, he and Eva Cavanaugh didn't see eye-to-eye on much of anything. If she'd stop trying to micromanage his life, that might change. His father, however, was a different matter. They got along fine, at least on the surface, though he felt he had never known what made Ted Cavanaugh tick.

In all fairness, his parents probably didn't know what made him tick, either. One thing he did know was they wanted him to marry Olivia Blackburn. No. They *expected* him to marry her, which was the same as waving a red flag in front of a bull. He didn't live by, or under, others' expectations. Besides, he didn't love Olivia. He'd made the mistake of falling in love once, and he'd never repeat it. Never.

Only problem was, he needed what Olivia could give him and that land she stood to inherit. His parents had deeded him the three hundred acres that adjoined their property, which he'd hoped would be enough to do most anything he chose in the way of ranching. But with his cattle business thriving, he needed more land.

That was where Olivia fit into his life so well. The acreage she'd inherit from her father would give him the room to expand his horse breeding business, a dream that hadn't yet come to fruition.

Ah, to hell with women and the garbage they dished out, his thoughts targeting Molly. What he needed was a drink, he told himself savagely. Something large and strong that would

cut through the constriction in his throat that had a strangle-
hold on him.

He was just about to accommodate himself when his phone
rang again. This time he did look at caller ID and saw that it
was his mother. He was tempted not to answer it, but he did.
Maybe she was canceling the dinner. A smirk crossed his
lips. Not a chance that would happen.

"Yo, Mother."

"Is that any way for a politician to answer the phone?"

"I'm not a politician. Yet." He was irritated and it showed.

"You will be," she said in her lofty tone. "Just as soon as
you throw your hat into the ring."

"I haven't decided to do that, either."

"I don't know why you take delight in being difficult."

"Mother, if you're going to get on your soapbox about
politics, then this conversation is over."

"Don't you dare hang up on me."

Not only could he hear the chagrin in his mother's voice,
but he could picture it in her face, as well. Although tall and
rawboned like himself, she was nonetheless a very striking
woman, with blond hair and black eyes, who commanded attention with her height and flare for fashion. But when she
was out of sorts, which she was now, her usually pleasant
features turned hard and unpleasant.

"I'll see you and Dad tomorrow night at Liv's around eight.
We can talk about politics then, okay?"

"That's not what I'm calling about."

Something in her voice alerted him to be on guard, that the
rest of the conversation would not be to his liking. Her next
words confirmed that.

"Why didn't you tell me?"

"Tell you what?" Worth's tone was as innocent as hers
was accusing.

"That Molly Bailey, or whatever her name is now, is at your ranch."

God, it didn't take long for news to travel, but then in a small town like Sky, Texas gossip was the most popular game in town.

"Because it's no big deal."

"No big deal." Eva's voice rose. "How can you say that?"

"Because it's true. She came to see about her mother."

"I understand that."

"So what's the problem?"

"The fact that she's staying at your place is the problem."

"Mother, I don't want to discuss this."

Eva went on as though he hadn't said a word. "A motel would've been just fine for the likes of her."

Although he had no intention of defending Molly—not for one second—his mother's words set him off like a rocket. It was all he could do to keep his cool long enough to get off the phone before he said something he'd be sorry for.

"Goodbye, Mother. I'll see you tomorrow tonight."

"Worth Cavanaugh, you can't hang—"

"Yes, I can. I've got to go now." Without further ado, Worth punched the red button on the phone and Eva's hostile voice was no longer assaulting his ear.

Women!

He'd had enough of them for one day. That stiff drink was looking more enticing by the second. He was about to walk back inside when he saw her strolling across the lawn. Alone.

Worth stopped in his tracks and watched. Molly was still dressed in the same jeans she'd had on earlier, jeans that fit her rear to perfection. Right now, it was her backside that held him captive—the sway of those perfect hips. Then she turned slightly, giving him privy to the way her full breasts jutted against the soft forest-green sweater.

For what seemed an eternity, his eyes consumed her. Then

muttering a harsh obscenity, he felt his manhood rise to the occasion. Even though he dragged his gaze away from the provocative thrust of those breasts and back to her face, that action did nothing to release the pressure behind his zipper.

She was such an awesome picture of beauty against the gold and orange leaves falling from the trees that his breath caught in his throat.

It was in that moment she looked up and saw him. For the second time in a day, their eyes met and held.

He stared at her, breathing hard. Then cursing again for the fool that he was, Worth pivoted on a booted heel and strode back inside, only to realize that he was shaking all over.

Three

Lucky for her it was Worth who looked away first. For some crazy reason, Molly couldn't seem to tear her eyes away from him, although he was several yards from her. Yet his tall figure appeared clear to her.

And threatening.

Even so, she had been held spellbound by his presence, though she knew that if she were close enough to read those black eyes, they would be filled with animosity.

Thank heaven the moment had passed and he was gone. However, she didn't move. Her body felt disassembled, perhaps like one of the many leaves that were falling from the trees, never to be attached again.

What an insane thought, Molly told herself brutally, storming back into her room. Besides, it was getting downright chilly despite the fact the sun was still hanging on. Once it disappeared, the temperature had a tendency to drop quickly.

By the time she closed the French doors, she was shivering all over. Not from the chill, she knew, but from her second encounter with Worth. She eased onto the chaise longue, the closest seat, and took several deep breaths to calm her racing heart, feeling lucky to be alone. Trent was with his grandmother who was happy as a lark reading to him. He had crawled into the bed with Maxine and was hanging onto every word she read out of the book.

Before she had ventured outdoors, Molly had stood in her mother's door and watched them, feeling a peace descend over her. Coming here, despite the obstacles, had been the right thing to do. Not only did her ailing mother need her daughter, she needed to get to really know her grandson. To date, Trent and Maxine hadn't had the opportunity to bond, to develop a close relationship that was so unique to grandparents and grandchildren.

Now, however, the doubts were once again creeping back into her mind, following that long distance encounter with Worth. Molly bit down on her lower lip to stop it from trembling while her eyes perused the room where she tried hard to concentrate on the rustic good taste that surrounded her.

She forced herself to take in, and appreciate, the cobalt blue walls and the big four-poster bed that was angled in one corner. The one thing that held her attention was the handmade quilt that adorned the bed. The coverlet picked up the blue in the wall, as well as other vivid colors, resulting in a stunning piece of art.

An armoire occupied the other side of the bedroom. The sitting area where the chaise resided held a desk and chair. No doubt, it was a place where she could be comfortable for a long period of time. But even if her job allowed that luxury, it wouldn't work.

Because of Worth.

Suddenly Molly felt tears fill her eyes, and that made her mad. Lunging off the chaise, she curled her fists into her palms and strengthened her resolve. She wouldn't let her emotions get the best of her again. She had indulged herself before she'd arrived, and that had to be her swan song. Otherwise, she wouldn't get through the quagmire that was already threatening to suck her under.

Yet seeing Worth again so soon after her arrival seemed to have imprinted him on her brain, and she couldn't let go of that image. What an image it was, too. She had never thought of him as handsome, only sexy.

Now he seemed both. He was tall and leathery thin, but not too thin, having toned his muscles to perfection riding horses and branding cattle—the two loves of his life. His short brown hair still had streaks of blond, but she could almost swear that some gray had been added to the mix. His face, with its chiseled features, was definitely more lined.

Neither change, however, was a detraction because of those incredible black eyes, surrounded by equally incredible thick lashes. They were by far the focal point of his face and his best asset.

And he knew how to use them. He had a way of looking at her like she was the only one in existence. And that was a real turn-on, or at least it always had been for her.

Until today.

When she had practically run into him upon her arrival, she'd seen none of that sexual charisma reflected in his eyes. Instead, she'd seen pure hostility and anger that bordered on hatred. Another shiver darted through Molly, and she crossed her arms over her chest as if to protect herself.

From Worth?

Possibly, because he was someone she no longer knew. More noticeable than the physical changes in him, were the changes in attitude. From the first moment she'd met him that fateful summer, she remembered him as having been rather cocky and self-assured for someone who was just twenty-nine years old. But she'd taken no offense at that attitude; actually that was one of the reasons she'd been attracted to him.

While both cocky and self-assured still applied, other adjectives now fit his personality. He appeared bitter, cynical and completely unbending. Though she didn't know the reason for such a radical change, she didn't like it, especially since it was directed at her.

After all, *he'd* been the one who had betrayed her. If anyone had an ax to grind, it was she. Admittedly she did, but she wasn't about to show her bitterness to the entire world.

Maybe she was just the one who continually brought out the worst in him. Around others maybe he was a kinder and gentler soul. That thought almost brought a smile to Molly's face. Worth Cavanaugh was a man *unto* himself, having carved an empire *for* himself in his early thirties. Kinder and gentler didn't make that happen. Hard and tough-skinned did.

Suddenly a sliver of panic ran down Molly's spine. What was she doing here? It wasn't going to work. She hadn't even been here one whole day, and thoughts of Worth had her by the jugular and wouldn't let go.

Molly swallowed convulsively as she eased back onto the chaise, vivid memories of the last time they were together rising to haunt her. If her recall served her correctly, she'd been in the barn that day, looking for Worth most likely.

The why actually hadn't been important. Once there, she'd climbed into the loft and plopped down in the middle of the hay. She remembered closing her eyes, taking a catnap during which she dreamed about Worth. When she finally opened her eyes, she was taken aback to find him leaning against a post, watching her with unsuppressed desire further darkening his eyes.

Since it had been summer and the temperature sizzling, she'd had on only the barest of clothing—a pair of blue jean shorts, a tank top without a bra and flip-flops. The way he'd stared at her, she might as well have been naked.

Heat pooled between her thighs as their eyes remained locked.

She saw him swallow with effort, causing his Adam's apple to bob up and down as he slowly, but surely pushed away from the post and made his way toward her, his fingers busily unzipping his jeans.

All of that seemed to take place in slow motion as she lay unmoving, her heart pumping so loudly she could hear it in her ears. By the time he reached her, Molly's eyes were no longer on his face but rather on the juncture at his thighs where his erection was thick and hard.

She couldn't speak; her mouth was too dry. She could only watch him lift his arms and pull off his T-shirt, then toss it aside. A gasp slipped past her lips as her eyes covered every inch of his big, beautiful body, settling on his erection that seemed to be increasing by the moment.

Blood pounded from her heart into her head at such a rapid rate that it made her dizzy. Yet she couldn't have removed her eyes from him if someone had threatened her life with a gun. It wasn't as if that had been the first time she'd seen him in the buff, either.

It hadn't. Far from it, actually.

Since her arrival that summer at his ranch, she and Worth had become an instant item. It had been lust at first sight.

When that lust had turned to love, Molly couldn't say. Maybe it had been after he'd taken her that first time. From then on, he hadn't been able to keep his hands off her and vice versa. With summer coming to an end, nothing had changed. Every time Worth looked at her, or came near her, her bones melted.

That day was no exception.

"You're a beautiful man," she said in her sultry voice that now had a crack in it.

He merely grinned, then knelt beside her and promptly removed her clothing.

"Not nearly as beautiful as you," he rasped, his gaze now covering every inch of her flesh.

He bent over and latched onto an already burgeoning nipple and sucked it until she couldn't keep still. Finally releasing it, he moved to the other one and did likewise. Only after he left her breasts and began to lick his way down her stomach did she take action, latching onto his erection, rubbing her thumb in and around the opening.

Worth let out a loud groan as he nudged her legs apart and gently inserted two fingers inside her.

"Oh, yes," she whimpered, her hips going crazy.

"Baby, baby, you're so wet, so ready."

"Please, now. Don't make me wait."

Propping himself on his hands, Worth leaned further over her, then entered her with unerring accuracy. For a moment he didn't move, seemingly to enjoy the way she formed a tight sheath around him, his eyes burning deeply into hers.

Then he pumped up and down until the fiery explosion hit them at the same time. Moments later he lay limp on her with her arms clasped tightly around him.

"Am I too heavy?" he whispered at last, his breath caressing her ear.

"No."

"Oh, but I am." He chuckled, then rolled over so that she was now on top of him.

She leaned down, kissed him, and said in an awed voice, "I can't believe you're still inside me."

"Me, either, especially since all the lead's gone out of my pencil."

She giggled and kissed him again.

Suddenly his gaze darkened on her. "Know what?"

"I know lots of whats," she said in a teasing voice. "One of them is that I love you."

"I love you, too, so much that I got carried away and didn't use a condom."

For several seconds, silence fell between them.

"Are you mad at me?" he asked.

"No," Molly responded, feeling her brows gather in a frown. "It takes two to tango, as the saying goes."

"Right, but I should've been more responsible."

"Shh. It's okay. It's not the right time of the month for me." Molly paused. "At least I don't think so."

"I'm sorry."

"Don't you dare say that. I loved every minute of it. There's nothing to be sorry about."

It was the thought of those words that jerked Molly out of the past back into the present. *Back to reality.* To the pain and hurt that had resulted from that passionate afternoon of lovemaking.

Knowing her face was drenched with tears, Molly went into the bathroom and wet a washcloth with cold water. Though the cloth felt like ice against her skin, it did what she'd hoped it would and that was clear her fogged mind.

She couldn't change what had happened between her and Worth. All she could do was change how she reacted to him now. Though the aftermath of their affair had left deep and lasting scars, she wasn't sorry because out of it had come the blessing of her life—her son.

For that she would never be sorry.

It was then that Molly suddenly heard the sound of an engine. Hurrying to the French doors, she walked onto the porch where she saw Worth sitting in his truck. She was still standing in the cold when the taillights disappeared.

With her teeth chattering, she went back inside, not stopping until she was in her mother's room, facing her son's animated face.

"Mommy, Mommy, come see what Granna gave me."

Squaring her shoulders, Molly shoved the past back under lock and key deep in her soul.

Four

"Oh, Doctor, thanks so much for returning my call."

"Not a problem," Dr. Roy Coleman responded. "I know you're concerned about your mother and well you should be."

Molly winced under the doctor's direct words, but then she was a nurse, for God's sake, so she shouldn't be surprised. Most doctors nowadays didn't tiptoe around the rose bush. They called the problem as they saw it and let the chips fall where they may. Her boss Sam Nutting was cut from that same bolt of cloth.

Somehow, though, she was reluctant to hear the truth because it was her mother, who had always been Molly's lifeline and still was. Her dad had died from heart failure when she was young, leaving them without ample resources. Hence, Maxine had had to work her fingers to the bone for other people in order for them to survive. However, she never forsook her daughter; Maxine always found time to spend with Molly no matter how exhausted she was, or how much she had to do.

"Are you still there, Ms. Bailey?"

The doctor's crisp voice brought Molly back to the moment at hand. "Sorry, I was woolgathering about Mother, actually. Now that I've seen her and the condition she's in, I'm really concerned."

"As I said earlier, you have good reason. She took a nasty fall, which did major damage to her back, as you already know, of course. The main plus, however, is that she has no fractures."

Even though Maxine had slipped in the hallway two weeks ago, it seemed much longer to Molly because she hadn't been able to leave work and come immediately. Her mother had insisted that she not, making light of the accident.

Only after Dr. Coleman talked with her, then sent copies of the MRI did Molly know the extent of the damage to her mother's back. Ergo, she lost no time in rushing to Maxine's side.

"I appreciate you keeping me posted at every turn, Doctor."

"Wouldn't have it any other way. As I told you, Maxine's special, a rare breed. I know she's in pain, yet she suffers in silence."

"Only that's not good."

"You're right. It's not. I don't want her in pain. But Maxine is one of—if not the most—hardheaded patients I have."

"That's why I'm here, Dr. Coleman, to see that she does like she's told and behaves herself."

He chuckled, and Molly liked that. Although she'd never met him, they'd had countless phone conversations. Each time she was more impressed with his sense of humor and his care of her mother.

"I'd like to get another MRI soon, so we can see if the severely strained muscles are beginning to heal on their own.

Meanwhile, I've ordered a corset for her to wear. In fact, I don't want her even sitting on the side of the bed without it, much less walking."

Molly tried to remain upbeat, but under the circumstances that was becoming more difficult by the second. "That sounds like she's going to be incapacitated for a good little while."

"Because of her osteoporosis, she will be."

Molly's heart sank. "So we're looking at long-term recovery instead of short-term." A flat statement of fact.

"Not necessarily. Maxine is so determined that she could rebound much quicker than most, I suspect." Dr. Coleman paused. "However, work of any kind is out for now."

"What about physical therapy?"

"That's coming, but it's too soon. The corset is enough for now."

Molly fought back the unknown fears that were festering inside her. For the moment, the picture was dismal. What if her mother never regained the full use of her body? Maxine had always worked, had always been full of energy. She didn't believe in resting on her laurels, she'd told that to Molly all her life. An honest day's work for an honest day's pay had been Maxine's philosophy.

"You're going to have to help me convince *her* that she can't work, Doctor. So far I don't think you've gotten that across to her. She thinks she'll be mopping floors next week."

"Someone will be mopping floors, but it won't be Maxine."

"Thank you for being brutally honest with me." Molly's sigh was shaky. "Now, I have to be brutally honest with her."

"If you want to wait, I'll drive out to the ranch. We'll gang up on her."

A doctor who made house calls? No way. Yet he had offered, though Molly wasn't about to take him up on that offer. She could handle Maxine, but it wouldn't be easy. No matter. Her mother had no choice but to comply.

"Thank you for your kindness, but let me have a go at it first. If she bucks me, you'll be the first to know."

"Call me any time."

When the conversation ended, Molly held the receiver for a few moments longer, then replaced it, feeling as though she was moving in a daze.

She had dreaded having this session with the doctor because she knew it wasn't going to be encouraging. Since her arrival yesterday, she had come to realize her mother was indeed in dire straits, with no easy fix.

Now this morning, she had the unpleasant task of breaking the bad news to her mother. Molly was just thankful Trent was with Maxine. Bless his sweet heart, he had rarely left Maxine's room since they had arrived, seeming to have forgotten the horses and cattle with which he'd been so fascinated. But then Maxine had played with him non-stop. Knowing Maxine was exhausted, Molly finally had to call a halt to their togetherness.

Putting off the inevitable wasn't going to make things any easier, Molly reminded herself. Squaring her shoulders with resolve, she left her room and headed toward Maxine's, though not without first taking a furtive look around. While she certainly didn't expect Worth to be lurking in the shadows waiting to pounce on her, she still found herself somewhat rattled every time she left her room.

She had no idea what time Worth returned home last night, but she knew it was late, having heard him open the door to his room. It didn't matter where he went or what he did. Their relationship was past history and she had no right or reason to care about his whereabouts. Her aim was to avoid him at all costs.

Only problem with that, she was staying under his roof.

Pushing that unsettling thought aside, Molly knocked lightly on Maxine's door, then went in, only to pull up short. Her mother was asleep while Trent lay sprawled beside her, coloring in his coloring book.

"Hi, Mommy," he said in a soft voice. "Granna felled asleep."

"It's okay, honey." She reached for him and lifted him off the bed, then gathered the books and colors. "I want you to go to our room and color there for a few minutes, okay?"

Trent made a face. "I don't want to."

She smiled. "I know, but again, it'll only be for a few minutes, then I'll come and get you. I want to talk to Granna alone."

"Why can't I stay?" he whined.

Molly gave him a stern look. "Trent."

With his bottom lip poked out, he took the stuff, and without further ado, made his way to the door.

"Don't go anywhere else. Stay put in our room."

"Okay," he mumbled.

Molly stood watch until he was down the hall and the door closed behind him. He was so precious. Rarely did she ever have to scold him, but she didn't want him to hear this conversation she was about to have with her mother. She feared Maxine's reaction would not be favorable.

"Mom," Molly said, gently touching Maxine on the shoulder.

Her mother's eyes popped open and for a moment, she seemed completely disoriented. Then when she apparently recognized Molly, she smiled in relief, only then to frown. "Where's Trent?"

"He's in our room. He'll be back shortly."

"What time is it?" Maxine asked, her frown deepening.

"Almost noon."

"Oh, dear. I can't believe I even went to sleep, much less for that long."

"It's okay, Mother. You need all the rest you can get."

"No, what I need is to spend time with my daughter and grandson before I go back to work."

Molly was quiet for a moment, her mind scrabbling for a way to tell her mother the truth without breaking her heart. "Mom—"

"You're going to tell me I can't go back to work any time soon, aren't you?" Maxine's eyes were keen on Molly.

"That's right," Molly declared with relief.

"No, that's wrong."

Molly's relief was short-lived. "I—"

"I'm going to be just fine. I know I pulled some muscles in my back—"

"That you did," Molly interrupted flatly. "And according to the doctor, your recovery won't be quick or easy."

Maxine's chin began to wobble. "I refuse to believe that."

"It's the truth, Mother, and you have to face it. More than that, you have to accept it. Now if you didn't already have osteoporosis, then maybe things would be different."

"But what about my job?" Maxine wailed. "Worth has been so good to me, but he'll hire someone permanently to take my place. He'll have to, only I can't bear that thought."

"Mom, let's not beat that dead horse again. Worth is not going to replace you."

"Has he told you that?" Maxine's tone held a bit of belligerence.

Molly hesitated. "No, he hasn't."

"So you don't know what he has in mind." Maxine's voice broke.

"Oh, Mom, please, don't worry. It's going to be all right." Molly caressed one of Maxine's cheeks.

"He doesn't know—" Again Maxine broke off.

"The whole story about your back," Molly cut in. "Is that what you were about to say?"

Maxine merely nodded.

"Ah, so you told him what you wanted him to know, what you thought he wanted to hear."

Maxine reached for a tissue out of the nearby box. "I can't believe this is happening."

"Look, Mom, it's not as grim as you think."

"That's because it's not you." Maxine paused, then added quickly, "For which I'm grateful. I couldn't stand it if it were you in this shape."

"Yes, you could. You'd just come and take care of me like I'm going to do for you."

"You can't," Maxine wailed again. "You have a child and a job. And your life. You can't—"

"Shh," Molly said softly. "Enough. I'm not going to give up my life, for pity's sake. Just rest easy, I have a plan."

"What?" Maxine's tone was suspicious.

"I'll tell you later." Molly leaned over and kissed her mother on the cheek. "Right now, I'm going to send Trent back in here unless you want to go back to sleep."

"Not on your life. I want to spend every moment I can with my grandson."

"By the way, I spoke to Dr. Coleman."

Maxine's chin wobbled again.

"Hey, stop it. I'll tell you about that later also. Meanwhile, keep your chin up, you hear? Everything's going to work out."

Maxine did her best to smile. "Send my boy back to me. I have plans that don't include you."

Molly smiled big, then sobered. "Don't let him wear you out. He can, you know."

"You let me worry about that."

When Molly reached her room, she realized tears were running down her face. Brushing them aside, she forced a smile and opened the door. "Hey, kiddo, Granna's waiting on you."

* * *

Would there ever come a time when she wouldn't react to him?

Yes, Molly told herself. As long as she didn't see Worth, life would resume its normal course. Or would it? Almost five years had gone by and never a day passed she didn't think of him. Residing in his house made a bad thing worse.

Right now she didn't have a choice.

As if he realized he wasn't alone, Worth swung around. When he saw who it was, his eyes widened, then a door seemed to slide over those eyes, blanking out his expression.

"Didn't anyone ever tell you it was rude to sneak up on a person?"

Go to hell.

She didn't say that, but oh, how she wanted to. To speak her mind in that manner, however, would only incite a verbal riot, and she didn't want that. Too much was at stake. She merely wanted to talk to him in a civil manner.

"Sorry," Molly finally said in a moderate tone.

"No, you're not."

She hadn't meant to sneak up on him without warning. She just happened to walk by the door leading onto the porch and saw him there, a booted foot propped on one of the iron chairs. He seemed to have been staring into the waning sun, far in the distance, as though deep in thought.

Molly guessed she should have coughed, or done something to reveal her presence, only she hadn't thought about it. She had just walked onto the porch and waited, seeing this as an opportunity she couldn't pass up.

"Look, Worth, I don't want to fight with you," she said at last. She'd meant what she'd said, too, especially when she watched him set the empty beer bottle down on the table, making more noise than he should have, which spoke volumes about his mood.

She couldn't let Worth see the effect he had on her. Not now. Not ever. And entering into another verbal skirmish with him would put the power in his hands, power that could end up destroying her and what she held dear. At all costs, she had to maintain her cool.

"Is that what we're doing?"

"I don't want to play word games with you, either."

He jammed his hands into his pockets which pulled the fabric tighter across his privates. For a moment, her gaze lingered on the mound behind the zipper. Then realizing what she was doing, she jerked her head back up to his face, praying that he hadn't noticed anything amiss.

If he had, he didn't acknowledge it. Instead, he continued to stare at her through those blank eyes.

"What do you want, then?"

"To take my mother's place."

His head bolted back at the same time he went slack-jawed. "As my housekeeper?"

"Yes," Molly said with punch in her tone.

He pitched back his head and laughed. "Get real."

"I'm serious, Worth," she countered with an edge in her tone.

"So am I, and that's not going to happen."

"Why not?"

He smirked. "Come on, Molly, you know why not. You're a nurse, and that's what you need to be doing."

"I can do both. I can take care of the house and my mother."

"What about Trent?"

"I'll put him in day care, and he'll be just fine."

"No."

She ignored that terse rejection and went on, "My mother's mind is her own worst enemy right now. She thinks you're going to replace her."

"That's hogwash. She has a job here as long as she wants one. And I'll tell her that."

"I appreciate that, but I still want to take her place. I can take care of Mom, encourage her and she will see that my job as housekeeper is temporary. This way she won't worry about someone permanently replacing her. She'll know I'm only filling in. Not only that, but I'm good. I grew up helping her clean houses."

Worth looked astounded. "Are you nuts? Besides, you don't have to do that anymore."

"I know I don't have to. I want to."

"Dammit, woman, you haven't changed a bit."

Molly raised her eyebrows. "Oh?"

"Yeah, you're still as stubborn as a mule."

She wanted to smile but didn't. Instead she held her ground. "So are you."

Worth cursed at the same time their eyes collided then held tighter than magnets.

Suddenly the oxygen in the air seemed to disappear, forcing Molly to struggle for her next breath. She could tell Worth was also affected as his face lost what little color it had left. And something else happened, too, though she couldn't identify it.

What it *hadn't* been was hostility. So had it been blatant desire? No. She'd been mistaken. He despised her and that wasn't about to change. She didn't want it to, either, she assured herself quickly, though the undertow of his sexy charisma was pulling on her.

Forcing her panic aside, Molly sucked in a deep breath and stared at him with an imploring expression.

"I'll think about it," Worth muttered on a sour note, cramming his hands further down in his pockets, which pulled his jeans even tighter across that area.

Molly averted her gaze and muttered, "Thank you."

He laughed, but again without humor.

Feeling heat rush into her face, Molly knew she should leave before insult was added to injury. She was about to do just that when his next words froze her in her tracks.

"Why did you run out on me?"

Five

She whipped back around and stared at him, feeling as though she were strangling. "What did you say?" she finally managed to asked.

"Don't play the deaf ear thing on me." Worth's tone was low and rough. "It won't work. You heard every word I said."

"I used to admire your badass attitude," Molly responded with fire. "In fact, I thought you were the stud of all studs because of it."

His eyebrows shot up as though that shocked him.

"But now I know better."

His features darkened. "Oh?"

"That attitude sucks big time."

The look that crossed Worth's face was chilling, and he took a step toward her, only to stop suddenly as though he were a puppet on a string and someone had jerked that string. She knew better. Worth was no one's puppet and never had been. Then she recanted that thought. His parents apparently knew how to pull his strings and get away with it.

"You know I really don't give a tinker's damn what you think about me or my attitude." Worth's voice had grown rougher.

"Then why ask me that question?"

"Curiosity is the only thing I can figure," he said in an acid tone, fingering an unruly strand of light hair that grazed his forehead.

Molly was suddenly tempted to reach out and push it back in place, something she had done on many occasions that long-ago summer. That sensual memory was so vivid she felt like a piece of broken glass was slicing through her heart.

"Your curiosity can go to hell. I'm *not* answering you."

He smirked. "That's because you don't have a satisfactory explanation."

"I have no intention of swimming through the muddy waters of the past. With your cynical judgment of me, I'd just be wasting my time anyway."

No doubt she was on the defensive and probably sounded as cynical as he did, but she didn't care. If she were going to survive and keep her secret from him and his parents, she had to best him at his own game, or at least match him.

Or she'd die in that muddy water.

"What's wrong?" His eyes consumed her. "You look like something suddenly spooked you."

Was that genuine concern she heard in his voice? Of course not. As before, her mind was playing tricks on her. He didn't give a damn about her. He was too much into himself.

"I'm fine," she bit out.

"Liar."

Her head kicked back. "What do you want from me, Worth?"

"What if I said *you?*"

Molly shook her head, trying to recover from the effect those words spoken in that toe-curling, sexy drawl had on her.

"I wouldn't believe you," she finally whispered.

Those dark pools roamed over her while the blood pounded in her ears like a drum. Oh, God, this kind of craziness had to stop or she'd be like putty in his hands again and wouldn't be good for any thing or any one. That was why she hadn't wanted to see him again. She was too weak, too vulnerable where he was concerned. She only had to be in the same room with him and she almost went to pieces.

"You're right, you shouldn't believe me," he said harshly and coldly, "because it's not true."

Molly sucked in her breath and tried to pretend that piece of glass hadn't taken another chunk out of her heart.

"Maybe you'll answer me this."

Molly barely heard him as she was striving to hold onto her wits and dignity under his attack, knowing that she should turn around and walk away, that nothing good would ever evolve from this conversation.

Why bother? She no longer gave a damn, either.

She simply didn't want to reconnect with that part of her life. Not only was it over and done with, it was way too painful to rehash, especially with him. What she and Worth had between them that summer was obviously dead, and to pull the past out of the dark into the daylight was futility at its highest degree.

"I have to go," she said in a halting voice, refusing to look at him.

"Do you love him?"

Shock caused Molly to blink. "Who?"

"Your husband. That Bailey guy who fathered your child."

Oh, dear Lord, if only she'd kept on going, hadn't sought him out on the porch, then they wouldn't be having this insane dialogue, making a bad situation worse.

"Yes," she lied.

His gaze dropped to her left hand. "Are you still married? I don't see a wedding ring."

"We're divorced." She hated lying, but right now it seemed her only recourse. He was like the Energizer Bunny; he just kept on going, kept on asking questions that were, frankly, none of his business.

If she didn't take charge, there might not be an end to his questioning. The more he knew, the more dangerous her presence became. And she was trapped. She couldn't leave because of her mother.

So they had no alternative but to work through their animosity toward each other, so she could remain on the ranch, ideally as his housekeeper. Maybe getting it all out in the open now, once and for all, was best for both of them. Then they could move on with the day-to-day grind of their lives and be less apt to meddle in each other's.

"I could ask you why *you're* not married," Molly blurted out of the blue, then was appalled. All she was doing was adding fuel to an already out-of-control fire. Would she ever learn to keep her mouth shut?

"Yeah, you could."

Silence.

"So why aren't you?" She paused. "I understand you're still seeing Olivia. I thought she would've dragged you down the aisle by now."

"Well, you thought wrong," he declared flatly, glaring at her.

Good. She'd finally hit him where it hurt, as he'd done to her so many times. Then she felt badly. She was above playing these hurtful games. Exchanging barbs only made the situation worse.

"If I'm going to stay here and work—"

"I haven't said you could do that yet," Worth interrupted, narrowing his eyes on her.

"I'm not leaving, Worth. I can't. My mother needs me."

He shrugged. "When it comes down to it, I really don't give a damn what you do."

"As long as I…we stay out of your way," she added, positive she had verbally expressed what he hadn't.

"You got it."

Ignoring the suppressed anger in his voice, she asked, "How about we call a truce? Do you think that's possible?"

"Do you?" His eyes were brooding.

"I'm willing to try."

He shrugged again, his eyes roaming over her, seeming to linger on his favorite spot—her breasts, which upped her heartbeat significantly.

"Whatever," he said without enthusiasm.

Molly gritted her teeth, but swallowed her sharp comeback. "Good night, Worth."

He didn't respond.

"I hope you sleep well," she added.

"Yeah, right," he muttered tersely, then turned his back on her.

Feeling the cold night air close in on her, Molly went back into the warm house, only to reach her room and notice that she couldn't seem to stop shaking.

"Hey, boss, what's up?"

Instead of going back inside the house, Worth had made his way to the barn. He hadn't expected to run into his foreman Art Downing, but then he shouldn't have been surprised. Art never seemed to know when to go home. He loved his job, especially caring for and working with Worth's stable of prime horseflesh. In fact, Worth had determined long ago that Art was more comfortable at the ranch than he was at home with his wife and kids.

Like him, maybe Art just wasn't cut out for family life.

"I was about to ask the same thing," Worth said.

Art lifted his massive shoulders that matched the massive girth around his stomach, and grinned. "Just making sure these beauties are settled in for the night."

All the while he talked, Art was busy rubbing one of the horse's noses.

"They're fine. Go on and get out of here."

"I will as soon as I check one more thing."

"And just what would that be?" Worth asked, glad to have something on his mind besides Molly who spelled trouble with capital letters.

"Making sure everything's ready for tomorrow's delivery."

Worth had bought another stud horse last week and the targeted arrival was the following morning. "Who you kiddin', man? You've had things ready since we bought him."

"You're right there." Art grinned, then rubbed his belly. "I am gettin' kind of hungry."

"Then get your rear home. And don't come back until it's daylight, you hear?"

"Yes, sir." Art tipped his hat then was gone.

Worth knew he might as well be talking to the air. His foreman would be here long before daylight, which made him more valuable to Worth than money could ever buy.

If he did as his parents wished and ran for political office, his time at the ranch would be limited. Thanks to Art, the ranch would continue to run smoothly.

After taking his own tour of the stables and rubbing all the horses and calling them by name, Worth made his way back to the house. Once there, he grabbed another beer out of the fridge, then headed to his suite. Glancing at his watch, he noticed he only had thirty minutes before he was due at Olivia's. She didn't like anyone to be late.

Dammit, he didn't want to go, not to a dinner party. Hell,

he'd just taken her to dinner the night before. However, he had made a commitment he couldn't break, especially as the gathering was designed to introduce him as a possible candidate for the Texas Senate. Still, it was too formal an affair for him. He knew Olivia expected him to dress for the occasion, which meant a sports coat and slacks.

He hadn't told her that wasn't going to happen. He planned on showing up in jeans, a white shirt and a leather jacket. If she didn't like it, that was her problem.

Instead of showering and changing his clothes, however, Worth plopped down on the side of the bed and guzzled half his beer. God, he was mentally tired, and he didn't know why.

Yeah, you do.

Molly.

Sparring with her on the porch had depleted his energy. He didn't know if he could take having her around here indefinitely, especially if she was working as his housekeeper. How ludicrous was that, anyway? So why had he mealy-mouthed around? He should have told her in no uncertain terms that was impossible.

But seeing her again had reopened the wound he thought had scabbed over. He supposed that was what he found most crippling. And frightening. With her arrival, it was like the messy tracks she had left on his heart had suddenly been covered by a lovely snowfall.

Which made him more of a fool than he'd thought. When it came to her, he couldn't use good judgment, and that made him madder than hell. At this point, he didn't need the aggravation of her presence back in his life.

Maybe if she'd still been married and brought her husband with her that would have made things easier. Like hell, he told himself with a snort, bolting off the bed and finishing his beer.

For a second he was tempted to grab another one and

maybe another after that. By then he'd be on his way to getting smashed. The thought of Olivia's reaction to him showing up three sheets to the wind brought a smile to his face.

Then he sobered. Right now he had nothing to smile about. Okay, Molly had upset his apple cart, so to speak, and he wasn't happy about that. But he remained king of this empire. No one told him what to do or how to do it.

So why had he suddenly gone soft?

The first time he'd laid eyes on Molly, she had managed to wrap him around her little finger. But after she had run off, married someone else and had his kid, Worth was so sure he'd feel nothing but contempt for her, if and when he ever saw her again.

Well, the contempt was sure as hell there, but so was another ingredient—an ingredient he refused to name, though it burned like a raging fire in his gut.

"Give it a rest, Cavanaugh," he muttered in a fierce tone, hurrying into the bathroom like a stampede of bulls were after him.

Only problem was, his mind refused to cooperate. In the shower, he squinched his eyes closed under the water, but it didn't help. Instantly, the image of Molly jumped to the forefront of his mind. She was standing in front of him, her eyes gleaming with desire, while she caressed his face, then his body.

Worth groaned, then gave in to the pain that momentarily paralyzed him.

Six

"Mommy, when can I ride a horse?"

Molly pursed her lips. "Oh, honey, I don't think that's going to happen."

Trent scrunched his face. "You promised."

"I beg your pardon, my sweet, but I did no such thing."

"I bet that man will let me."

Molly almost smiled. "Are you talking about Worth?"

"No, that other man."

Molly thought for a moment, then realized Trent was talking about Art, Worth's foreman. She had always thought he was such a nice man and that Worth was lucky to have him, especially when Worth would get upset about something. Art never seemed to take it personally. Instead he would listen, then take care of the situation.

"I saw him on one of the horses from Granna's window." Trent's voice held excitement.

"That's great, but you don't know a thing about riding a horse."

"I could learn," Trent said with a protruding lower lip.

"We'll see, okay?"

"I—"

She gave him one of her looks. "I said we'll see."

Although he didn't respond, Molly knew he wanted to. His lower lip was now protruding and trembling. "I'll talk to Mr. Art tomorrow, but I'm still not making any promises, young man. Is that clear?"

Trent's face instantly changed, and he ran and gave her a hug.

"Come on, big boy, it's time for your bath, then bed."

Again, Trent looked as if he wanted to argue, only he didn't, as though he realized he'd pushed his mother far enough.

Long after Trent was in bed Molly stood at the window, staring at the cantaloupe-shaped moon and Venus close by. What a lovely clear night, she thought. And chilly, too. She turned and glanced thankfully at the gas logs with their bright, perky flames.

Considering the way Worth felt about her, he sure had given her nice quarters. But then the entire ranch house was nice, built for guests and entertaining, which, now that she was old enough to think about it, rather surprised her. Worth wasn't the entertaining type, didn't have that personality, or at least not the Worth she'd known and loved.

Apparently, that Worth was no longer in existence. If anything, he was more self-centered, more spoiled than ever, an entity unto himself, definitely someone she no longer recognized or wanted anything to do with.

On second thought perhaps now she was seeing the *real* Worth Cavanaugh. Maybe back then, she'd been so young, so impressionable, so inexperienced, she simply hadn't recognized those flaws.

Besides, she'd been madly, and obviously *blindly*, in love.

Since that was no longer the case, she had to do what was necessary for her mother, then leave ASAP.

Thinking about her mother suddenly made Molly long to see her. She checked on Trent one more time, then went to Maxine's room. Thankfully, her mother was still awake.

After she had made both of them a cup of flavored decaffeinated tea, Molly eased into the chair by the bed and said without preamble, "I plan to enroll Trent in a day care facility in town."

"What on earth for?" Maxine asked in an astonished voice.

Molly hesitated, which gave her mother time to voice her displeasure.

"Since you're not going to be here long, I want Trent to stay here." Maxine struggled to sit further up in bed, then winced from the exertion.

Molly hurried to her side only to have her mother hold out her hand. "I'm okay. The sooner I learn to move on my own the sooner I can get up and get back to work."

"That's not going to happen any time soon, Mother, and you know it."

"I know no such thing."

"Please, let's not argue about that again."

"Who's arguing?"

A short silence followed her mother's succinct words.

"So back to why you want to put Trent in day care," Maxine said.

"I'm staying."

When Molly's bluntly spoken words soaked in, Maxine gave a start. "What does that mean?"

"It means that I'm not leaving any time soon."

"But I don't understand. What about your job?"

"For now, I have a new one."

Maxine's eyes widened. "Pray tell, girl, you're not making a lick of sense. What are you talking about?"

"I'm going to take your place here as housekeeper."

Maxine gasped. "No, you're not."

"Mother."

"Don't you Mother me in that tone, young lady."

Molly almost swallowed her tongue to keep from making a sharp retort.

Not so with Maxine. She hammered on, "Why do you think I worked my fingers to the bone all these years?" When Molly would have spoken, Maxine held up her hand again. "No. You hear me out. I did that so you wouldn't have to do manual labor, though don't get me wrong, working for Worth is wonderful. The best job I've ever had, not to mention he's the best person I've ever worked for."

Boy, did that admission ever surprise Molly. She would have thought the opposite, but then maybe it was when he was around her that Worth took on a different personality. No doubt, he abhorred the ground she walked on. Well, the feeling was mutual.

Liar, her conscience whispered before she shoved that thought aside and concentrated on what her mother was saying.

"But that doesn't mean I want you doing that kind of work."

"I'm not above doing that kind of work, as you call it," Molly said flatly. "I'm quite good at it, actually, since I grew up helping, and learning, from you."

"That's beside the point." Maxine glared at her. "I'd rather Worth fire me and hire someone else than for you to give up your job in Houston."

"I never said I was giving up my job. I'm just taking my sick leave and vacation time. Once you get your brace and start physical therapy, you'll be good as new in no time. Then I'll be out of here."

Her mother grunted in disbelief, then said with despair in her tone, "I'm afraid I'll never be the same again. What if those twisted muscles don't straighten out and I have to have surgery? If that happens, then I won't be able to walk across the room without a cane or walker. Worth will surely replace me then."

"There you go borrowing trouble again."

"No, I'm just being realistic, something you young people are not."

Molly rolled her eyes in frustration. "Talk about me being hardheaded."

"If I can no longer cut it," Maxine argued, "then what's to keep him from making me second in command?"

"Mom, we've been over this issue several times already."

"I know, and I'm sorry for beating that dead horse," Maxine said in a petulant tone.

"If I take your place, your job won't be in jeopardy."

"No matter. I'm not about to let you do that."

"Too late," Molly said flatly. "It's a done deal."

"I can't believe Worth would approve that. I need to talk to him."

"I'll admit he wasn't overjoyed at the prospect, but I think he'll come around."

"After I get through with him, he won't," Maxine said.

"This is between Worth and me, Mother."

"Please, Molly, don't do this." Maxine's tone had a begging edge to it.

Molly sat on the bed beside Maxine, leaned over and kissed her on the cheek. "Please, *let* me do this. Don't fight me. You've always been there for me, never judged me for shaming you by getting pregnant before I married, then immediately divorcing. It's my turn now to pay you back."

Maxine placed her palms on either side of Molly's face, looked into her face with tear-filled eyes and said in a torn voice, "You're my child, my baby. That's what mothers do—love unconditionally."

Molly fought back the tears. "And that is what daughters do, too."

Maxine dropped her hands and fell back against the pillow. For a long moment both were silent, seemingly lost in their own thoughts.

Maxine was the first to speak. "I thought you were going to marry Worth, you know." Her mother's voice was weak and far off.

Molly almost choked on the pain that suddenly squeezed her heart. "I did, too, Mom, only it didn't work out."

"You never told me what happened." Her mother's eyes drilled her.

Molly licked her dry lips. "I know."

"It's okay." Maxine reached out and grabbed one of her daughter's hands. "If you ever want to tell me about it, I'm here. I've never been one to pry and I'm not about to start now. You've got a precious child and a wonderful career, so it's best to let sleeping dogs lie."

Molly tasted a tear. "You've been the best mother ever and still are." She sniffled, then smiled. "Perhaps one day I'll be able to confide in you."

"But it's okay between you and Worth now, right?" Maxine asked with concern. "I guess what I'm asking is do you still care about him in that way?"

"Absolutely not," Molly responded vehemently. "Granted, we'll never be friends, but we're okay around each other."

Here she was lying to her mother again. But she couldn't help it. Once she had almost blurted out the truth concerning her and Worth, but the words had stuck in her throat. After that, she had talked with a minister in Houston when she'd found out she was pregnant, then entered counseling.

While some people might judge her harshly for her silence concerning the baby's father and fact that she'd lied about marriage, she felt her mother never would, even if she were to learn the truth. Still, there was a part of Molly that just couldn't unburden her heart to her mother, or anyone else.

For now, no loved one or friend was privy to her heart's secrets.

"My, but you're quiet all of a sudden."

Molly shook her head and said, "Sorry." Then she leaned her head sideways and added, "Have you thought about going to a facility while you're recuperating?"

"Have you gone daft, child?"

Molly chuckled. "No, but I had to ask."

"If I have to leave this place, I would go to Houston with you."

"That's certainly an option."

"Only not now. I want to stay right here, get well, then go back to the job I love."

Molly stood and gave a thumbs up. "Together we'll make that happen."

"I knew you were stubborn—" Maxine's voice played out with a forlorn smile.

Molly chuckled again. "I'm going to bed. We both need our rest."

However, when she returned to her room the sound of a car door slamming pulled Molly up short. Without thinking, she dashed to the window, knowing it was Worth returning from another night out. Probably with Olivia again, though she didn't know that for sure. Still, she didn't move, continuing to track his movements, hoping he couldn't see her because the room was practically dark. Only a small lamp burned in one corner.

Molly glanced at the clock on the bookshelves and saw that it was past midnight. If he'd been with Olivia, had they made love? Suddenly her stomach clenched. The thought of his hands and mouth caressing another woman like they had hers didn't bear thinking about. In fact, it made her flat outright sick to her stomach, which was in itself *sick*.

Of course, he'd made love to Olivia, if not other women, as well. After all, it had been almost five years since she'd seen him. A man like Worth, with a heightened sexual appetite, or at least it had been that way with her, wouldn't have remained celibate all that time.

Dammit, it didn't matter, she told herself. But it did, though she was loathe to admit it because such an admission was dangerous to her peace of mind and threatened her sanity.

If she was going to go through with her plan to work for him—and she was—then she'd have to corral her mind and not let it wander down forbidden paths.

When Molly realized she had been indulging, she blinked just in time to see him saunter toward the house. He was halfway there when he looked up at her bedroom.

Feeling her heart leap into her throat, Molly jumped back, out of sight. Had she been in time? Had he seen her watching him? If so, what must he think?

When she mustered up the nerve to peek again, he was gone. Then disgusted with herself and her juvenile antics, she mentally kicked her backside all the way to bed.

She heard the grandfather clock in the hall chime three o'clock, realizing she had yet to close her eyes.

Damn him!

He had seen her all right. And for a second he was tempted to say to hell with everything, stride inside and bound down the hall to her room. Then what? he asked himself.

Make mad, passionate love to her?

Sure thing, as if she'd let him cross the threshold much less touch her. God, what was he thinking when he let his mind and emotions have free rein? Dwelling on the impossible was crazy. More to the point, it made *him* crazy.

Why he hadn't sent her packing was beyond him. It wasn't too late, he reminded himself as he grabbed a beer, then made his way to his room, making sure he didn't pause in front of hers.

But sleep was impossible. He'd already had too much to drink. He'd used the boring dinner party as an excuse to get partially plastered, much to Olivia's chagrin. Boring though it was, something good had come out of it. The man Olivia had invited as a potential backer for his campaign turned out to be someone he'd instantly liked and to whom he could relate.

Ben Gibbs seemed to have felt the same way about him. They had talked at length, and Worth had come away from the conversation positive Gibbs would back him if he chose to run against the incumbent. He had also spoken highly of Worth's parents, which was another good thing.

Other than Gibbs, the rest of the evening had been only tolerable. After everyone had left, Olivia had wanted him to stay. He made up some lame excuse, which didn't sit well with her, and left.

Now, alone in his bed with only his tormented thoughts, Worth almost wished he'd spent the night with Olivia, so he wouldn't think about *Molly* and that kid of hers. For some reason, he couldn't get the boy off his mind.

If only *he'd* gotten Molly pregnant that summer day in the barn when he hadn't used protection, how different his life would've been. He'd have a child—a son no less.

Now, he'd probably never have that opportunity even if he wanted it. According to the doctor, he'd be damn lucky if he could father a child. A horse had kicked him in the groin shortly after Molly had run out on him.

At the time, he'd been so busy nursing his anger and bitterness against Molly the diagnosis hadn't registered.

Having anything to do with a woman after that had been disgusting to him. The emotional wounds Molly had left had been open and oozing.

Now, after having seen her son, the enormity and repercussions of his accident rose up and hit him in the face like the chill from a bucket of ice water. To make matters worse, he hadn't even told his parents. To this day, they still didn't know that he might not ever give them the grandchildren they so coveted.

Dammit, by all rights Trent should have been his.

"You're full of it, too, Cavanaugh," he said out loud, followed by an ugly laugh.

He drained the remainder of his beer, then tossed the empty bottle on the floor at the same time the room swam. Good. Maybe he was drunk enough to fall asleep. Without removing his clothes, he fell across the bed, trying to forget he was nursing a hard on.

For Molly.

Seven

"Mommy, these pancakes are so good."

"I'm glad, honey, but don't you think you've had enough?" Molly smiled at her son. "Five is a lot, even for a growing boy. But you do need to finish your milk."

"Your cakes taste just like Granna's."

Noticing that Trent's mouth was smeared with syrup and butter, Molly grabbed a paper towel, moistened it, then wiped his entire face, while he squirmed. "Be still. You can't go to day care dirty."

"I'm not dirty."

"Yes, you are," she corrected him with a broader smile. "Go brush your teeth, then we'll go."

"Where's he going?"

Stunned that Worth had pulled her stunt and made an appearance without her knowledge sent her heart into a tailspin. Striving to cover that fact, Molly pulled in a deep breath, and looked at him, which only added to her trepidation. It looked as though he'd just gotten out of the shower as his thick hair was still damp and slightly unruly, which always made her want to run her hands through it.

But it was what he had on that had her heart in such a dither. His flannel shirt was tucked into worn jeans that fit his long, muscled legs like a second skin, especially over his crotch, leaving nothing to the imagination.

For a moment her eyes honed in on that private area and set up camp. Then realizing what she was doing, she jerked her head up at the same time she felt heat flood her face.

To make matters worse, she knew what he was thinking. The lines around his mouth deepened, his eyes turned into banked down coals of desire. Their gazes met and held for what seemed an eternity, but in reality was only seconds.

Bless Trent. He was the one who broke the tension that sizzled between them.

"Hey, Worth."

Her son's words brought Molly back to reality with a thud. "Mr. Cavanaugh to you, young man."

"It's okay. He can call me Worth. I want him to."

Trent turned his eyes tentatively to his mother, as if seeking her approval. "Whatever," she said without conviction.

"I love your cows and horses," Trent said to Worth. "I wish I could ride one of your horses," he added down in the mouth.

"Trent." Molly's tone was reprimanding.

Trent pawed the tile floor with a booted foot, his lower lip beginning to stick out. "I didn't do nothing, Mommy."

"He sure didn't." Worth squatted in front of him. "How 'bout I start teaching you to ride today?"

"No," Molly exclaimed in horror.

Both looked at her like she'd just sprouted two heads.

"I'm about to take Trent to day care."

"Why?" Worth asked, standing, his gaze pinning hers.

Though she wanted to squirm, she didn't. She met him eye for eye. "Because I can't see about him and the house, too. And Mother's not able."

"Kathy can watch him."

"I need her to help me."

A grim look crossed Worth's face, especially his lips. "I don't want you doing that."

Molly glanced over at Trent, then back to Worth, as if to say now's not the time to have this discussion."

"Mommy?"

Without taking her eyes off Worth, she said to her son, "Run brush your teeth."

After looking from one adult to the other, Trent trudged off, his little shoulders slumped.

"He's not a happy camper," Worth said into the tension-filled silence.

"He'll get over it."

"Let him stay here, Molly. I'll hire someone to watch him."

"I can't allow that."

"Why the hell not?"

"I'm responsible for running the house—your house—and I don't want to be worried about Trent and what he's into. Furthermore, it's not your place to hire someone to watch my son."

"For God's sake, Molly, that's all the more reason to put an end to this nonsense. I don't want you running my house."

"Are you backing out on your word, Worth?" She glared at him.

His eyes narrowed on her. "Unlike you, I don't do that."

She wasn't stupid; she knew where that remark originated. He had just taken another potshot at her for when she'd walked out on him. "Contrary to what you might think, I don't do that, either."

He sneered, then muttered something under his breath.

She didn't want to know what it was because it would add coals to an already smoldering fire that simmered between them. Until her mother was up and about, Molly reminded herself she must contain her tongue and hold her counsel, or else she wouldn't survive this jungle she'd reentered.

"I was serious when I offered to teach him to ride," Worth said in a more conciliatory tone than she'd heard in a while. "But I was more serious about him staying here."

Fear burgeoned inside her. "Why do you care?"

"He seems to be a good boy, and I know how much Maxine enjoys his company. She talks about him all the time, how much she misses seeing him."

"My mother told you that?"

"You act shocked," he remarked in a dry voice.

"I guess I am." Molly's tone was confused.

"Obviously you don't know it, but I have a great deal of respect for your mother. She's not just my housekeeper. She's a friend and part of my family."

"I appreciate that, Worth," Molly said in a halting voice as she shifted her gaze. "I really do. I know she feels the same about you."

"That she does."

"Again, I so appreciate your patience with her injury."

"When she hurt her back," Worth responded, "her mind must've conjured up the worst possible case scenario because I never had any intention of letting her go."

"She definitely went into the panic mode."

"Under those circumstances, my suggestion is that you spend time working with, and caring, for her, and let the house go."

"I can't do that, Worth. Even though I'm a nurse, and a good one I might add, I'm not a physical therapist. Too, it wouldn't be good for Mother and me to be together that much. Too much togetherness can be a bad thing."

"Don't I know that," he muttered again.

"Speaking of togetherness, how are Eva and Ted?" Not that she cared, she told herself, stunned that she'd even inquired.

Worth shrugged and gave her a strange look. "Same as always—great."

"I'm glad," Molly acknowledged in a stiff tone.

"You never did like them and still don't." A flat statement of fact.

Molly deliberately changed the subject. "When I get back from town, I need to talk to you about upcoming events. I know about the day-to-day run-of-the-mill things. Mom told me your schedule, more or less, that you—"

"Dammit, Molly, put a stopper in it, okay?"

Her mouth clamped shut at the same time her temper flared. "Don't you dare talk to me like that."

"Sorry," he muttered again, shoving a hand through his hair, clearly indicating his irritation.

"Look, Worth, we can't go on like this."

"And how is that?"

"You're being deliberately obtuse, but for the moment I'm going to let that pass."

Worth eyes darkened on her. "Okay, you win."

Molly's breathing slightly accelerated. "On both Mother and Trent?"

"On one."

"And that is?"

"The house."

Her anger rose. "You have nothing to say about Trent."

"Don't you want him here?"

"Of course," she admittedly tersely.

"Then let him stay. I know someone who's perfect to look after him."

"And I'll pay them," she said in an unbending tone.

After having said that, she experienced a hollow feeling in the pit of her stomach like she'd done something terribly wrong and didn't know how to fix it.

Worth and Trent should not be a pair, but if she continued to remain unmovable, then it might raise a red flag, giving Worth cause for thought. She couldn't allow that. Hence, she'd try Worth's plan. If it didn't work out, then she could always insist on reverting to *her* plan and to hell with what Worth said or thought.

"That's fine by me," he said on a sigh.

"So can we get down to other business now?" she asked.

He made a face, then peered at his watch. "Now's not a good time for me. I have to meet with a breeder. How 'bout later, maybe this evening?"

Before you go see your lover. I don't think so. Appalled at her catty thoughts, Molly felt the color drain from her face as she turned quickly around, praying that he hadn't read her thoughts through her eyes.

"Molly?"

The crusty edge in his voice brought her eyes back around. "What?"

For another long moment, their gazes held.

Worth cleared his throat, then said in an even crustier tone. "Will that be okay?"

"I guess so," she responded in brittle tone.

Worth gave her another long look out of suddenly vacant eyes, then left the room. Once alone, Molly sank against the kitchen cabinet for support, wondering how she was going to survive staying there even one more day.

He just couldn't keep a lid on it.

It was as though he'd suddenly developed diarrhea of the mouth. He shouldn't have interfered with her plan to put the kid in day care. The last thing he wanted was to be saddled with her brat.

Not true.

He liked the boy, and that was the problem. He should leave them both alone, have as little to do with them as possible. Only that wasn't *possible* since Molly insisted on working for him.

Damn her lovely hide.

Only she wasn't to blame. He could have put his foot down and said an emphatic *no* and meant it. She wouldn't have had a choice but to comply. After all, she was on his turf with no alternative but to do as he said.

But again, he'd wimped out, and let her have her way, at least on one account.

Worth let go of a string of expletives that did little to relieve that gnawing in his gut. If only she didn't look so good or smell so good, having her around would be easier.

This morning when he'd walked into the kitchen and saw her dressed in those low cut tight black jeans that hugged her butt and legs to perfection, and the white T-shirt that also hugged her breasts and stomach with the same perfection, he wanted to grab her and punish her with hard, angry kisses for the havoc she was wreaking in his life.

Of course, he hadn't made such an insane move, didn't plan to, either. He aimed to keep as wide a berth between them as possible. With that kind of rationale, he'd be fine, or so he hoped. To think she'd only been there four days. That already seemed an eternity.

Realizing he was almost at his parents' house, Worth gave his head a fierce shake to clear it. Molly was poison and he had to stop thinking about her, *stop wanting her.* Around his parents, he had to be constantly on guard; they were much too inquisitive and much too intuitive.

They had never liked her and had made that quite clear. But he hadn't given a damn. He'd liked her. Hell, he'd *loved her,* and would have married her if she hadn't left him.

Bitterness rose in the back of Worth's throat in the form of bile. Swallowing deliberately, he concentrated on maneuvering up the circular drive in front of his parent's antebellum home. About that time, his father walked onto the porch.

Olivia's father, Peyton Blackburn, stepped out, too, just as Worth braked his truck, killed the engine and got out.

He didn't have anything against Blackburn except that he thought he was better than most, but then that seemed a characteristic of many of the well-to-do families in this town. He was sure people said the same about him and his parents.

"Hey, son, your timing's perfect."

At sixty Ted Cavanaugh still posed a striking figure, Worth thought. Tall and slender with a thatch of silver hair and blue eyes, his good looks had turned many ladies' heads. But as far as Worth knew, he'd never looked at another woman besides his mother. From all appearances, they seemed to adore each other.

"What's up, Dad?" Worth asked, then let his gaze wander to Olivia's dad who posed an unstriking figure. Blackburn, in his middle sixties, looked his age, sporting a paunch around the middle and deep grooves in his face. But the main reason Worth thought him unattractive was the scowl that rarely left his face.

Even now, when he appeared to be smiling, he wasn't. Yet when he spoke, his voice was pleasant enough. "We're working a deal, young man," he said to Worth. "It concerns you."

Worth paused, shook Peyton's outstretched hand, then patted his dad on the shoulder. "How so?"

Ted smiled a huge smile and was about to speak when Peyton jumped in. "No, let me tell him."

"Suit yourself," Ted exclaimed in an amicable tone.

"Tell me what?" Worth was curious and it showed.

"I've decided to go ahead and deed Olivia that parcel of land that adjoins yours."

Good for Olivia, Worth wanted to say, but didn't. What he did say was, "That's great, but what does that have to do with me?"

Ted and Peyton both looked at each other, then back at him, stunned expressions on their faces.

"What?" Worth pressed, getting more agitated by the moment.

"It's got everything to do with you, son, since you're going to marry Olivia."

Worth felt his jaw go slack.

Eight

"Dad, we need to talk."

Worth knew his blunt words bordered on rudeness, especially since he'd totally ignored Ted Cavanaugh's comment about marriage. But he didn't give a damn. Who he married was none of his parents' business, and he wasn't about to let them think it was—rude or not.

Blackburn shifted as though uncomfortable, then said, "Ah, look, I'll leave you two alone. I know you've got lots to discuss, especially with all this political stuff brewing."

"Thanks for stopping by, buddy," Ted responded absently.

Blackburn tipped the brim of his hat to both men, then spoke to Worth, "You take care, you hear? We'll talk about the land and the race later."

"Thanks, Peyton," Worth said, "we'll keep in touch."

Once he'd driven off, Ted said, "Come on in. Your mother's waiting to see you. I think she's made breakfast."

"Mother cooking?" Worth asked in a light voice, purposely masking the fury that was churning inside him.

"Hannah's on vacation," Ted said by way of explanation. "Anyway, we figured you'd be by, so…"

Worth's father let the rest of the sentence trail off as they made their way inside, straight to the kitchen, where the smell of bacon and sausage put Worth's stomach on edge. His mother was in the process of setting the table. When they entered, Eva looked up and smiled, then walked over and gave Worth a cool peck on the cheek.

Like his father, she didn't look her age, continuing to hold her beauty. Although tall and rather strapping, she had beautiful skin and hair, hair that held its true color, a natural blond. But there was an air about Eva that was also off-putting.

"You're shocked, I know," she said, waving her hand across the bar where an array of food was set.

"You got that right. How long has it been since you've made a meal?"

"I'd rather not say," Eva replied in a coy tone. "If you don't mind, that is."

Although she smiled, Worth noticed it never quite reached her eyes. Suddenly Molly's face rose to the forefront of his mind. When she smiled, every feature lit.

Now where the hell had that come from? Dammit, Molly should be the furthest thing from his mind.

"Get a plate and chow down, son, then we'll talk."

The last thing Worth wanted to do was chow down. After the comment his father had made in front of Blackburn, his stomach remained in no mood to tolerate food, even if it smelled divine. In order not to hurt his mother's feelings, he filled a plate and forced himself to swallow as much as he dared.

A while later, after the plates had been cleared and the cups refilled with freshly brewed coffee, Ted asked, "Did I open my mouth and insert my foot in front of Blackburn?"

Worth didn't pull any punches. "You sure as hell did."

Eva's eyes sprang from one to the other. "What's going on?"

Ted told her what he'd said.

Her eyes drilled her son. "I don't see anything wrong with that. You do intend to marry Olivia, don't you?" She paused, then went on before Worth could answer. "Although I am surprised she doesn't have a ring and that a date hasn't been set."

Worth barely managed to keep a lid on his temper. "Marriage is not in the cards for me," he said, "at least not any time soon." Probably never, he wanted to add, but didn't. No use throwing gasoline on a burning fire.

"And just why not?" Eva pressed in an irritated tone. "To be a more viable candidate for office, you need a suitable wife. And Olivia is certainly that."

That lid was jarring loose. "Don't you think that's my call, Mother?"

"What about the land?" Ted chimed in. "I thought you wanted to increase the size of your herd of horses."

A vein in Worth's neck beat overtime. "I do, Dad."

Had his parents always been this steeped in his business and he just hadn't realized it? If so, perhaps that was because he was an only child, and they doted on him. No excuse. He refused to let them live their lives through him.

"Look, Art and I are trying to figure out a way to utilize the land I already have," Worth explained. "We're not there yet, but we're making headway."

"Why would you do that when more land is being offered on a silver platter?" Eva asked in that same irritated tone.

"Because I'm not ready to marry Olivia."

"If your tone of voice is anything to judge by, you won't ever be."

"That's entirely possible," Worth quipped.

His parents looked at each other, then back at him. But again, it was his mother who spoke. "Is it because *she's* back?"

Here we go again, Worth thought with disgust. Same song, second verse. "No, it's not because Molly's back."

"I just don't understand you, Worth." Eva's tone was as cold as the look she gave him.

He refused to take the bait, so he kept quiet.

Eva's generous lips thinned. "You know we're concerned. You should respect that."

"That's right, son, you're not being fair to us."

Worth stood abruptly. "The fact that Molly has come to see about her mother is none of your business."

Eva's gaze tracked him. "I still can't believe you'd let her back in your house after what she did to you."

This time Worth's lips thinned. "Don't press it, Mother. I told you Molly's off-limits."

He might as well have been talking to the wall for Eva steamrolled right on, "You never said how long she plans to stay."

"Mother!"

Eva's hand flew to her chest as though terribly offended. "That's a perfectly legitimate concern I would think."

"She's taking her mother's place as my housekeeper." Hell, he might as well drop the bomb now as later, and let the debris fall where it may.

Ted and Eva gasped simultaneously, then they both started talking at once, which turned into a bunch of gibberish.

Worth held up his hand. "Don't say another word, either of you. I've made my decision and it stands."

"As my son," Eva said with a quiver, "I gave you more credit than that."

"Sorry to disappoint."

"I understand she has a child."

Worth shrugged. "So she has a child."

"I can't imagine her with a brat."

That nixed it. Suddenly fury was an invisible malignancy that threatened to devour him. Yet somehow he managed not to throttle his own mother. "His name is Trent."

"Then he's with her." Eva pursed her lips.

"Yes," Worth said in a tired tone.

"You don't still care about her, do you?" Eva asked in a softer, gentler tone as though realizing she pushed as far as she could without completely alienating her son.

"No." Worth's voice was clipped. "If we don't change the subject, I'm out of here. Is that understood?"

Eva sighed as she cast another look at her husband who merely shrugged his shoulders as if to say, what choice do we have.

"So, Dad, do you really think I have a chance to win the Senate seat if I decide to toss my hat into the ring?"

Ted's heretofore glum features returned to life. "You betcha. Dan Elliot has lost his popularity with his constituents, which means you've got a clear shot at taking the nomination, if not the election."

Worth rubbed his chin in an idle fashion. "I guess the next step is to have a gathering of supporters and test the waters."

"Now you're talking, son," Eva put in. "Once you win that Senate seat, perhaps you'll become so addicted you'll keep right on climbing the political ladder."

"Hold on, Mom. I'm not even sure about this race, much less anything else."

"I think a barbecue would do for starters."

Worth thought a moment. "That sounds so trite and typical, but I guess that's still the best way to go."

"You need to get Maxine—" Eva paused midsentence,

then made a face. "Oh, dear, for a moment I forgot she's out of commission."

"Not a problem. I've got it covered."

Eva's mouth looked pinched. "Well, I doubt that Molly's capable—"

"Mother!"

"Sorry," she said, compressing her lips.

Worth knew she wasn't in the least sorry, but nonetheless she had the sense to let the subject drop. Suddenly he felt the urge to get out of his parents' house before he completely blew his temper and said things he'd regret, not that he had any intention of defending Molly because he didn't. Still, it bothered him that they looked on her as someone they had carte blanche to belittle and get by with it.

Since he had no intention of defending her, he had no alternative but to keep his mouth shut. He couldn't have it both ways.

Suddenly Worth felt like he'd stepped in a bed of quicksand and was being sucked under.

"Look, I gotta go," he said, lunging to his feet and heading for the door. Then he turned and said to his mother, "Thanks for breakfast. I'll be in touch."

By the time he reached his truck, he slammed his hand down on the top and cursed a blue streak.

Believe it or not she had been at the ranch a week. Since Maxine still needed her, she intended to stay on a while longer. To her relief, the last few days had passed uneventfully.

Molly had gone about her business of taking care of the household duties. With Trent content and happy, watched by a young lady named Tammy Evans, she was free to do what needed to be done. With Kathy's physical help and Maxine's verbal input, Molly was pleased.

The house was lovely and her mother had apparently taken

great pride in keeping it that way, which made things easy for Molly. In the beginning, she'd been leery of her temporary position. But after the first day, Molly realized she actually enjoyed doing something different.

Working with the public, especially the *ill* public, was a far cry from working with inanimate objects such as dishes and crystal. Cooking was the part she liked least, never having mastered that craft like her mother. But she guessed it didn't matter because Worth apparently hadn't wanted her to cook for him.

It seemed as if they had fallen into a pattern of avoiding each other, which was just fine with Molly. Oh, they passed in the hall and at those particular times, their gazes never failed to meet, then tangle. Most times she couldn't read his response unless his features were pinched in anger.

She knew he continued to resent her presence, but that couldn't be helped, she told herself as she went about slicing some fruit for lunch. But she knew sooner or later, they would have to talk, not only about the house, but about upcoming parties or events.

In fact, word had gotten around that a barbecue for potential political backers was on the horizon. In due time she supposed he would speak to her about that.

Meanwhile, she would continue to divide her time between her chores, her mother and her son, all of which were full-time jobs. However, she wasn't complaining; the setting was too perfect. Not only did she work inside, but she worked outside, as well. If she had a hobby, it was growing plants. And her green thumb was evident, especially at this time of year. The multileveled porch was ablaze with potted plants filled with vibrant fall colors.

Now, as she continued to slice the fruit, Molly gazed through the window into the bright sunlight, admiring her handiwork.

She wondered what Worth thought, or even if he'd noticed the added pots of plants.

"You've done a great job with the porch."

Molly's heart went wild. Was that mental telepathy or what? She swung around and faced Worth who looked like he'd been ridden hard and put up wet. The lines on his face seemed deeper; his hair was disheveled; his jeans, shirt and boots were covered in dust.

"What happened to you?" she blurted out.

"Art and I have been clearing land."

"Must have been some task."

"It was that and more."

"You look exhausted."

"I am. But it's nothing a shower and a glass of tea won't cure."

She immediately crossed to the fridge and opened it.

"You don't have to wait on me, you know?" His voice was low with a moody edge to it.

She looked back at him, then swallowed. "I know, but I don't mind." Before he could say anything else, she latched on to the pitcher of tea, poured him a glass, then held it out to him.

As though careful not to touch her, he took the glass, then without taking his gaze off hers, put it to his lips and took a big gulp. His stare was all consuming.

Molly wanted to look away, but couldn't. She was mesmerized by the unexpected heat in his eyes and the way he smelled—manly—like clean sweat. Suddenly her palms went clammy and her mouth went dry.

Before he realized the impact he had on her, she whirled around, went back to the cabinet, picked up the knife and began cutting more fruit. It was in a split second that it happened.

The knife slipped and instead of slicing the apple, it sliced her. "Oh!" she cried, just as Worth reached her side, grabbed her finger, and squeezed it until the blood stopped.

"Dammit, Molly," he said in ragged voice.

"Why are you yelling at me?" she cried, looking at him only to realize his lips were merely a heartbeat away from hers, his eyes seemingly dark with need.

She knew in that second he intended to kiss her.

Nine

Only he didn't.

Worth swore, then focused his attention back to her finger that he now held under the faucet, rinsing off the blood. Molly looked on in shocked silence—not because she'd injured herself, but because she had wanted him to kiss her. Disappointment washed through her in waves.

No! her conscience cried. That was insane. She never wanted him to touch her. Physical contact of that nature was forbidden and out of the question. Again, keeping her distance was her only method of survival.

And her hand in his was *not* keeping her distance.

"It's okay," she murmured, tugging at her hand, only he wouldn't let go.

He grabbed a paper towel and gently touched the wound.

"Ouch," Molly exclaimed before she thought.

"Sorry." Though Worth's tone was gruff, his touch was

gentle, which made her quiver all over, especially since he continued to examine the wound at close quarters. Much too close.

When he finally raised his head and looked at her, Molly was hit with a sizzle of electricity. For a second the world seemed to tip on its axis. Clearing his throat, Worth moved his head back.

"I think you're going to live," he said in a husky tone.

Molly managed a shaky smile. "You think so?"

A semblance of a smile reached his lips, which warmed her insides even more. God, she couldn't let herself fall under this man's spell again. She couldn't. It was just too painful. He ripped her soul out once already and stomped on it. She couldn't allow him to do it again. If it were just her—maybe she'd go for it. But it wasn't just about her.

Trent.

He was the one she had to think about. With that sobering thought, Molly jerked her hand out of his, which in turn dislodged the tissue, causing the cut to start bleeding again. Without thinking, she stuck that finger in her mouth.

"Don't do that," Worth all but snapped.

She removed her finger and stared at him. "A little blood never hurt anyone."

"I'll get some ointment and a Band-Aid."

"That's okay. It'll eventually stop bleeding."

"Until it does, what are you going to do?"

She couldn't believe they were having this rather inane conversation about a cut that was certainly not serious. A big to-do about nothing, actually. "Ah, good question," she said at last.

"I'll be right back."

After he had gone, Molly wrapped another paper towel around the wound and leaned against the cabinet, realizing her legs suddenly had the consistency of Jell-O.

As promised, Worth returned in record time and without asking, reached for her hand. If he held her hand a bit longer than necessary to administer first aid, they both chose to ignore it.

Maybe that was because Trent came dashing through the door about that time, only to pull up short, his eyes widening on the scene before him. Instantly, Molly reclaimed her hand and stepped a safe distance from Worth.

Trent's eyes went straight to the bandage. "Mommy, did you hurt your hand?"

"Yes, honey, I did, but it's okay."

"Did Worth fix it?"

Molly forced a smile. "He surely did."

"But you're a nurse."

Worth chuckled, which instantly drew her gaze and made her catch her breath. It had been so long since she'd heard him laugh, her body went into meltdown. He was sex personified, and she couldn't stop herself from reacting no matter how hard she tried. If she weren't careful, she'd be drooling, for heaven's sake.

"You'll learn one day," Worth said to Trent, "that nurses and doctors are the worst patients ever."

Trent's eyes got big again. "Really?"

Worth winked at him. "Really."

"Okay, you two, enough," Molly put in, then focused on Trent. "Go wash your hands. Lunch is almost ready."

Trent hesitated, cutting his gaze to Worth. "Will you eat with us?" he asked.

Stunned at her son's bluntness, Molly immediately said, "I'm sure Worth has other plans. I'll—"

"No, I don't, except to wash up a bit."

Silence fell over the room at the same time Molly darted her eyes back to Worth. He returned her gaze with one as innocent as a new born babe's. Damn, she thought, now what?

She had planned to take her mother lunch, and she and Trent would join her while she ate. Worth had certainly usurped those plans. Not necessarily, she told herself. She could say no to Worth, tell him what she'd had in mind. If the truth be known, he was probably wishing he'd kept his mouth shut. Wonder why he hadn't?

"Oh, boy," Trent said, racing for a chair.

"Hey, slow down," Molly reprimanded. "You know not to run in the house. Any house."

"Sorry," he muttered, his eyes on Worth, who once again had something akin to a smile on his face.

Trent smiled back and Molly's stomach did a somersault. For a brief moment the resemblance between father and son was so obvious she could scarcely breathe, anxiety having another field day with her stomach.

"Molly?"

Worth's voice brought her out of her trance. "What?" Even though she answered, she knew she didn't sound like herself.

"Are you all right?"

"I'm fine," she said stiffly, groping to cover her tracks. "Why do you ask?"

Worth's dark eyes narrowed, but then he shrugged, glancing quickly at Trent whose eyes were ping-ponging between them, as if sensing something was going on.

"No reason," Worth finally said, then changing the subject asked, "What's for lunch?"

"Roast sandwiches, chips and fruit."

Worth winked at Trent. "Sounds like a winner to me. How 'bout you, son?"

Son.

Don't call him that, Molly wanted to scream. He's not your son—he's *mine*. All mine, she told herself savagely and desperately, as she looked out the kitchen window into the meadow, the sun creating a beauty that miraculously calmed her fractured nerves.

"Mommy, I'm hungry."

"Ah, sorry, honey. I'm coming."

Worth shoved back his chair and walked toward her. "Tell me what I can do."

"Nothing," she said in an obviously cold tone.

He paused midstride, his eyebrows kicking up and a scowl darkening his features. "Excuse me," he muttered, then pivoted on one foot and made his way back to the table.

Molly released a pent-up breath, knowing that Worth was not used to having someone give him orders. That was his job, and he expected everyone, especially hired help, to hop to it. The long hot days of their summer together taught her that.

However, for some unknown reason, he didn't make an issue out of her bossiness, most likely because Trent was there, which was a good thing. She wasn't in the mood to take any of his high-handedness.

"What do you guys want to drink?" Molly asked, making her tone as pleasant as possible, mostly for her own sake. She had to prove to herself that she could be with Worth and behave like a rational, in-control woman. No matter what, he must not rattle her.

Several minutes later, the goodies were on plates, on the table and the tea glasses filled. Though they ate in silence, Molly was aware of Worth, how much he turned her on and how much he provoked her. A double-edged sword, on which she hopefully wouldn't fall.

She sensed he was aware of her, as well. When she accidentally looked at him, he was watching her with a mixture of desire and anger.

"Mommy, I'm finished."

Thank God for her son's perfect timing. "I made cookies

for dessert," she said in a higher than normal voice. "You want one?"

"Can I have two?"

Molly cocked her head, then smiled. "I guess so, since you were such a good boy and ate all your sandwich."

"Mr. Worth, you want some, too?" Trent asked.

Molly couldn't help but notice that her son looked at Worth like he was a hero. She could understand that. As always, Worth looked the consummate cowboy, dressed in jeans, white shirt, and boots, and hat.

It was at that moment that she regretted letting Trent remain at the ranch. She should have insisted he go to day care, eliminating the chance of Worth and Trent becoming too chummy.

But it was too late to renege and too late for regrets. She'd just have to be sure to keep them apart as much as possible.

"You bet, I do," Worth said. "Who in their right mind would pass up homemade cookies?"

"Especially the ones my mommy makes." Trent grinned. "They're yummy."

"Thanks, sweetie," Molly said. "Before you dig in, why don't you and I take Granna's meal to her?"

"I want to stay here with Mr. Worth."

Worth raised his eyebrows. "Unless you need the help, we'll stay and eat our cookies."

Which was exactly what she didn't want. Since she'd seen the likeness in them, she couldn't bear the idea of leaving them alone together. Yet she couldn't make a scene about it, either. She might possibly raise a red flag, something she still did not want to do.

"That's fine," she muttered, grabbing her mother's tray and making her way out of the room.

Five minutes later she walked back in the kitchen to find

Worth seemingly hanging on every word Trent was saying. Panic almost paralyzed her, but she rebounded, saying to her son, "Hey you, it's your nap time with Granna."

"Aw, Mommy, I don't want to take a nap. I'm too big. Tammy doesn't make me."

"Since Tammy's off today, you're out of luck." Molly gave Trent a pointed look. "So don't start whining."

He made a face, which she ignored. "I'll join you and Granna in a minute, after I clean up the kitchen." Molly paused and ruffled his hair. "First, though, tell Worth bye."

Reluctantly, he did as he was told.

"See ya, fellow," Worth said. "Hey, how would you like to look at some of my horses, say maybe tomorrow?"

"Oh, boy," Trent shouted, his gaze landing on Molly. "Could I, Mommy? Could I?"

It was on the tip of her tongue to say not only no, but hell no. She didn't say either. "We'll see. Okay?"

Trent knew not to argue, but his reply was glum. "Okay."

Once he left, a silence fell over the room. At last, Worth broke it. "Come on, let's get this mess cleaned up."

"I don't need your help," Molly said in a stilted tone, then realizing how she must have sounded, she softened her next words. "But thanks, anyway."

"Suit yourself," Worth almost barked.

She turned her back and went to the sink, thinking he would leave, only to have him say, "When you finish, I'd like to talk to you."

Molly swung around, her breasts rising and falling rapidly. For a millisecond, his gaze honed in on her chest, which created more chaos inside her. "Ah, can't you talk to me now?"

"No. I want your full attention." His tone was thick and low. "I'll be in the sunroom."

The entire time Molly cleaned up the kitchen, dread hung

over her. And panic. Had Trent said or done something that had made Worth suspicious? God, she hoped not. But Worth had sounded so serious she couldn't help but worry.

By the time she joined him, Molly was a bundle of nerves. "So what did you want?" she asked without preamble.

His eyes seemed like black holes as they pinned her, as though her directness pissed him off. "Sit down. Please."

"I'll stand, if you don't mind."

"If you're trying to test my patience, you're doing a damn good job of it."

"Sorry," she whispered, hoping for the best but preparing for the worst.

"I'm sure you've heard that I've been considering having a political rally here. Anyhow, I've decided to have it and I want to do a barbecue."

Feeling slightly shell-shocked, she peered into his face, knowing her eyes would rival the size of silver dollars. "Is that what you wanted to talk to me about?"

"Yes," he said in a clipped tone. "What else?"

"Ah, nothing. I'll take care of it."

"No, you won't."

"Excuse me?"

"I don't want you messing with all that. Hire someone to cater it."

"Why?"

"Because I said to."

They glared at each other.

"That's what I was hired to do."

He laughed without humor, which raised her ire to the next level. "If my mother were still in charge, would you hire an outsider?"

Worth didn't hesitate. "No."

"Point taken, I hope."

Faster than a streak of lightning on a stormy night, Worth crossed the room and grabbed her arm.

The very air around them seemed to have dried up, making speech impossible.

"Did anyone ever tell you you've got a smart mouth?" he asked.

"Let me go," she demanded.

"When I'm ready," he shot back.

Molly parted her lips just in time to collide with his mouth in a raw, wet, hungry kiss that sent her senses reeling. She clung to him for dear life.

Ten

From some foreign place in her mind, Molly heard Worth groan, then the next thing she knew he had shoved her at arm's length. With his breaths coming in shuddering gulps, he stared down at her, a dark, tortured expression on his face.

Molly couldn't move. She couldn't even breathe. Like him, she was too stunned at what had just taken place. Thank goodness, he hadn't abruptly released her, or she would have fallen to her knees. They were weak and trembling just like the rest of her body that still felt the imprint of his lips adhered to hers. To make matters worse, she continued to feel the way he'd pushed into her, making her aware of his hard and urgent mound. To her horror, it had felt so good, she had pressed back.

What on earth had she done? *The unpardonable.*

As though he read her mind, Worth muttered in a low, agonized tone, "I must have lost my mind."

Those cold, harsh words were the catalyst Molly needed

to strengthen her body and her resolve. She jerked herself free and gave him a bitter look. "How do you think I feel?" she flung back in much the same tone.

"Okay, so it was a mistake," Worth responded, his tone bordering on the brutal. "Still, I'm not going to apologize."

Molly laughed, but it, too, was crammed with bitterness. "You apologize? The great Worth Cavanaugh." She laid the sarcasm on so thick a sharp knife wouldn't have cut it. "Why, that thought never crossed my mind, not for one second."

"Dammit, Molly."

"Don't you dare damn me. You're the one who—" She stopped suddenly, hearing her voice—along with her control—crack. She could easily go to pieces right in front of his eyes. As it was, she was barely keeping body and soul together. But she couldn't let him know that. She feared he would use that weakness to his advantage.

After all, he was fighting on his home turf, which definitely gave him the upper hand.

"Kissed me," Worth finally said, finishing the sentence she'd started earlier.

"That's right," she countered with spunk.

"And I don't know why the hell, either."

"I hope you're not asking me."

"Maybe I am."

"You're wasting your time."

"I'm not so sure about that." He paused and their hostile gazes collided. "You damn sure kissed me back."

"That I did," she admitted, then felt heat seep into her face and scorch it. He was right. She had kissed him back. Had she ever, and even though it had been so long, Molly felt like she had just reentered the gates of heaven. But again, she didn't intend to share feelings so personal even she was having trouble digesting them.

She had tried so hard to keep from stepping into this hornets' nest and getting stung, but she had failed miserably. The truth was, she hadn't stepped in; she'd jumped in.

Jamming a hand through his already mussed up hair, Worth stepped further back, though he continued to stare at her under hooded eyes. "Maybe you shouldn't stay here."

Molly panicked, widening her eyes. "Are you kicking me out?"

"I didn't say that," he said tersely.

"Then exactly what did you say?"

"Dammit, Molly."

"That's the second time you've damned me."

He blinked.

"That's right, and I don't like it. It takes two to tango, Worth. So maybe you should stop damning me and take a look in the mirror."

She watched the color drain from his face as he took a step toward her, only to pull up short when Trent came bounding in.

"Mommy."

Her son certainly had a knack for timing, for which she was grateful. Reclaiming her composure was difficult, but she managed to do it. "What, honey?"

"Granna she needs you."

"I'll be right there."

"I'll go back and tell her."

Molly forced her gaze off Worth and onto her son. "No, that's not necessary. I'm on my way."

"Can I stay with Worth?" Trent asked out of the blue.

Worth's eyes darted to hers, a question in them.

"No, Trent," she said in a scolding tone. "You know better than to ask."

She felt Worth's gaze purposely pull at her. "It's okay. I don't mind if he comes with me."

"Well, I do."

"Mommy, please," Trent begged, pulling on her hand.

"I said no, Trent."

His chin began to wobble, but he didn't say anything. Instead, he turned and ran back down the hall.

No doubt about Worth's reaction to the rejection, either. His features were taut as their eyes sparred. "In that case, I'm outta here."

"No, please, wait."

He pulled up and whipped around, his jaw clenched, indicating he was pissed. Well, so was she, but they both had to get over this incident and move on, or else she *would* have to go.

"I'm waiting," he said in a ragged voice.

"We need to talk specifics about the barbecue."

He gave her an incredulous look. "You've got to be kidding me."

She ignored that, and enunciated her words very carefully. "No, I'm not kidding you."

"Look, I really don't give a damn about the particulars." His gaze held her captive. "Especially right now."

"You know," she spat, "you really can be a bastard."

"So I'm told."

"I'm not going to disappear."

He looked taken aback, then recovered. "What does that mean?"

"It means I'm not leaving." Her tone was soft yet her eyes drilled him. "Short of you kicking Trent and me out, that is."

A scowl twisted his features. "You make me sound like some kind of monster."

"No, I believe I said bastard."

He looked like he wanted to strangle her, probably thinking she'd crossed way over the line. Frankly, she didn't care what he thought. Even for Worth, his obnoxious behavior was a bit over the line.

She was about to make another suitable retort when she was interrupted by Trent.

"Mommy! Granna wants you. She says she's all hot."

"Go see about your mother," Worth said brusquely. "Let me know what's going on, and if she needs anything."

"Now, Mommy."

"I'm coming, son."

At the door, Worth turned. "Call if you need me."

Molly's eyebrows rose at the concern she heard in his voice, but didn't say anything.

"Later," he muttered and walked out.

Molly turned and practically ran to her mother's suite, certain something was wrong, making her feel badly about dallying with Worth. Suddenly, she wanted to yell at someone; she didn't care who. She'd known coming back here would be difficult. She just hadn't known how difficult until now, still feeling the brutal, yet hungry imprint of Worth's lips on hers.

What had she done?

"Mom, are you okay?" The instant Molly asked that question upon entering Maxine's room, she knew the answer. Her mother's face was extremely red, like she'd been stung by fire ants.

Without saying anything further, Molly raced into the bathroom, grabbed a rag and wet it with cold water. Then racing back into the room, she bathed her mother's face. Then she folded the cloth and laid it across Maxine's forehead.

On the beside table was a bottle of Tylenol. She grabbed two tablets, then proceeded to give them to her mother.

"Mom, do you hurt anywhere, like your stomach, for instance?"

"No," Maxine responded weakly. "Just tired."

"I'm calling the doctor. He may have to make a house call."

Five minutes later she was off the phone, assured that if Dr. Coleman was needed, he'd be here, but that he thought Maxine had probably just picked up a bug and would be okay in twenty-four hours or so.

Molly's thoughts ran along the same line, but she'd still wanted the doctor's opinion. By the time their conversation ended, Maxine felt less feverish, and she'd fallen asleep. However, Molly did not leave, choosing to remain in the sitting room with Trent in her lap, reading to him.

It was only after her mother's fever broke entirely and she was feeling much better that Molly left with Trent in tow to find Worth. Whether he liked it or not, she was determined to get his input concerning the upcoming barbecue, as well as her mother's. A week was not long to make plans, and her personality didn't lend itself to waiting until the last minute.

Besides, she wanted to make a good impression. Worth was convinced she couldn't do it. She was convinced she could. Another battle of wills. Besides, proving him wrong would certainly buoy her battered spirits.

"Mommy," Trent whispered, "I like Mr. Worth."

"I'm glad."

A moment of silence followed. "Why don't you like him?"

Molly's chest constricted, and she had no comeback.

She was the stubbornest, most hardheaded female he'd ever known. He'd thought Olivia had that top honor, but she couldn't hold a candle to Molly. After all these years, he had never quite figured her out. Maybe that was one of the reasons she still interested him.

"Get a life, Cavanaugh," he muttered savagely, kicking at a clod of dirt with the toe of his boot. He'd made the rounds of the stables, met with Art and was now heading to the new barn. He hated that his other one had burned down, but since it had, he'd built a state-of-the-art one this time.

It was his pride and joy, too. He loved to spend time there, and he loved to show it off. In fact, he would like to live in it. If he were truly a free spirit, he could move in and be perfectly content.

He liked his home, too. After all, he'd designed and built the sprawling ranch house with the help of Art and several subcontractors. But again, there was something unique about the barn. Perhaps that was because it was spacious and smelled of hay and horseflesh.

Whatever the reason, the massive structure—painted red, of course—had become a sanctuary when he needed it. Like now.

It would be a perfect place to have his barbecue. Thinking about that stopped him in his tracks, and he muttered a curse. He'd been excited about entertaining until Molly took over the housekeeping duties.

The thought of her working as a maid still soured his stomach.

She should have been his wife, not his housekeeper. Suddenly, he upped his pace, like the seat of his pants was on fire.

By the time he made it to the barn, his heart was pounding unusually hard, though he prided himself on being in great physical shape. Emotionally, though, he was a cripple— thanks to Molly. She apparently still had the power to turn him like a combination lock, thus exposing his emotions so easily.

He gritted his teeth, picked up the nearby pitchfork, and began spreading hay that didn't need spreading. But he needed something to do with the overabundance of energy raging inside him.

He'd lost his mind.

That was the problem. He'd kissed her. Hell, he hadn't just kissed her; his mouth had practically raped hers, especially when he'd felt the lush roundness of her breasts poking his chest. To make matters worse, his hands had dropped to her hips so that she'd feel his arousal, which made it even harder to let her go.

She'd tasted so incredibly good, smelled so incredibly good, felt so incredibly good that he'd lost all perspective, his body wanting a satisfaction it wasn't getting.

Just when he'd realized what he was doing and was about to thrust her away, she had gone limp in his arms, and had begun returning his wet, savage kisses. She'd even gone so far as to entwine her tongue with his.

Yet he'd eventually done what he'd had to do and that was to put her at arm's length. But that small endeavor took every ounce of fortitude he had in him.

Looking back on it now, he didn't know how he'd done it. Without thinking, his eyes dipped south and he let an oath rip. Whenever he thought about her, or she was around, he went hard. Somehow he had to figure out a way to stop this crazy rush of blood to his groin.

Maybe what he needed was Olivia. She could give him what he wanted in the way of sex. But the thought of touching her after Molly was repulsive and not going to happen.

That added to his fury and frustration. How dare she come back into his life, wagging some other man's kid, and tormenting him this way?

How dare *he* let her?

Eleven

"Mom, how are you feeling?"

Her mother tried to sit up. Molly placed a hand on her shoulder and stopped her. "Don't. I'll do the sitting."

"I'm fine."

Molly rolled her eyes. "Yeah, right."

"Don't use that high-handed tone with me, young lady." Maxine's smile took the sting out of her words.

"Yes, ma'am," Molly countered with mock severity at the same time she felt her mother's forehead and it was indeed cool to the touch.

"See, I told you I was fine. My fever's gone."

Molly smiled her relief. "Guess it was just a twenty-four hour bug, after all."

"Where's Trent?" Maxine asked, looking around.

"He's with Tammy, running around outside."

"My, but that boy seems to have taken to this place like ducks to water."

Molly gave Maxine a suspicious look. "Don't let those wheels of your mind turn in that direction."

Maxine huffed, as though insulted. "I don't know what you're talking about."

"Damn straight you do."

"Why, Molly Bailey, I don't recall ever hearing you say that word."

"I don't often." Molly paused for emphasis. "Unless it's called for, or I need to make a point."

Maxine picked at the blanket on the bed. "So what's wrong with me wanting you and Trent closer?"

Feeling like a terrible daughter, Molly clasped Maxine's hand. "Nothing, Mom, nothing at all."

"Then why won't you consider it?"

"Why don't you consider moving to Houston?"

Maxine went stark-eyed. "And leave Worth?"

"Yes, and leave Worth," Molly replied in a pointed tone.

"Why, he…he wouldn't know what to do without me," Maxine stammered, seemingly appalled that Molly would even think such a thing.

"I'm sure Eva and Ted would help him out."

Maxine narrowed her eyes. "My, but you sound bitter. What have they ever done to you?"

"Mom, look, I don't know how this discussion got started, but let's can it, shall we?"

Maxine looked taken aback and Molly sensed she'd probably hurt her mother's feelings, but she couldn't help it. At this point, she was doing well just to survive remaining on the ranch, especially after what had happened yesterday between her and Worth.

Because of that kiss, her heart remained sore to the touch. And to think she'd convinced herself that Worth couldn't cause her any more pain.

Apparently, she still had a lot to learn about herself.

"I didn't mean anything by that, Molly. Since you've been here, you've seemed different. Uptight might be the word I'm searching for."

"Mother—"

Maxine went on as if Molly hadn't spoken. "I know things didn't work out between you and Worth, and I hate that because I thought you two were crazy about each other."

She paused and took a breath. "And maybe things didn't turn out the way you wanted, getting married, then divorced, but that shouldn't have a bearing on your attitude toward Worth and his family. Frankly that puzzles me, because you don't have a mean-spirited bone in your body."

Before she found herself getting further tangled in that bed of thorns, Molly forced a laugh. "My, but you must be feeling better, Mother dear. I've never heard you deliver such a long speech."

"If you weren't grown, girl, I'd turn you over my lap and give you a good spanking."

Molly laughed for real this time and gave her mother a big kiss on the cheek. "I love you, even though you nose around where you don't belong."

"Huh! There you go, insulting me again."

"Oh, Mom, I'm okay. But you and this place have been a bit of a strain on me, I'll admit."

Maxine's features became whimsical for a moment. "I just wish I knew more about what makes you tick. You're my only child, but sometimes I feel like I don't know you at all."

"Mother, enough."

"Please, just let me get this off my chest, okay?"

Molly held her council.

"You were married and divorced, and I never even met the man."

"That's all water under the bridge."

"To you, maybe, but not to me. He was Trent's father, for Pete's sake. And I don't even know him." Maxine's words ended on a wail.

Oh, but you do, Molly wanted to shout.

Instead, she grabbed her mother's hands, squeezed them, then peered closely in her eyes. "You and Trent mean more to me than anything or anyone else. I know I've brought you pain by not explaining everything to you. But one day, I promise I will. I just can't say when."

Maxine's eyes filled with tears as she squeezed Molly's hands even harder. "Until that day, I promise I'll try to keep my mouth shut and not bug you."

Molly grinned. "Bug me. Mmm, that sounds like you've been around your grandson."

"Speaking of my grandson," Maxine injected on a lighter note, "you've done a splendid job raising him."

"The raising's just getting started, actually."

"Well, so far, so good, my child."

"Thanks, Mom," Molly said in a slightly choked voice. "Now that you've mentioned that boy, I'd best go see about him. First though, there's a matter I need to discuss with you."

"Okay."

"Tell me how I go about planning a barbecue without any help from the host."

Maxine threw her head back and laughed. "First off, you don't ask him. He doesn't have a clue."

"I suspected that."

"Nor does he want one."

"I suspected that, too."

Maxine chuckled again, then sobered. "If only this old back would straighten up, I could have everything done in no time at all."

"Sorry, you're stuck working through me."

"Not to worry. We'll make a great team. It'll be a rally people will talk about for a long time."

"The gossip flavor of the month, huh?" Molly said with a twinge of bitter humor.

"That's right, honey."

Molly got off the bed, leaned over and kissed her mother's still cool forehead. I'll check on you later."

"Send Trent to see me."

"Will do."

Trent and Tammy were walking toward the house when Molly walked out the door. Trent ran to her. "Mommy, can we go to the barn?"

"Oh, Trent," she said with exasperation.

"You promised."

"I did no such thing."

"I saw Worth go in there, but Tammy wouldn't let me go."

"Tammy did the right thing."

The young girl smiled her sweet smile, showing off dimples that made a plain face almost pretty.

"Thank you for today, Tammy," Molly said. "We'll see you tomorrow."

"Yes, ma'am." She turned to Trent who was pouting. "See you, buddy."

"I'm not your buddy."

"Trent! Your manners."

"Sorry," he muttered.

Tammy merely smiled again, then strode off.

When Molly turned toward Trent again, he was making a beeline for the barn. Her anger flared. Since coming here, he'd turned into a wild child.

"Trent!" she called. "Stop right where you are."

He did, but ever so reluctantly. When he stared up at her, he had a belligerent look on his face. They were really going to have to sit down and have a talk. She couldn't allow his insubordination to continue unchallenged.

"Mommy, are you mad at me?"

"Yes, I am."

"I'm sorry.

"You should be," she said, catching up with him.

That was when she realized the barn was in sight. She pulled up short. Would Worth still be there?

"I don't wanna go back inside," Trent muttered, sounding down in the mouth.

Molly thought for a long minute instead of just blurting out, *too bad,* which turned out to be her downfall.

Trent grabbed her by the hand, "Please, don't make me."

"All right, you little scoundrel, you win. We'll go see what Worth's up to. Maybe he'll let you rub an animal."

"Oh, boy!" Trent jumped up and down. "Come on, let's hurry."

"Hold on. There's no need for that."

Still, it was an effort to keep up with her son. By the time they covered the remaining distance to the barn, Molly was out of breath. She grasped Trent's hand tighter in hers, stopping him.

He gazed up at her with a question in his eyes. "What?"

"We can't just go barreling in there like we've been invited because we haven't. That's not nice."

"I got invited yesterday," Trent said in his big-boy voice. "'Member, Mommy?"

"Ah, right." Molly paused, then digging for courage, she called out, "Worth, are you in there?"

"Yeah. Come on in."

The second she saw him, Molly stopped in her tracks, thinking how sexy he looked leaning on the pitchfork with several twigs of hay stuck in his hair. Sheer willpower kept her from walking over to him and pulling them out.

Totally unnerved, her body broke out in a cold sweat. She shouldn't have come here, especially not with him watching her with eyes that seemed to seduce her on the spot.

"Wow!" Trent said in awe, looking around.

Molly dragged her gaze off Worth and stared at the premises herself. "I second that wow."

"You like, huh?" Worth asked, clearing his husky voice.

"It's great." She took a chance and looked at him again. The desire had been tempered. Actually, his features were blank. "But what about the old one?"

"It burned."

Her voice transmitted her shock. "Burned?"

"To the ground."

"Aw, man," Trent said.

Her son's comment was lost as her mind slid back to that summer, to the old barn where they made love for the last time. She could tell from the change in Worth's features that he, too, was thinking about that day.

The day she'd gotten pregnant.

Feeling dizzy, she closed her eyes. When she opened them again, Trent and Worth had gone ahead.

After a few moments, Worth paused and turned. "You coming?"

"Where are we going?" she asked in a slightly quivering voice.

He stared at her for a long moment. "To show Trent some of my prize horseflesh."

"Okay."

She followed, but didn't really get into the scene like the two of them. After she'd seen several horses, they all started to look alike, with the exception of their color.

"I'm sorry if we're boring you."

Molly almost visibly jumped at Worth's rather harsh and unexpected voice, definitely taking umbrage to what he said. "I'm not bored."

His eyebrows shot up. "Couldn't have proved it by me."

"Mommy, aren't you having a good time?" Trent chimed in as they made their way back to the main section of the barn, as if sensing the sudden undercurrent that ran between the two adults.

"I'm having a great time, honey. Only it's time we head back to the house. I have to make dinner and you have to get a bath."

"Is your mother all right?" Worth asked, changing the subject.

"She's fine. I guess it was just a twenty-four hour virus."

"Again, anything she needs, you just let me know," Worth said almost fiercely. "Anything."

"Thanks," Molly said, thinking at least he thought a lot of her mother. Too bad… She slam-dunked that thought before it could take a life of its own.

Worth had rejected her, not the other way around. She had to keep that in mind.

"Hey, buddy, that's off-limits."

Worth's louder-than-usual voice jerked Molly back to the moment at hand to find Trent on the first rung of the ladder leading up to the hayloft.

"Trent!"

He froze.

"Don't you dare go a step further," Molly said. "You have no business up there."

Hanging his head, Trent turned around.

Molly grabbed his hand. "Come on, let's go."

When they made it to the door, she forced herself to look back at Worth who was once again leaning on the pitchfork, staring at her with that smirk of his. Ignoring him, she said, "I'm about to make supper. Will you be joining us?"

"Nope."

His gaze looked her up and down, which made her body grow hot. "I suppose you're going out again." God, what made her say that? Even to herself, her tone sounded waspish. And jealous. Dear Lord, what must he be thinking? Probably that she cared about what he did, which couldn't be further from the truth.

His eyes burned into hers. "As a matter of fact, I am."

"Fine," she said in a prim tone, then walked out, silently cursing herself all the way back to the house.

"Ouch, Mommy!" Trent cried. "You're pulling my arm off."

"Be quiet, and keep up," she demanded, her breath coming in spurts.

Twelve

Molly almost wept with relief.

The shindig was in full swing without any glitches. *So far,* she reminded herself, tamping her excitement because things could change in the blink of an eye. The day after the debacle in the barn, Molly had finally pinned down Worth as to a date, time and guest list for the barbecue.

She couldn't have put the trimmings in place, of course, without her mother's help, especially since they'd had only a week to get ready. But that had been enough time since Maxine was a pro at planning last-minute parties.

As promised, she had directed traffic, so to speak, from her domain, as Molly fondly called her mother's suite.

Surprisingly, Maxine's back had improved much quicker than first expected. The brace and physical therapy combined seemed to be doing the trick. Molly was a bit disappointed, however, that Maxine couldn't join the festivities even for a little while. But the doctor had been afraid it might be too exerting, and Molly had agreed.

Now, as she looked around the premises, Molly was astounded at the number of people who had attended, just about everyone who had been invited. Yet Molly had been prepared. Her mother had warned her and she'd listened.

Most of the guests were now gathered on the multilevel porch, laughing and talking. At various points, tables were set up and decorated, awaiting the arrival of plates filled with all kinds of barbecued meat.

A band set up by the pool was doing its thing. The singer, belting out a country western song, had drawn a crowd. Other attendees were eating, drinking and being merry, which was exactly what the Cavanaughs wanted.

The hired help aimed to please.

Then kicking herself for that sarcastic thought, Molly forced her mind onto more pleasant things, such as the beauty that surrounded her. Yes, God had definitely smiled on the day. She looked up and didn't see one cloud in the sky.

Talk about great temperature. One couldn't have asked for better. Cool, but not cold—light jacket weather—perfect for an outside event.

Tammy was watching Trent, freeing Molly to take care of anything that might arise and might keep things from running smoothly. But she didn't mind the hard work. It kept her from thinking about Worth, looking at Worth and wondering about Worth.

Forbidden.

All the above fit into that category for her. Suddenly Molly felt a pang near her heart that she couldn't ignore. Stopping and closing her eyes, she took a deep, shuddering breath. When she opened them Worth was looking straight at her.

For an instant, she stood transfixed. He was leaning against a tree, seemingly totally relaxed, surrounded by several men who were talking non-stop—probably trying to convince him what a great politician he'd make.

She agreed.

As usual, he had on a starched white shirt, black jeans, dress boots and a George Strait Resistol. He was total eye candy, of which she couldn't seem to get enough.

Although she was sure he'd shaved that morning, his chiseled features no longer bore that out. He had the beginnings of a five o'clock shadow, which merely enhanced his sexy good looks.

Her heart began pounding like she'd been hiking a mile straight uphill. He broke loose from the posse and strode toward her, his gaze never wavering.

She wished she had the nerve, no, the willpower, to turn her back and pretend she hadn't seen him. Even though that wasn't going to happen, she nevertheless stiffened her spine, preparing herself for the worst.

The last few times their paths had crossed the exchanges between them hadn't been pleasant—anything but, actually.

It seemed as though every time he saw her, he was in an angry mood. Yet he looked at her with anything but anger. Desire and fire often lit his eyes, which kept her on edge. Despite the fact that he despised her, he wanted her. He didn't try to hide that. She suspected that was what kept his anger boiling.

She was sure today was no exception. By the time Worth reached her, his features looked like they were carved out of stone, though his tone was surprisingly soft. "Have you sat down at all?"

"No, but then, I'm not supposed to."

"Hogwash."

Her eyes widened.

He leaned in closer, which called attention to his cologne.

God, he smelled so good. For a moment, Molly's head spun, and she wanted to rest her head against his chest and say to hell with everything and everybody. Then reality hit her in the face, and she literally jumped back.

A dark frown covered Worth's features. "For heaven's sake, I'm not going to touch you."

"I know that," she snapped, crossing her hands over her short pink jacket that barely topped the waist of her low cut jeweled jeans. In doing that, she knew she'd slightly bared her waist as her white camisole underneath was also short. Even when Worth's eyes dropped there, and she saw desire heat his dark eyes, she made no effort to lower her arms.

"Then why did you jump?" His muttered question was spoken in a guttural tone.

"Does it matter?" she asked, thinking she should be ashamed of herself for purposely allowing him to see her naked flesh, knowing what it would do to him. What was happening to her? Once aroused, Worth was like a lighted stick of dynamite; he could go off at any moment.

Instead of that frightening her, it excited her.

As if he could read her thoughts, he stepped closer and whispered, "You'd best be careful how you look at me."

Color flooded Molly's face and she turned away, but not before saying, "Ah, I'd best get back to work."

"I want to talk to you."

She whipped back around, careful her facade was back in place and asked, "What about?"

"To tell you what a great job you've done on such short notice."

"Is that a thank-you?"

"You betcha."

His praise took her so by surprise that her mouth flew open. Her reaction brought an unexpected smile to his lips, which made her heart beat that much harder. It had been a long time since he'd smiled—or at least at her. It seemed as if the sun had broken through a dark cloud.

She smiled back.

He rolled his eyes, though his smile widened. "You're a piece of work, Molly Whoever."

She almost giggled at his unwillingness to say her last name, then caught herself, especially when their gazes tangled and held, while sexual tension danced all around them. For a breathless moment, he looked as if he might actually grab her and kiss her again.

She'd like nothing better.

Appalled anew at her thoughts, Molly shook her head at the same time he shook his, putting everything back on an even keel. "I'm glad everything's going well."

"That's because of you."

"And Mother."

"Of course."

For another moment silence surrounded them.

"I want you to sit down, even have a beer."

"Why, Worth Cavanaugh," she said in her most southern drawl, "you know that wouldn't be good 'cause I can't handle spirits all that well."

He threw back his head and laughed. "Don't I know that. The drunkest I've ever seen you was that night—"

As though he realized what he'd said and where this conversation was headed he broke off abruptly, a scowl replacing the laughter. "Dammit, Molly," he said in a savage tone, "you almost ruined my life."

She gave back as good as she got. "And you almost ruined mine."

Another silence.

"Hey, Cavanaugh, get over here. Rip wants to talk to you."

The moment was severed, never to be repaired. Without looking at her again, Worth turned and walked away. Thank God, a table was near by so she could sink onto the bench, or she might have sunk to her knees. Every bone in her body was quivering.

Every nerve.

Molly couldn't let him paralyze her. Wouldn't let him do that to her. The best antidote for her heavy heart was a dose of her child. Trent had a way of putting things back in perspective. Molly was well on her way to finding her son when she almost ran head-on into Eva and Ted Cavanaugh.

"Oh," she said in a faltering tone, quickly moving back. "Sorry."

Though Molly hadn't seen them since her return to the ranch—she'd purposely kept her distance at the barbecue, too—she knew sooner or later her luck would run out. The inevitable had happened. After her encounter with Worth, meeting them face-to-face couldn't have come at a worse possible time.

With them, there was no good time, she thought, feeling a pinch.

The intervening years had been kind to Eva. Oh, she was maybe a bit heavier and had a few gray hairs now mixed in with the blond, but amazingly her face remained virtually unlined. She still carried her large frame with the same confidence as always.

Aging had also been kind to Ted. He was still tall and good-looking, especially dressed in jeans and boots. She couldn't tell if he was losing his hair since he had on a Stetson.

"Hello, Molly," Eva said in her usual haughty tone, which had always irked Molly and still did.

Ted chimed in, "Yeah, Molly, it's good to see you."

Maybe he had a little too much enthusiasm in his voice to

suit Eva because she shot him one of *those* famous Eva looks, indicating he had done something to displease her. Molly knew that when it came to her just being on planet Earth was displeasing to Eva.

Once she had cared. Now she didn't. And the *didn't* felt damn good.

"I hope you two are well," Molly said out of politeness more than anything else.

Eva inclined her head and ran the tip of her tongue across her lower lip. "Do you really care how we are?"

No. As far as I'm concerned, you can butt a stump and die. Molly smiled her sweetest smile. "Of course."

"How much longer do you intend to stay here?"

"As long as it takes."

"For what?"

Eva knew, so Molly wasn't about to indulge her. Now that she was older and wiser and knew the vicious games these two played, she was not about to take a ticket. When the situation called for it, Molly could be a bitch, as well.

"Her mother, Eva," Ted put in, apparently embarrassed by his wife's open hostility.

"By the way, how is Maxine?" Eva asked, though her tone was devoid of empathy.

"You know very well how she is," Molly said without mincing words. "I'm sure Worth keeps you informed."

"Actually," Ted said, "we don't see that much of our son."

Although Molly was shocked at that disclosure, she didn't let it show. Besides, she felt a tad sorry for the elder Cavanaugh. When he was not with his wife, he was a nice man. That summer he'd treated her with dignity and respect until—

"I'm talking to you, Molly."

Molly clenched her hands to her side to keep from slapping both of Eva's cheeks. She was the rudest person she'd ever known and Molly would be damned if she apologized for woolgathering. "What did you say, Eva?"

"I said you're not wanted here."

"Eva!" Ted exclaimed, giving her a hard look. "Now's not the time for this kind of conversation."

"That's all right, Ted, I don't mind." Molly forced a smile. "Eva should feel free to say what she wants."

Eva laughed though it fell far short of humor. "Mmm, not the same cowed young girl you used to be, huh?"

"That's right."

Eva leaned in closer, her features hard. "Make no mistake, honey. You're no match for me and never will be."

"That thought never crossed my mind," Molly drawled in her sweetest tone yet.

Ted pulled on Eva's arm and said between his teeth, "Let it go, dammit."

Whipping her face around to her husband, Eva said, "If you don't like what I'm saying, you can leave." Her glare harshened. "But you ought to be right in here with me. For our son's sake, if nothing else."

"Eva," he said again with considerably less confidence, as though he knew he was fighting a bear using only a switch.

"It's all right, Ted." Molly gave him a real but halfhearted smile. "I'm no longer that young, stupid girl I once was. I can take care of myself."

"Molly, I'm sorry."

"Don't you dare apologize to her," Eva flung at him viciously.

Ted merely held up his hands, then stepped aside.

She'd had enough of Eva Cavanaugh, too, and was close to telling her so. Only her mother and her condition kept her quiet. She didn't think Worth would take any rash action like asking her, Molly, to leave, but when it came to his parents, she wasn't sure. That summer had taught her how much he depended on his parents and how much influence they had on him.

"Molly, one more thing."

"I'm listening, Eva," she said calmly, knowing that would get Eva more than anything else.

"I'm sure you know that Olivia and Worth are soon to be married."

"Not to worry, Eva." Molly smiled. "She's welcome to him. They'll make a perfect couple."

With that she walked off.

Thirteen

The party was winding down and for that Molly was grateful. She knew it had been a smashing success, if the mood of the guests was anything to judge by. Everyone seemed to have had their fill of the best barbecue in east Texas and all the booze they could want.

And the hottest band in the county was still playing.

The guests who remained behind were the really happy campers; her instincts told her they had talked Worth into finally throwing his hat into the political ring. Of course, she didn't know that for sure, not being privy to that information.

The way John Lipscomb, Worth's wannabe campaign manager, was slapping Worth on the back was the best indication that changes were in the works.

Molly still felt like Worth would make a good politician, not that her opinion mattered; it didn't. Still, after musing about it, she sensed he'd make a good one. He was such a take-charge person, one who made decisions and stuck to them. Honesty was another *must* quality. Despite his having been less than honest with her, she felt that didn't apply to his day-to-day dealings. In her book, a politician should have those assets and more.

A sigh split Molly's lips as she looked over the grounds and spotted a table with leftover debris scattered over it. She had just taken steps in that direction when a hand caught her arm.

Knowing that touch above all else, her heart lurched and she swung around to face Worth.

"How 'bout a dance?"

For a split second, shock rendered her speechless, then she stammered, "I…I don't think so."

"Why not?" Worth held on tightly, staring at her out of naked eyes.

"It wouldn't be appropriate," she whispered, feeling her insides go loose.

"Baloney."

"Worth."

"If you don't dance with me, it's because you don't want to."

"I—"

He didn't bother to let her finish the sentence. He grabbed her, pulled her close and they began to do the Texas two-step in perfect unison, which wasn't surprising. That summer they had danced many a time together, and Molly had reveled in each step. Perhaps that was because she was in his arms where she had longed to be.

Now, she'd just gotten into the beat of the music when the song abruptly ended.

"Damn," Worth muttered.

She wanted to mutter hallelujah, knowing they were being watched by the remaining guests, his parents and his lover. Not a good thing.

"Look, I need to get back to work."

"You know how that pisses me off."

"What?" she asked innocently.

"Telling me you have to work when you don't."

"Go ask Olivia to dance," Molly said in a weary tone, gently moving out of his arms, then she hurried to the table where the centerpiece was just short of becoming airborne. She had the object in hand when she felt the hairs on the back of her neck stand on end. Someone was behind her.

She whirled around and stared into the lovely face of a strange woman.

"I'm Olivia Blackburn," she said bluntly.

Molly schooled herself to show none of the myriad of emotions that charged through her. God, what had she done to deserve attention from both Worth's parents and his girl in one afternoon?

"Hello, Olivia," she said with forced politeness, having to admit that the woman was lovely in the truest sense of the word. Her hair was red with blond highlights, and her eyes were blue—a rare combination—but a stunning one, nonetheless. And she had a figure to die for. Though short and trim, she had oversized breasts that emphasized her tiny waist.

She would be just the right person on Worth's arm when he did his political thing.

"If you don't mind, we'll dispense with the pleasantries," Olivia said into the heavy silence, her tone nasty.

Molly took offense, but she kept her mouth shut. If Olivia had something else to say, then so be it. She couldn't care less, one way or the other.

"I know why you've come back."

Molly shrugged. "Good for you."

"You're fooling no one. It's for Worth."

"Oh, please," Molly exclaimed in disgust.

"When you two were dancing, I saw how you looked at him."

"Then you saw wrong."

"No way." Olivia's tone now reeked of sarcasm.

Molly sugar-coated her smile, then said, "Surely you noticed, he's the one who pulled me onto the dance floor."

That blunt statement seemed to rob Olivia of words, but only for a second. She rebounded with the force of an alley cat fighting for survival. "You're not wanted here."

"Trust me, I wouldn't be here, if I had a choice."

"Oh, I know you're saying you came back because of your mother, but I know better."

"Really, now." Molly made her tone as insulting as possible, plus she plastered on a fake smile, both of which seemed to spark Olivia's eyes.

"You're nothing but a slut, Molly Stewart, or whatever the hell your name is, and you'll never be otherwise."

"Now that you've gotten that off your chest, is there anything else?" Molly was determined to keep her voice stone-cold even. She wasn't about to let this vindictive witch rattle her cage.

Only she had, Molly admitted silently, feeling perilously close to tears and hating herself for it.

"As a matter of fact there is. Worth is mine, and I intend to marry him."

"Good for you."

Olivia smiled an evil smile. "You're not fooling me. You'll never get Worth back, so you might as well pack your bags, get your brat and leave town."

"Stop it!"

Olivia blinked, clearly taken aback by Molly's sharp tone and words. "Despite what you think, you're no better than me. As for my son, you leave him out of this." Molly took a heaving breath, then hammered on, "As for Worth, you're welcome to him." She paused again. "To my spoils, that is."

Olivia gasped while her hand flew to her chest as though she might be having a heart attack. While Molly didn't wish that, she was glad she'd pierced Olivia's hard heart with an arrow much the same as Olivia had pierced hers.

Olivia's recovery was quick. Stepping closer to Molly, she hissed, "No one talks to me like that and gets away with it. Trust me, you'll pay."

Molly didn't bother to respond. Instead, she whipped around and walked off, not even aware of where she was going until she reached the cool, shadowed barn. For a second, she was tempted to crawl into the loft and sob until she couldn't sob any more. But giving in to her heartache would only make her feel worse.

Suddenly she felt trapped, wanting to flee Sky, Texas so badly her stomach roiled. Leaning against a post, she surrendered to her pain, letting the tears flow.

"Are you okay?"

Fear froze her insides, especially when she realized her intruder was none other than Worth himself. After those rounds with his parents and his woman, *he* was the last person she wanted to see, especially since her face was saturated with tears.

Would this nightmare ever end?

Before she faced him, she dabbed with a tissue she fished out of her pocket. Maybe in the shadows, he wouldn't be able to tell she'd been crying.

Wrong.

"You're not okay," he said more to himself than to her, as he made his way further into the barn.

Panicked that he wouldn't stop until he was within touching distance of her, which she couldn't handle, Molly turned with her arms outstretched. "Don't."

Worth stopped instantly, though she knew taking orders from her, or anyone, went against his grain. Too bad. She'd had it with the entire Cavanaugh clan.

"Leave me alone, Worth," she said in a low voice, feeling drained to the core.

"No."

"No?"

"You heard me."

"I can't take any more," she said, hearing the crack in her voice and knowing he did, too.

He took two long steps, which put him within a hairs-breadth of her. However, he refrained from touching her.

"I know what's going down."

"I don't think you do."

"I'm not blind, Molly."

"It doesn't matter," she countered in a resigned tone.

"Mother and Dad cornered you." A flat statement of fact.

"I don't want to talk about it."

"Well, I do," he said flatly.

Silence.

"What did they say, dammit?"

Anger suddenly flared inside her. "In a nutshell, I should get lost."

He muttered some of the foulest words Molly had heard in a long time. "They don't speak for me."

"Couldn't prove that by me."

Ignoring that shot, he went on, "I also saw Olivia talking to you."

"She also told me to get lost, that you belonged to her."

Another string of curses flew out of his mouth, then he said, "Contrary to what she said, there's no wedding in the offing."

"Maybe there should be. She'll make the perfect politician's wife—all show and no do."

That muscle in his jaw jerked, indicating that he hadn't liked her remark, but he didn't respond.

"I need to go," she whispered, feeling more drained by the moment.

"Despite what you think, they—Mother, Daddy, Olivia—don't speak for me."

"Like hell they don't," she said, whipping her head back and glowering at him. "From the outside looking in, it appears the monkeys run the zoo, not the zookeeper."

"Damn you, Molly." His nostrils flaring, he grasped her by the arms, hauled her against his chest and peered into her eyes.

"I told you not to touch me." Her teeth were clenched so tightly her jaw throbbed.

"Not in those words, you didn't."

"Then I'm telling you now."

"What if I like touching you?"

She struggled. "Let me go."

"No."

"Worth." Her voice broke.

"Worth what?" His also broke.

"This is crazy."

She swore she could see the blood heat up in his eyes as they held hers captive. "God, Molly, I can't think of anything but you."

"Stop it, please," she pleaded, fearing not so much what he would do but what she would do. Right now, she needed to be held and loved, having been battered and beat up since the moment she'd arrived.

Kindness towards her now would surely be her undoing. It would lead to the one thing she could only dream of, but never have.

Him.

"I can't," he whispered, his agony evident.

Then he did what Molly most feared. He sank his lips onto hers in what was a hot, savage kiss that seemed to rip her soul out of its socket. At first, she fought him, then when his tongue warred with hers, she lost all will and gave in.

As the kiss deepened, their bodies went slack until their knees met the floor of the barn. That was when she felt him reach under her camisole and cover a breast. She moaned and without thinking, dropped her hand to his zipper, feeling him enlarge under her hand.

"I want you," he muttered. "I have to have you. Now." It was when he began to unbutton her jeans that she came to her senses, crying out. "No. I can't do this."

One hard push was all it took for him to lose his balance and fall backward. That was all she needed to scramble to her feet and flee from the barn, his string of curse words following her.

She placed her hands over her ears and ran for dear life.

Fourteen

"Well, son, are you, or aren't you?"

Worth rubbed his stubbled chin. He had gotten up and come to his parents' place before he'd showered and shaved. He'd at least taken time to brush his teeth.

"How 'bout a cup of coffee first?" Worth asked, continuing to massage his prickly chin.

"Eva is the coffee brewed?" Ted called out from his place at the breakfast room table.

"Coming."

Worth still didn't know what the rush had been about to get over to his parents' ranch. His mother had called earlier and said they wanted to talk to him over coffee ASAP. He'd just rolled out of bed, bleary-eyed from having drunk too much the night before, trying to forget Molly was down the hall and that he wanted her more than he'd ever wanted anything in his life.

Yet, she was off limits to him.

Someone who gave her word then went back on it was something he couldn't get past or tolerate. Besides, he believed in the old adage that you can never go back and pick up where you left off. It almost never worked.

However, that didn't stop him from craving the pleasure of Molly's company in his bed. He nursed one particular whisker on his chin, letting his imagination run wild. If she were willing to have sex with him, what would it hurt? A good lay for old times' sake?

Wonder what Molly would think about that? He knew. She'd tell him to go straight to hell in a handbasket, and he wouldn't blame her. After all, he hadn't exactly made her stay at the ranch a bed of roses. In fact, he'd been a thorn in her side at almost every turn.

But dammit, she'd deserved it, he kept telling himself. Still, that didn't absolve his conscience, and he didn't like that. Guilt was not even a word in his vocabulary, and he wasn't about to add it now.

"Ah, thanks, Mom," he said, peering up when Eva set steaming mugs of coffee in front of him and his dad.

"Hannah made some scones and blueberry tarts, your favorites." Eva smiled as she leaned down and grazed her son's cheek. "I'm warming them even as I speak."

Worth shook his head with a frown. "Ah, Mom, thanks, but I'm not hungry."

"Sure you are," she said. "Or at least you will be when you smell them. I think they are Hannah's best efforts yet." She paused and smiled her confident smile. "And Lord knows she aims to please you. Above all."

If only his mother would stop her prattle. If not, Worth wasn't sure he could hang in for very much longer. His head was hurting like someone was beating on it with a jackhammer and his stomach was pitching. If he choked down even a morsel of food, and it stayed down, it'd be a bloody miracle.

But how could he tell his parents he'd gotten dog drunk because he wanted to sleep with a woman who had betrayed him, and whom they held in such contempt? He wouldn't, mainly because it was none of their damn business.

"So tell us what you're thinking."

"Yeah, right," Worth mumbled into his mug.

Eva's eagle eyes honed in on him, before saying bluntly, "You look dreadful."

He put his cup down and peered up at her. "Thanks."

"Well, you do."

"Thanks again." Sarcasm lowered Worth's voice.

"Don't play dumb, Worth," Eva said in a scolding tone.

He rolled his eyes. "Let it go, Mother. I'm not in the mood."

"When are you ever in the mood?"

"What the hell does that mean?"

Ted waved his hands. "Hey, you two, time-out. We're a family who's supposed to be civil, right?"

"I'm going after the goodies," Eva said, exasperation evident in her tone.

"Don't pay any attention to your mother," Ted said, his features scrunched in a frown. "She's obviously in one of her moods. It'll pass."

"It had better," Worth countered without mincing words. "I don't like her in my face, Dad."

Ted's lean face drained of color. "I know, son. Just bear with her. She only wants the best for you, and she thinks that's in politics."

"What if I don't agree?" Worth asked.

Eva walked back into the room and placed a plate of piping hot goodies in the middle of the table. Worth swallowed hard and tried not to look at them. Even the smell turned his stomach, but he decided to keep that to himself. Maybe later, he'd try a bite or two, to keep his mother off his back, if for no other reason.

"Want me to help your plate?" Eva asked with a smile, certain she'd won her son over.

"Not right now," Worth responded. "I'm still enjoying my coffee." Which was a lie. Right now, all he wanted was to go back to his ranch, shower and hit the sack.

"So back to what I asked earlier, son, have you made up your mind?"

Worth heard the anxious note in his father's voice and sighed. His mother, for the first time was quiet, as if holding her breath until he answered. "Nope."

Both gave him a stunned look.

"I can't believe you're still dallying," Eva said, anger deepening her voice. "Even though the rally was only yesterday, you still should make a decision."

"It's not that easy. For me it's a huge decision and a huge commitment."

"Why should that bother you now?" Ted asked, his brows drawn together in a frown. "You've never backed down from a challenge yet."

"You know my heart's really in expanding my horse business," Worth pointed out. "Both would be a bit much to tackle at the same time."

Eva flapped her hand. "The chance to breed horses will always be there. Your political chances won't."

"I'm well aware of that, Mother."

Eva's face took on a pinched look. "Are you also aware that if you don't hurry up and marry Olivia you might lose her?"

That was the straw that broke the camel's back. Worth lunged out of his chair, which caused his parents to jump. "I'm not marrying Olivia."

His mother's hand flew to her throat. "What?"

"You heard me."

"Not ever?" Eva asked, her voice coming out in a squeak.

"Not ever," Worth responded in a tired voice.

Silence filled the room for a moment while Eva and Ted stared at each other, their faces registering perplexity and dismay.

"It's her, isn't it?" Eva asked in an acid-filled tone.

Worth folded his arms across his chest. "I don't know what you're talking about."

"Like hell you don't."

"Eva," Ted said, glaring at his wife.

"Well, it's the truth. He hasn't been the same since Molly came back."

"Leave Molly out of this." Worth's tone brooked no argument. "And while we're on that subject, stay away from her. I know both you and Olivia took your shots at her at the barbecue." Worth transferred his gaze to his dad. "That goes for you, too."

Ted flushed while Eva ground her teeth together.

Finally Eva said, "We have every right—"

Worth cut her off. "You don't have any rights when it comes to speaking for me. Neither does Olivia."

"Worth, you're upsetting me," Eva said, "making me fear things that I shouldn't have to fear."

"If it has to do with Molly, you can stand down. Trust me, she hates me and can't wait to leave here."

Eva released a huge breath. "Thank God for small favors."

Worth drained his cup and put it down. "Thanks for the coffee."

"You mean you're leaving?" Eva demanded, wide-eyed.

"That's right. I'll talk to you later. Meanwhile, try to stay out of my life."

He didn't turn back around, but he knew both their mouths were gaped open.

* * *

Molly tiptoed into her mother's room that same afternoon and saw that Maxine was sleeping. She stood by the bed for a second and peered down at Maxine, feeling herself smile. Her mother was definitely on the mend.

The shots the doctor was injecting into her back had worked wonders. Of course, Maxine hadn't been released to do any housework yet. However, her mother was up and walking, alternating between a walker and a cane, which was a praise. It wouldn't be long now until Molly and Trent could leave.

Thinking of her son sent her to the window where she peered outside. She expected to see Tammy and Trent playing, and she did. What she didn't expect to see was Worth.

Only there he was. With them.

He was dressed in old jeans riding low on his hips, hugging his powerful legs and an old cutoff T-shirt that exposed his washboard belly and his navel. In truth, he was a gorgeous specimen.

And the effect on her was galvanizing as she watched the scene play out before her. Worth had brought a colt from the stable and was letting Trent rub on it. But it was Worth on whom she was concentrating.

As soon as possible, she had to get out of this house, out of *his* life for good, which meant she never intended to set foot on this ranch again. Her mother would just have to come and visit her.

Deciding the panacea to her tormented thoughts was work, she turned her back on the window. When called for, Molly could be a lean, mean, cleaning machine. Today was one of those days. Cleaning things, polishing things, making things sparkle not only occupied her mind, but her hands, as well.

Molly had just changed into some grungy jeans, and a T-shirt without benefit of a bra to encumber her efforts. She had pretty much cleaned the downstairs yesterday until it glowed. She felt the upstairs was entitled to the same treatment.

Suddenly, Molly paused in her thoughts, wondering if Worth had decided to run for office, or not. Of course, she would be the last to know unless he confided in her mother, which was possible.

She was delighted Worth and Maxine had such a good rapport. When the time came for her to leave, it would be with a clear conscience, knowing Worth would never let her mother want for anything.

Worth didn't like many people, but to the ones he did, he was loyal to a fault. She was grateful Maxine fit into the latter category.

She just wished she did.

"Can it," she spat out loud, then cut her gaze to the bed to see if her outburst had awakened Maxine. It hadn't. She turned then and went back to her room. The instant she walked in, her cell phone rang.

Surprised but glad at the caller, Molly said with enthusiasm, "Why, hello, Dr. Nutting."

"Hey, kiddo."

His familiarity was just the balm she needed for her battered senses. While he was the consummate elderly doctor in looks, with a thatch of white hair, delving blue eyes and an ever-ready smile, that wasn't his only claim to fame. He was one of the best and most renown doctors in the south, especially when it came to cardiology.

She'd been thrilled and honored when he'd chosen her as his head nurse. Now that he was willing to send her to school to become a physician's assistant, she was humbled and even more eager to please.

"I'm so glad to hear from you, Doctor."

"Same here, young lady." He paused. "So how are things?"

Molly gave him a quick rundown of her mother's condition.

"Ah, so you may be returning sooner rather than later."

"Sounds like you miss me," Molly said in a teasing tone.

"You have no idea. I've come to depend on you too much, I think."

Instantly Molly felt a bout of homesickness come over her. "Is everything going okay? I hope my absence hasn't created undo hardship in the office."

"Nah, but it'll be good to have you back."

"It won't be long now, I promise. I'll keep you posted."

Dr. Nutting chuckled. "I guess I just wanted to hear your voice and hear you say that. Now, I'm feeling much better."

"Me, too," Molly said with a smile and tears on her cheeks. "Thanks for calling. I'll be in touch."

Once the cell was flipped closed, Molly wiped her face, dashed to the laundry room, grabbed her tray of cleaning supplies and headed to Worth's room. Usually, Kathy maintained his space, but since Kathy was off ill and had been since the barbecue, Molly felt she had no choice but to tackle it herself.

Besides, it was a wreck. She'd passed his room earlier, paused and took a quick look inside, having no idea what possessed her to do such a thing. Maybe it was because Worth's bed was a mess, like he'd wrestled with a bear and lost.

Whatever, the room needed attention, and she was the only one available. With her Sony Walkman attached to her jeans and her earplugs in, she cleaned his bedroom proper, then moved to the bathroom.

After everything was shining there, with the exception of the shower, she stepped into it and began scrubbing. Although she didn't get wet, she came close to it, her T-shirt anyway. It got damp and, therefore, clung to her breasts like a second skin.

After finishing that job, she removed her ear plugs just in

time to hear a sound, a sound she couldn't identify, though she panicked. Surely it wasn't Worth having come back in. She was positive she'd be in and out of his room before that happened.

Brightening, she told herself she was just hearing things. Still, Molly didn't see any reason to tarry any longer. That was when she opened the door and stepped out, only to freeze in horror.

"You."

She wasn't sure if she spoke the word out loud or not, so shocked was she to see him naked as the day he was born, standing in front of her, staring at her with fire leaping from his widened eyes.

For a moment, they both just stared, him at her breasts with their rosebud nipples thrusting forward and her at his huge, beautiful, growing erection.

"Molly," he said in a voice that sounded like he'd been gutted, then he reached for her.

But she was too fast for him. Before he realized what was happening, she turned and ran out of the room.

"Molly!"

She ignored the plaintive cry she heard in his voice and kept on running. *Out of harm's way.*

Fifteen

Out of sight; out of mind.

She wished.

Worth had been gone for three days, and the thought of seeing him when he returned gave Molly the weak trembles. Realistically, there was no way to avoid the inevitable, and she knew it. He'd at least told Maxine he was going to Dallas to look at some horses. She hadn't expected him to tell her, of course, nor was she complaining. The less she had to do with Worth, the better.

Still, she found herself jumping when she heard a door open or close, which was ludicrous. On this ranch, someone was coming or going all the time.

But she knew from past experience she would look up, turn a corner or walk into a room and there he'd be.

In the glory of his magnificent manhood.

Only clothed, she prayed.

Whenever she thought about that encounter in his bath, she almost lost it. Her breathing turned labored, her limbs trembled and her mind spun.

None of which was good. Or sane.

In fact, since that incident she'd been a basket case. Oh, she'd done what she was supposed to do, probably to perfection because she was so determined to concentrate. She'd taken care of the house, her son and her mother. Yet she'd felt as if it were someone else doing those things—as if she existed outside herself.

Right now Molly found herself pausing and leaning against the cabinet for support, feeling slightly dizzy. Stress. That was all it was. She was under so much pressure that she felt her insides might explode at any second, which was horribly unfair to her son and to her mother.

She had let Worth get under her skin. *Again.*

The sight of him naked had made her crazy with an aching need that wouldn't go away. Although she knew it was wrong to want him to make love to her, she couldn't control her mind. It seemed to have taken on a life of its own.

She didn't know what to do; that was the problem. The more she was around the ranch, the more under Worth's spell she fell. She couldn't leave. Not yet. But soon.

Meanwhile, she would continue to remind herself what Worth had done to her, how he had ripped her heart out and trampled on it. Now that she had Trent, she couldn't dare let that happen again. Even though he had denied it, she felt sure he would eventually marry Olivia. And she was yearning to make love to him.

What kind of woman had she become?

Since she couldn't bear to answer that question, Molly went back to polishing the piece of silver. She was just about finished when Trent rushed into the room.

"Mommy, Mommy!"

"What, darling?"

"Mr. Worth's back."

Molly's heart took a dive, though she kept her tone even and cool. "That's great, honey."

"He wants to take me riding."

Molly panicked. "Oh, Trent, I don't think that's a good idea."

He scrunched up his face.

"You've never ridden a horse, and Mommy's afraid."

"I'm not," he responded with belligerence. "I'm a big boy. You're always telling me that."

"You are a big boy."

His eyes brightened. "Oh goodie, I can go."

"Whoa, cowboy. I didn't say that."

"Mommy! You're being mean."

"Trent," she responded in a stern tone.

"What's going on?"

If she hadn't had such a tight grip on the piece of silver, she would have dropped it at the sound of Worth's voice. The time she'd been dreading had come. He was back, and as suspected, in full sexual glory, sending little tremors of shock to her chest.

"Mommy says I can't go," Trent said to Worth, his lower lip twice its normal size.

"I—" she began.

"I won't let anything happen to him, Molly."

She didn't want to look at Worth, especially with him standing in front of her, staring at her through eyes that were thankfully unreadable. She just hoped she could do the same thing. She'd rather die than to have him know she'd been thinking about how awesome he'd looked naked.

"Molly."

Feeling like her face had just caught on fire, she drew a ragged breath then forced herself to meet his gaze.

"I said I'd take care of him." While his voice had a gruff edge to it, his eyes didn't. They seemed to have suddenly ignited with heat that told her he wasn't as cool and in control as he appeared, that he, too, was remembering the episode in the shower.

And what could have happened, but didn't.

"I just don't think—" Molly's voice played out under that hot, probing gaze.

"Pease, Mommy," Trent begged.

"Oh, all right. Just don't keep him out long, Worth."

"Your wish is my command."

The old sarcastic Worth was back, but she ignored that and added, "I mean it." She knew she sounded unreasonably controlling, but she didn't care. The thought of the two of them alone was like a knife turning in her heart.

But why punish her child for her sins? She couldn't. Besides, she would be leaving soon, and she wouldn't have to worry about those unexpected twists and turns.

"Yippee!" Trent cried, zipping around and running toward the door.

Before Worth followed, a smile almost broke through his tight lips. "I'd say he's excited."

Molly wanted to respond in kind, but her lips felt glued together.

Worth cocked his head to one side. "By the way, I'm having my parents, Olivia and John Lipscomb over tonight."

"For dinner?" Molly asked in a business tone.

"No. Just for snacks and drinks."

"Consider it taken care of."

Worth deliberately perused her body with that cynical curl to his lips. "I never doubted that." He then tipped his hat. "See ya."

Molly attacked the next piece of silver with such vengeance, she almost broke her hand.

* * *

He'd had a great time with the kid, which was both good and bad. The good was that Trent made him laugh, something that he rarely did anymore. It seemed like the laughter had left his body at the same time Molly had left his life.

That kind of thinking was as crazy as it was untrue. Still, more often than not, he realized he walked around with a surly look on his face.

The bad was that the boy made Worth yearn for a son of his own, a gift that would never be his.

Muttering a sailor's curse under his breath, Worth strode into his room where he shed his clothes. It was much later than he'd thought; hence his parents, et al. would soon be arriving. He prided himself on punctuality; this evening was no exception, even if he dreaded what lay ahead.

Lately, his parents got on his nerves big time. Olivia, too. John Lipscomb, his potential campaign manager, was the only one he looked forward to seeing. Suddenly, Worth felt the need for a beer. Maybe that would put him in a better frame of mind.

But since he was naked, he could forget that. *Naked.* He groaned, that word bringing back memories of that bathroom debacle. He laughed without mirth. Who was he kidding? That memory had never left him; since it had happened, it had haunted him day and night.

Even this afternoon, when he'd seen Molly in the kitchen, polishing silver, he could barely remember what she had on, though he figured it was her usual work attire—a pair of low-cut jeans, belt and tight-fitting white shirt.

In his mind, *she* was naked.

Envisioning her perfect breasts, perfect tush, perfect legs, perfect skin and perfect lush lips had shot his libido into overdrive at the same time his control took a kamikaze dive. His body so burned to take her, he'd barely been able to contain himself.

Worth licked his dry lips, wanting a beer more by the second. Again, he glanced at his watch and noticed he scarcely had time to get a shower and dress before the guests arrived. But this was his house, and if he was late, then so be it.

He *needed* a drink.

With that, he slipped back into his jeans and made his way into the kitchen where he pulled up short. Molly was still there—working.

"What the hell?" he said in a rougher tone than he meant.

"Good evening to you, too."

Though he heard the sting in her voice, she kept her gaze averted. He wondered if that was on purpose since she probably saw, out of her peripheral vision, he was only half-dressed.

"Sorry," he muttered, charging for the fridge and grabbing a beer.

"No, you're not." With her head lowered, Molly never stopped arranging fruit on a tray.

He pulled in his breath and stared at a spot where her hair didn't quite touch her collar, thus exposing a bare place on her neck. He clenched his fists, longing to lean over and lick that soft skin, knowing it would feel like velvet under his tongue.

Then realizing what she'd said, he made a face. "What does that mean?"

"You might say you're sorry, but you're not, especially when it pertains to me."

He was about to open his mouth and tell her that was a damned lie. But then he slammed it back shut, knowing she was right. He wasn't sorry he'd spoken harshly to her. Any contact with her now seemed to bring out the worst in him.

Worth wanted what he couldn't have, and that was her. Every time he saw Molly that fact ate a bigger hole in his gut and made him angry to boot, an anger he took out on her. What a freakin' mess.

"You're right, I'm not sorry."

"What do you want?" she asked in a tired voice.

"A beer, which I got." He paused, then added, "You look ready to drop in your tracks."

"I'm about finished."

"Good Lord, Molly, we're not feeding five thousand tonight."

"I haven't fixed for five thousand, either." Her tone was hostile.

His gaze perused the table full of food. "Sure appears that way to me."

She merely looked at him.

Worth shrugged his shoulders. "Okay, so I don't know a damn thing when it comes to entertaining."

"Enough said," Molly responded with a wry tone.

He took another swig of beer before he asked, "Is Kathy helping you serve?"

"No, she's not feeling well."

"Dammit, Molly, you're not superwoman."

Her head popped back. "Who told you that?"

She sounded so serious that for a second, he was so taken aback, he actually laughed.

It was then his eyes trapped hers and the room seemed to tilt. In one giant step Worth ate up the distance between them and was about to reach for her when she skirted around him and dashed for the door.

He muttered an oath.

At the door, she turned but couldn't seem to say anything, which told him she was as shaken as he, especially since her chest was heaving.

Finally, though, in a surprisingly neutral tone, she said, "Thanks for taking Trent riding. He had a great time."

Worth bowed, then responded in his most cynical tone, "My pleasure."

"Dammit, boy, you beat all."

"Now, Dad, if you don't calm down, you're going to have a heart attack."

"No, he isn't," Eva said. "He doesn't have a bad heart. But he might, if you don't stop playing cat and mouse with your future."

"Your mother's right, Worth," John pitched in, his features and voice filled with undisguised concern. "Push has come to shove. You have to make a decision."

His guests had just arrived, and he was already eager for them to go home. The moment after they were seated in the living room and ordered their drinks, they had done nothing but rap on his ears about whether he was going to run for office or not.

The bad part about it was they were right. If he was indeed going to enter the race, he needed to make up his mind and make it up now. But there was just something inside him that kept him from saying the word *yes* and meaning it definitively.

Which probably meant he didn't have the heart of a politician.

"I'm with them, Worth," Olivia said, sidling up closer to him on the sofa, and grabbing his hand, then bringing it up to her lips. For some reason, his gaze went straight to Molly, who was at the bar mixing John a drink. If she saw Olivia's intimate gesture, she chose to ignore it.

No matter. Worth removed his hand with as much grace as possible, suddenly repulsed by Olivia's touch. God, everything that he'd once held near and dear seemed to have gone down the tubes.

Once Molly had handed John his drink, she said, "Is there anything else I can get you?" She paused and smiled. "As you can see, the table is filled with hors d'oeuvres and plenty of sweets."

"Thank you, Molly," Eva said in a stilted tone. "You've done a great job."

Worth knew Molly well enough to sense she was having difficulty keeping a straight face. He also knew that Molly thought his mother was a snob in the truest meaning of the word.

It was in that moment that his and Molly's eyes accidentally met. Later, he told himself he was nuts, but at the time he could've sworn she had winked at him, as though she knew he'd read her mind.

Then Molly smiled again and said, "I'll be back shortly to check on you."

"That won't be necessary," Eva said, turning to Worth. "We won't need her anymore, as we have private matters to discuss. Right, son?"

Worth gave his mother a withering look as he opened his mouth to refute her words. He never got the chance to speak.

Molly beat him to the draw. "Fine, Eva. I'm sure they can depend on you to mix and serve their drinks."

With a horrified look on her face, Eva opened her mouth to speak only nothing came out.

That was when Molly smiled her sweetest smile yet and spoke in her syrupiest southern drawl, "Good night y'all. I sure hope you have a pleasant evening."

Sixteen

Man, he was glad that ordeal was over.

Then Worth felt his conscience pinch him. Those were his folks he was thinking ill of, and the woman he'd been squiring around. Even though he had no intention of marrying her, he should still treat her with respect. As for John, there was no problem. He was a good friend and seemed to want only what was best for Worth.

The others—well, Worth wasn't so sure. That was why his feet were heavy as he made his way toward his bedroom. He paused in his thoughts, toying with the idea of grabbing another beer. Since he'd already had more than his share, he kept going.

His parents and Olivia had tried to pin him to the wall the entire evening, but he'd held firm in his convictions. He still hadn't made up his mind about running for office, which was not like him. *Waffling* was another word that normally wasn't in his vocabulary. Again, until he was fully committed and excited himself, he wasn't going to sign on just to please others.

While the political pressure hadn't been comfortable, it hadn't bothered him nearly as much as his mother's put-down of Molly. When Eva had all but dismissed her as nothing more than a servant, Worth had been furious. Yet he'd kept his mouth shut, which made him despise himself. But what could he have said that wouldn't have sent up a smoke signal? And for what purpose?

He wanted Molly, wanted her so badly he could taste it. But his bodily needs and cravings were nobody's business but his. Besides, nothing would ever come of his hot, scorching desires.

He'd already suffered third-degree burns at her expense, and he didn't have that much skin left to spare. Besides that, she was no longer a road he wanted to travel.

He was certain Molly didn't want to relive that pain and heartache, either. Yet if she didn't hurry up and leave, he wasn't sure he could keep his hands to himself. God, he ached to touch her, to taste her, to…

"Stuff it, Cavanaugh," he muttered, upping his pace down the hall. He was one tired mother and the sooner he got to bed, the sooner his mind would find relief.

He almost laughed at that thought. Since Molly had entered the door of the ranch house, sleep had escaped him, except for short catnaps. Thank goodness, he was lucky he didn't need much shut-eye to keep going.

It was when he passed Molly's room that he heard a sound, a sound he couldn't identify. Not at first, anyway. He paused outside her door and listened.

Sobs.

Muffled.

But gut-wrenching sobs, nonetheless.

Worth continued to stand as though cemented to the spot,

not knowing what to do. Then, as if his hand had a mind of its own, he slowly twisted the doorknob.

She hated them all, especially Eva.

Molly had never been vindictive and didn't think of herself as that now. But she'd had enough of those people and could not wait to get out of their sight, determined never to see them again.

When she'd been dismissed like a piece of garbage by that conniving, mean-spirited mother of Worth's, she'd almost packed her bags, put her son in the car and hauled it out of there.

By the time she returned to her room, took a hot shower, slipped on a silk nightgown and crawled into bed, she had calmed down. But not much. Now, as she lay in a fetal position, resentment and anger welled up inside her, so much that she wanted to scream. Instead she cried.

Molly didn't know what she'd expected after the attack in the living room. Yes, she did. She had expected Worth to defend her, to take up for her. Then she realized that was not only crazy, but it wasn't going to happen.

After all, he was the leader of the pack against her. From the get-go, he'd resented the hell out of her—first, for returning to the ranch and second, for staying. The only reason he tolerated her was because of her mother's health problem.

Another sob stuck in her throat as she curled tighter. If only she didn't care what Worth thought or did. If only she didn't care he hadn't come to her rescue verbally.

But she did care, and that was what was killing her.

Trapped.

She felt like a trapped animal, and that didn't sit well with her. The Cavanaugh clan had already wreaked more havoc in her life than anyone or anything ever had. And they were continuing to do so, which made her feel badly about herself.

Especially since she still wanted the one man she could never have. Worth, she had decided, was in her bloodstream, and she would never get rid of him. No matter where she was, if he came around, she would want him. She had decided that would never change. But that didn't mean she had to give in to that desire, that craving of her body.

Once she left the ranch, she would lick her wounds. Time would take care of much of her pain. Too, she had Trent. From the day he was born, he had been the main focus in her life. Once they arrived at the ranch, Worth had cluttered her mind. Once they were back in Houston, Trent would take top priority again.

Her son and her job.

An awesome combination. With both, she could be happy and content once again. She didn't need a man, certainly not one who didn't want her or he wouldn't have let his parents send her away.

She just had to keep Trent and the secret she bore up front in her mind, and she would prevail. Those two things gave her the courage to uncoil her body and try to get some sleep.

Molly had just tossed the blanket back, the gas logs burning low, making cover a bit much, when she heard what sounded like the knob on her door turning. She stilled herself and held her breath.

"Molly?"

Worth!

Oh, God, what should she do?

"Are you all right?"

She could barely hear him as he was as close to whispering as his deep voice would allow.

Pushing the panic button, she remained silent, hoping he'd get the message she didn't want to be disturbed, especially by *him*.

Her ploy failed.

Then the door opened more, and he walked into the shadowy room. Her heart jumped into the back of her throat making speech impossible. Once again her silence backfired, seeming to give him courage to forge forward until he reached the side of her bed.

Molly squeezed her eyes tightly together, praying he would think she'd fallen asleep. She realized, however, that the fresh tears saturating her cheeks said otherwise. When she felt the mattress give beside her, her eyes flew open.

"Worth," she said in an aching tone.

"Shh, it's okay." His voice literally shook with emotion as he stared down at her in the glow of the fire.

"No, it's not," she whimpered, feeling a new set of tears cloud her vision.

"You're right, it's not," he acknowledged in that same emotional voice. "I should've kicked some ass tonight, mine included."

"I want to go home." Her tone was so low, she wasn't sure he had heard her. He had.

"I don't blame you," he said, letting out a shuddering breath.

Another silence.

"You…you should go," Molly whispered, starting to curl into that fetal position again.

"No."

The edge in his voice stopped her cold.

"I want to look at you." His voice now shook. "You're even lovelier than I remembered."

Without thinking, Molly lowered her gaze and saw that her breasts and nipples were swollen and pushing against the silk. When she raised her eyes, fire burned in his, especially when he reached out and removed one strap, exposing one full breast.

His breathing faltered, and he closed his eyes for a moment.

If only she hadn't let Trent spend the night in Maxine's room, she'd have a valid excuse for calling a halt to this madness.

"Molly...please don't send me away."

"Worth, you're not playing fair." She felt desperate not to give in to his pleading, but she felt herself weakening.

"Tell me you don't want me, and I'll go."

"I don't want you."

Worth focused on her with piercing intensity. "Do you really mean that?"

"No...I mean..." She couldn't go on, not when his hand cupped that exposed breast and a moan of despair escaped her.

"God, Molly," he ground out, leaning over and tonguing that bare flesh until the nipple was ripe and pulsating. "I can't leave you now."

In that moment, she was lost. It was beyond her capacity to do anything more than lay there and let him have his way with her. After all, that was what she'd been wanting since the day she'd arrived and had seen him.

Like she'd admitted, he was in her blood and she would never cease to want him. Now was her chance to love him one last time. And she wasn't going to pass it up—right or wrong.

Molly trembled all over when he lifted his face and their eyes clung. Sensing she was his for the taking, Worth cradled her face between his palms and tilted her head toward him. "I need you so much," he said in a low, shaky voice.

She believed him because she felt the same hot need blazing inside her. That summer with him had been the happiest of her life and it had given her the gift of a lifetime— her son. Despite knowing what she knew now, and what she'd been through these past few weeks, she would let him make love to her, even if it put her soul in jeopardy.

He bent to kiss her, and her lips parted to the wet thrust of his tongue as it plunged deeply into her moist cavity. She clutched at him while his hands wandered over her body. It was after she felt a slight chill that she realized he had removed her gown, leaving her naked before him.

Without taking his eyes off her, he stood and removed his clothes, giving her the exquisite luxury of perusing his nakedness. So as to make room for him on the bed, Molly scooted over, and he lay beside her, drawing her to him—flesh against flesh.

His hands circled her back, drawing her close against him, the surge of his manhood waging war against her lower stomach. "You are still the loveliest creature on earth," he told her huskily before his mouth returned to hers with feverish urgency.

She rejoiced in the feel of his lips tangling with hers, especially after he sucked on her tongue, further deepening and lengthening the kiss. Only after they couldn't breathe any longer did he come up for air.

His eyes were glazed with passion, he reached for her leg and swung it over his hip, giving him access to her most sensitive place that he instantly covered with the palm of his hand, then inserted a finger into its warmth.

"Ohh," Molly cried, bouncing her buttocks up. It had been so long since she'd felt this emotion, this high, that only his touch could bring her. Not only did she want his fingers to work their magic, she wanted him inside her, pounding her until she was spent.

And satisfied.

Realizing she was ready for him, she heard his breathing quicken at the same time the burgeoning thickness of his erection tangled in the curls at the entrance to her moist core.

Then it hit her that neither were protected. She drew back.

"Molly?" he asked in a guttural tone. "Please…"

"We…you don't have any protection."

"It's okay," he ground out. "I promise."

"If you say so," she responded in a frantic tone, revealing

how much she wanted him whether he spoke the truth or not. Besides, getting pregnant twice, accidentally, with the same man, was not about to happen, whether it was the right time of the month or not. Fate had to be on her side this time.

She didn't want to think about that now. She only wanted to think about how it would feel to have his hard flesh invade her softness. With only that in mind, Molly reached down, clutched his erection and guided its big, velvet-smooth tip into her aching flesh.

"Oh, my, Molly," he groaned, shoving himself into the heart of her.

She couldn't help but gasp, having forgotten how big he was. Still, her muscles contracted around him; and because she was so ecstatic he was inside her, she framed his face with her hands, bringing his eager lips to hers, where they clung.

She had thought this one last invasion into her flesh would be enough to last her for the rest of her life. She knew better now. When he began to move, and his breathing grew hoarse and labored, she realized she wanted more.

She wanted him forever.

Because that couldn't be, when she felt him empty in her, and she climaxed like never before, she buried her face against his chest so tightly it took her breath.

"Oh, Molly," he cried, shuddering in the aftermath of that awesome coupling. "My Molly."

After it was over, he kissed her all over her face. With him still inside her, he brushed her lips with his, then they both closed their eyes.

And slept.

Seventeen

Molly awoke with a start, especially when she felt her leg entwined with a hard, hairy one. Outwardly, she remained immobile, but inside her was a mass of quivering nerves.

Worth.

Had they made hot, torrid love all night? Surely not. Surely it was only the middle of the night, or earlier. That was why he was still with her. She stole a glance at the clock; it told an entirely different story. It was almost six o'clock. Suddenly she felt like a giant hand was squeezing the life out of her heart.

She could be pregnant. *Again.* Although last night, when they had briefly discussed the fact that no protection was in the offing, he had told her not to worry, and she hadn't. That was because she'd been in the throes of passion and nothing had mattered except feeling Worth inside her.

But with the dawn came reality and with reality came fear.

Yet she didn't want to think about those emotions, especially with Worth's warm body still wrapped around her like a blanket.

Yet she had no choice.

"Worth," she whispered, nudging him awake.

His eyes popped open, and she realized that for a second he, too, was disoriented. Then it apparently hit him where he was; the muted groan against her neck told her that.

"No," she said in a desperate tone.

He paid her no mind, continuing to nuzzle and lick.

Oh, dear Lord, Molly thought, feeling her body weaken then ache for him to make love to her again. But she couldn't allow that, not with Trent having jumped to the forefront of her mind.

"Stop it," she whispered again, this time with more force.

Worth pulled back, confusion mirrored in his eyes. "What's wrong?"

"It's nearly six."

"In the morning?"

"Yes."

"So?" he muttered, still making no effort to dislodge himself.

"You have to go."

"Why? It's my house." Propping himself on his elbow, Worth leaned over and gave her a raw, devouring kiss.

When he pulled his lips off hers, she was as breathless and rattled as she'd ever been. Damn him. He refused to play fair, having stirred her body back to life.

"I loved making love to you," he said in a lazy tone.

Her gaze was intense. "Me, too."

"It was even better than I remembered."

His eyes had turned into banked down coals of fire as she felt him harden against her leg. Somehow she had to get him out of this room, but first she had to know what he'd meant last night when he'd promised she wouldn't get pregnant.

"Worth?"

"Mmm?"

He sounded like his mind was a million miles away, only it wasn't. It was on getting himself inside her again, as he was busy urging her legs apart.

"Why are you so sure I couldn't get pregnant?"

His body went stiff as a plank, and for the longest time he didn't say anything. Then he got back up on his elbow and stared into her face, his features contorted. "Not long after you left I had an accident."

A feeling of dread spread through her. But she didn't say anything. It was up to him to tell her what he wanted her to know, not that it would make any difference, she assured herself. They were destined to live separate lives.

"A horse kicked me in the groin. Kicked the hell out of me, actually."

She winced. "I'm so sorry." And she was. Even though he had hurt her to the core, she didn't wish him any ill will, not when it came to his health.

"Me, too," he said, his tone bleak. "As a result, I probably can't father a child."

Molly almost freaked out, which made speaking, or anything else, impossible.

Only you do have a child, a precious son named Trent.

For the first time since the birth of their son, she yearned to share that news with Worth, to take away the pain she heard in his voice and read in his face.

Only she couldn't.

For her own self-preservation that was impossible, especially with his parents in the picture. However much they might despise her, if they *knew* she had their grandson, they would pull out all the stops to take him away from her. And they had the money and the power to do just that.

As for Worth, she had no idea how that would affect him. She suspected he would follow their lead. Hence, she had no choice but to keep her mouth shut and guard her secret more now than ever.

Which meant she needed to leave ASAP. Today wouldn't be too soon. Knowing that wasn't going to happen, she would be forced to sharpen her acting skills.

She refused to give up Trent or share him with the man who had broken her heart, who was well on his to way to doing it again.

Fool!

"Molly?" he asked in a sandpaper-like tone, placing his lips against her forehead.

"I'm not asleep, if that's what you're thinking."

"Now you know why we can make love all we want to and don't have to worry about it."

She stared at him wide-eyed. "That's where you're wrong."

It was obvious he picked up on the censure in her tone as he pulled his head back, not bothering to mask his confusion.

"This was our swan song, Worth," she said with emphasis.

His jaw went rigid with fury. "So this was our goodbye nookie, huh?"

She knew that crude statement stemmed from the fury that rearranged his features. But she was furious, too, scooting away from him. "Please go," she said in a terse tone.

He reached for her. "Molly, I didn't mean that."

"It doesn't matter," she replied in a dull voice. "This was a mistake and we both know it."

He sighed, but didn't argue, which cut her deeply again. It was then she wondered again how she could have ended up in such a position. But when it came to Worth, she had never used good judgment, and time and years apparently hadn't changed that. But it didn't sit well with her or make her proud of herself. On the contrary, it made her sick to her stomach.

Suddenly thoughts of Trent popped back into her mind.

He was usually a late sleeper. But since he was with her mother, she couldn't make that call. If he were to simply wander back into their suite...

The repercussions of what would happen if he chose to do that this morning didn't bear thinking about. As far as she knew the door was not locked.

Great.

"Worth."

"I'm going, Molly. You've made it quite plain how you feel."

The bitterness was so thick in his voice that for a second she felt sorry for him. Then she mentally kicked her backside for that thought. If it hadn't been for him and his betrayal of her years ago, both their lives would've been different.

Now it was too late.

She would soon go her way and he his.

Jerked back to the moment at hand by him rolling out of bed, Molly found herself gawking at his backside, mainly his buttocks, which were firm and perfect—buttocks she had caressed at will.

When he swung around and stared down at her, she swallowed a labored gasp. Pain was evident in his eyes and face. Only she wasn't looking at his features, God help her. Molly's eyes feasted on the rest of his body, equally as perfect—the muscled arms and chest, the dark hairs—just the right amount—that covered his stomach, down to his fully aroused manhood.

Hot adrenaline rushed through Molly as that turgid flesh made her ache to reach out, and not only caress its big, smooth tip, but surround it with her mouth.

"God, Molly," he whispered in an agonized voice. "If you don't—"

Feeling a flush steal over her face, she quickly averted her gaze and said, "Please leave."

He didn't move immediately; he was too busy uttering harsh obscenities. Then moments passed, and she finally heard the door open and close. Only then did she grab the pillow, hug it close to her chest and let it absorb the tears that freely flowed.

Recriminations?

That soul-searching time had come. Surprisingly, though, she had no regrets. She refused to beat up on herself for letting her body overrule her mind, since she knew it would never happen again.

And for that she was as sad now as she had been the day five years ago she had walked out of his life.

Worth rode the horse until both were tuckered out. Although he hadn't covered anywhere near all of his property, he had achieved his goal.

Riding had definitely tempered the anger that threatened to blow his insides to smithereens. Before Molly had come back to the ranch, he'd been at a crossroads in his life, trying to decide whether he wanted to be a full-time horse breeder or a full-time politician.

Now he was more mixed up and uncertain than ever before. He still wanted to breed horses, but without Olivia's land it wouldn't be on the scale he'd envisioned. And he wanted to run for office, though the fire in his belly still wasn't there.

He was in one big mess.

He blamed Molly. From the moment she had walked in the door of his ranch house, she had screwed with his mind. After yesterday, it was more than his mind. She had screwed with his body. She'd screwed *him.* Not true, he told himself. What they had done had been more than simply screwing. They had made love in the truest sense of the word.

As a result, Worth didn't know how in the hell he was going to keep his hands to himself now that he had gotten another taste of Molly's sweet, succulent flesh.

What awesome, heady stuff. Not only had his body exploded, but his mind, as well. And he wanted more, dammit. But she had made it clear that wasn't going to happen.

Soon she would be gone. That thought made him nudge the horse in the side and send him galloping once again. However, nothing worked to remove the thought, the smell, the feel of Molly from his mind. It was as if she'd been permanently implanted there.

If that were truly the case, then he was in big trouble. This time she would leave and never return. So what could he do about it? Ask her to stay, a little voice whispered, which would be the height of insanity. He couldn't trust her. Hell, she'd run off once. What was to keep her from doing the same thing again?

Nothing.

That was why he couldn't take a chance on exposing his heart and having it broken all over again. Ergo, he had to let her go. And get on with his life.

Some things he could change and some things he could not.

Molly happened to fit in the *could not* category.

"Trent," Molly called from the porch, "it's time to wash up for dinner."

Her son didn't answer right off as he was playing with a ball, pretending he was one of the Harlem Globetrotters, and seemed to be having the time of his life. Since it was near dusk, she didn't like him outside alone, and Tammy had already gone home.

"Aw, Mommy, I wanna play a little longer."

"Trent."

"I'll watch him."

As always the sound of Worth's unexpected voice never failed to slam-dunk her nervous system. Dammit, she wished he'd stop appearing out of nowhere.

"Oh, boy, Mommy! Can I stay with Worth?"

She wanted to yell no, but she didn't. Again, why punish her child for her misdeeds? What difference would it make anyway? Their time was on the downhill slide, as her mother was getting better, and stronger, every day.

Their departure couldn't come soon enough because she was beginning to take a trip down Guilt Lane, to beat up on herself, something she had promised she wouldn't do. But Trent needed a father and she knew it.

All boys need a father.

Trent had one he would never know. Suddenly, that thought was overwhelmingly depressing, thinking how much Trent loved this ranch. Not only was she robbing him of his inheritance, she was depriving him of his father.

But if she told the truth, *she* would lose her son.

That couldn't happen.

"Mommy!"

"All right, Trent. You can tag after Worth until supper's ready."

With that she turned and went back into the house, hoping that decision wouldn't come back to haunt her.

Thirty minutes later, Molly returned to the porch and only caught a glimpse of Worth. A frisson of uneasiness ran down her spine. "Worth," she called.

He stopped in his tracks and swung around.

"Where's Trent?"

He made his way closer to her, his features pinched. "I don't know."

"What do you mean you don't know?" Her voice had reached the shrill level.

"Hold on. I'm sure he's okay. I turned my back for a second, and he was gone."

Molly leapt off the porch and ran to Worth. "Where have you looked?" she demanded, trying to keep her panic at bay.

"Everywhere but the barn. That's where I'm headed now."

"Trent!" Molly yelled over and over. No answer.

By the time they reached their destination, Molly was beside herself; her mind had become her own worst enemy. And Worth. She could have gladly strangled him, but since that wasn't possible, she kept her mouth shut, almost choking on her suppressed fury.

"I'm sorry, Molly," he said, entering the shadows of the barn.

She merely flung him a go-to-hell look.

He blanched, but didn't say anything back.

"Trent, are you here?"

"Mommy, Worth, look."

Both pair of eyes shot up to the hayloft. Trent was standing near the edge of the loft that overlooked the cement below. Fear, like poison, spread through her as she stared at Worth. He, too, looked green around the gills, though when he spoke his voice was even and cool.

"Stay where you are, Trent. Don't move."

"Wanna watch me walk—"

"No!" Molly and Worth cried in unison.

The boy froze.

"I'm coming up to get you," Worth said. "Meanwhile, stay right where you are, okay?"

"No, I'll come down."

"Trent, no!"

The boy paid no heed. He turned, then slipped, miraculously falling straight into Worth's outstretched arms.

For a moment no one said a word. It was as though they were all paralyzed. Finally, Trent rallied and said, "Are you mad at me, Mommy?"

"Put him down, Worth," she said with a quiver in her voice. Worth did as he was told.

Pointing at her son, Molly added, "You go straight to your room and wash up. I'll be there shortly."

Trent hung his head. "Yes, ma'am."

"Go. I'll be watching until you get inside."

As if glad to be away from his mother's wrath for a few minutes at least, Trent took off in a dead run.

Once he disappeared into the house, a heavy silence fell over the barn.

Worth was the first to break it. "You're pissed, and I don't blame you."

"Pissed is too mild for what I am." Her voice dripped with icicles.

"He's okay, Molly. Besides, he's a kid, a boy. They try daring things like that."

"Don't you dare tell me about kids. Especially mine."

"Well, excuse me." His hands clenched. "I told you I was sorry. What more do you want?"

"I don't want anything. Your behavior just proves that your word is as worthless now as it was when you asked me to marry you five years ago."

"What the hell are you talking about?"

"I think we're past the pretend stage, don't you?"

"If you have something to say, then spit it out, 'cause I still don't know what the hell you're talking about."

"Your parents."

"What about my parents?"

"Are you saying you didn't send them to me to try and buy me off?"

Worth rocked back on his heels as though she'd sucker punched him in the gut. "I didn't send them anywhere, and certainly not to talk to you."

"You told me you loved me and wanted to marry me, only to then back out."

"I did no such thing. You're the one who lost your nerve and ran off like a scalded dog."

"Only because of your parents. After they came to me and expressed your feelings, telling me that you didn't love me, but didn't want to tell me for fear of hurting me worse."

Worth's expression turned dark as a thunder cloud.

"Oh, and to further insult me," Molly drilled, "your parents offered me money, lots of money, to get lost."

"That's a lie. You're making all this up to appease your conscience. My parents wouldn't do such a thing."

"Are you calling me a liar?" Molly retorted hotly.

"For God's sake, Molly—"

"Ask them." Her gaze, filled with disdain, wandered over him. "If you've got the guts, that is."

Eighteen

"Son, what a delight," Ted said, opening the door wide enough for Worth to stride through. "You're just in time. Supper will be ready in a few minutes."

"I don't—" Worth never got the rest of the words out, as his mother came around the corner into the living room, a smile on her face.

"What a nice surprise, darling." Eva gestured toward the plush leather sofa near the gas-burning fireplace. "Have a seat," she added with a wink. "I have a feeling you've come to tell us something that will call for a celebration. What can I get you to drink?"

"Nothing, Mother. Please, just sit down and stop talking."

Eva put a hand to her throat. "Why, that's not a very nice way to talk to your mother."

Worth cut his eyes to his father who no longer had that warm look on his face. In fact, his features appeared rather grim, as if he sensed something was terribly wrong. "You, too, Dad. Sit."

Eva's eyes widened. "What on earth is wrong with you? You're acting so unlike yourself." Her frustration and anger seemed to be gaining speed. "You can't just come in here and order us around. This is our house."

"Mother," Worth hissed, "be quiet."

Eva sounded as though she might strangle trying to get further words out of her mouth. Then Ted glanced at her and shook his head, frowning.

Worth watched his mother toss him a go-to-hell look, but she didn't say anything else, thank God. Though she was his mother, he was as close to choking her as he'd ever been in his life.

That was not good, but his fury factor was off the charts, although he was trying his best to keep his emotions under wraps. After all, Molly could be lying to cover her own skin, but his gut told him that wasn't so. Otherwise, she wouldn't have demanded he face his parents.

Besides, he'd reached the end of his rope, and there was nowhere else to go, or anyone else to rescue him—except himself.

"I guess you're not running for office, son," Ted finally said into the uncomfortable silence.

"The election's not why I'm here."

"Then why are you here," Eva demanded in a cold voice, "especially with that mean attitude?" She grabbed a tissue and dabbed at her eyes.

Worth rolled his. "Spare me, Mother, you're mad not sad."

"Stop talking to me like that, Worth Cavanaugh. I've taught you to have respect for your elders, especially your parents. What on earth have we done to make you look at us like you despise us?"

"Does the word *Molly* give you a clue?"

"What about her, son?" Ted asked in a guarded voice.

"Oh, please," Eva put in with added dramatics. "Do we have to talk about her?"

Worth didn't mince any words. "As a matter of fact we do."

"What then?" Eva demanded in a resigned, but sharp tone.

"Did you two have a conversation with her before she left that summer?"

The room got funeral-home quiet.

"I don't know what you're talking about," Eva finally said in her lofty tone. "We had several conversations with that girl."

Worth's ire rose, but when he spoke he still held onto his cool. "That girl, as you call her, was my fiancée."

"Oh, Worth, for crying out loud." Eva flapped a hand with perfectly manicured nails. "She was just your play toy and we knew it."

Worth clenched his teeth, reminding himself that she was his mother, though at the moment he wished he'd never been born to these two selfish snobs.

He couldn't change that, of course. What he could change was the here and now. *And the future.* No more messing around with his life.

"Did you talk to her?" Worth asked again, his gaze including both of them. "And don't lie to me, either."

Eva whipped her head around to Ted who actually looked like all the blood had drained from his face. Worth watched him nod to his wife.

She in turn, faced Worth, her lips stretched in an unbecoming tight line at the same time her eyes sparked. "Yes, we talked to her."

"What did you tell her?" Worth stood and loomed over them. "The exact words."

"Will you please sit down?" Eva asked, clasping her hands together in her lap. "You look like a panther about to pounce, and frankly, that makes me nervous."

"Mother!"

"All right." She raised her eyes to Worth. "We told her you didn't really love her, and that you didn't want to marry her."

An expletive shot out of Worth's mouth.

Eva's head flared back, and she glared at him. However, she seemed to know better than to reprimand him.

"Go on." Worth could hardly get the words through his lips; they were so stiff and his mouth so dry.

"Well, we told her she wasn't good enough for you, but that you didn't want to tell her yourself, so you asked us to do it."

Another string of expletives followed.

Both Eva and Ted sucked in their breaths and held them, staring at him as though their son had suddenly turned into some kind of monster they didn't recognize.

"We…we thought we were doing what was best for you," Eva said in a tearful voice. "We didn't think she was good enough—"

"Your mother's right," Ted chimed in. "We thought we had your best interest—"

"Shut up! Both of you."

Eva's and Ted's mouths dropped open, but they shut up.

Worth leaned in further and spoke in a low, harsh tone. "I loved Molly and intended to marry her. As a result of what you did, you've cost us five miserable years, and the two of you ought to be horsewhipped."

"My God, Worth," Eva cried. "Listen to what you're saying."

He paid her plaintive cry and words no mind. "But because you're my parents, I hope I can find it in my heart to forgive you. Only not now. I don't want to see either of you, so stay away from me, you hear?"

He turned, strode to the door and slammed it behind him with such force, he figured he shattered the expensive glass.

So what? He'd never felt better in his life. Yet he still had a major task in front of him.

Molly.

Despite the chill in the air, sweat broke out on his forehead and his knees threatened to buckle. He had to find Molly and make things right.

"Mama?"

Maxine smiled and patted Molly's hand. "You haven't called me that in a long time. Usually it means you're upset about something."

Molly pulled at the sheet on her mother's bed and finally looked her in the eye. "It's time I left."

Maxine frowned. "That's fine, honey. I'm so much better. In fact, I was thinking about—"

"No. The deal is this. Only if you let me hire a private nurse will I leave."

"I don't need one. I already have a therapist."

"With me gone, you need both. And Worth needs to hire another temporary housekeeper. You have to tell him that. He'll do it for you."

Maxine blew out a frustrated breath. "I sure reared a stubborn child."

"That you did. Those shots in your back, combined with physical therapy, have done wonders. You've made tremendous progress. It's just a matter of time until you'll be your old self."

"Only I'm not quite there yet, right?" Maxine asked with raised brows.

"Not quite."

"While I can hardly bear the thought of you and Trent leaving, you know I understand. On second thought, maybe I don't."

"I just need to get back to the office."

"I think there's more to it than that," Maxine said, then paused. "It's Worth, isn't it?"

Molly could only nod; her throat was too full to speak.

"If he hurt you again, I'll strangle him myself."

"It's okay. It's just time for Trent and me to leave. You love it here. Worth loves you, and I don't want to mess that up."

"I still say you two should've married."

"Well, it's too late for that now," Molly said bitterly.

"It's never too late for happiness, my dear. If it's pride we're talking about here, then let it go. It can bring down the biggest and strongest."

"Mama."

Maxine held up her hand. "I'll say no more. When you're ready to talk, I'm ready to listen. Nothing you've ever done, or could ever do, is unforgivable in my sight. Remember that. I love you more than life itself."

"Oh, Mama," Molly sobbed, leaning over and holding her mother close. "You're my rock and always have been. Maybe it's time I shared my heart."

Maxine reached up and trapped a tear running down her daughter's cheek. "I'm listening, my sweet."

Holding tightly to her mother's hand, Molly began to talk.

She was all packed and ready to go.

Yet she hadn't called Trent. She hadn't had the heart to do so yet as he and Tammy were somewhere on the grounds, running and playing.

She had just walked out on the porch, searching for fresh air that would hopefully calm her nerves, when she heard a knock on the door. She didn't bother to turn around.

"It's open."

When no one said anything, she made her way back inside.

Worth stood leaning against the door frame. Her stomach did its usual thing, and the saliva in her mouth dried up.

"I know I'm the last person you want to see," Worth exclaimed, his gaze zeroing in on the bags on the floor.

"That's right," she said, feeling goose bumps dance up and down her skin.

"I spoke with my parents."

She merely shrugged.

"You were right."

His face seemed to have sunk so that its bones took on new prominence and his voice had a crack in it. That was when she met his tormented gaze head-on.

It was in that moment that Molly knew she still loved him, that she had never stopped and that she would love him until the day she died.

"I'm so sorry they interfered," Worth said, tilting his head as though to keep it above water. "You've got to believe I had no idea any of that garbage had gone on behind my back."

Suddenly a ray of hope burst through the dead spot in Molly's heart, and she saw the possibility of swallowing her pride, like her mother said, and starting anew. If he were willing, that is.

"But that doesn't excuse what you did, Molly."

In one instant, Worth brutally dashed that ray of hope. "And just what did I do?"

"When you left me, you obviously married the first guy you met and screwed his brains out."

For the longest time Molly couldn't speak. The pain and humiliation were so severe, it put a vise on her throat. Finally, though, she rallied and spat, "How dare you say a thing like that to me? Have you no shame?"

"Tell me it isn't true." Worth's tone remained unrelenting. "And I'll take it back."

"Of course, it's not true."

His features contorted. "Then, dammit, what is the truth?"

Almost choking on her words, Molly lashed back, "I never married. I made up that story for my and Trent's protection."

"Okay, so you never married. You just screwed his brains out!"

"No, I didn't!" Molly cried out in fury.

"Well, you obviously let *someone* have your body," Worth said with a sneer.

Molly felt her fury rise to a new level. How could the man she loved say such awful things to her? She felt her face heat as words came screaming from her mouth. "No man has ever touched me but you!"

God, how could she have said that? She clasped her hands over her mouth to stop a wail from escaping. Molly knew the answer, and it made her sick at heart and sick to her stomach. She had been goaded into revealing the one secret she had sworn to take to her grave. But words, like arrows, once released, could never be recalled. The damage had been done.

Standing stonelike, she watched Worth's face as her words sank in. A myriad of emotions crossed it, none of which she could read. Was he already planning how he was going to rip Trent out of her arms and claim him as his own? With his money and power, Worth certainly had the means and power to do so.

Molly grasped her stomach, giving in to the fear that stampeded through her.

Worth, meanwhile, crossed the room with lighting speed, grabbed her arm and demanded in a raspy voice, "Did you say what I think you said?"

She could only stare at him, searching frantically for the words to right a wrong. She could deny what she'd said, or she could remain mute and let her words speak for themselves.

"God, Molly, please tell me. Is Trent my son?" Worth moaned softly. "But even if he isn't, it doesn't matter. I don't think I can live a moment longer without you."

Without thought, Molly's hands came up, encased his face and delved deeply into his eyes. "We—Trent and I come as a package deal," she murmured around the tears clogging her throat.

"So, he is my son," Worth said, his voice husky with emotion.

"Yes," Molly whispered. "Trent's your son."

He rocked back on his heels, his breath coming in heaves. Molly instinctively reached out a hand. "Worth?"

Worth clasped her hand and said, "Trent's really mine?" This time awe filled his voice and tears filled his eyes.

She pulled back and peered into his contorted features. "Yes, yes, yes."

"Oh, God, Molly, I can't believe that."

"Do you hate me for not telling you?"

He didn't hesitate. "I could never hate you for anything," he said fiercely. "I love you too much. In fact, you're the only woman I've ever loved."

"And you're the only man I've ever loved," she replied breathlessly.

"Molly…" He pulled her into his arms and simply held her for the longest, sweetest time. Then peering down at her, he said, "I want you. I need you. But most of all I love you, and I'll never let you go again."

He kissed her, then, so hard, so long, and so deep and held her so tightly, she couldn't tell whose heartbeat was whose. It didn't matter; in that moment they became one.

One Year Later

"Oh, yes, Molly, don't stop."

"As if I would," she whispered, atop Worth, continuing to ride him, slowly, then faster, until they climaxed simultaneously.

Exhausted, she fell onto his chest, hearing their hearts beat as one.

Moments later, Worth maneuvered so that he could get to her lips, giving her a long, tender kiss. Only he didn't stop there; he lifted her a little more and put those lips to one breast, then the other, and sucked.

"Ohh," Molly whispered. "You're about to get something started again."

Worth chuckled at the same time he rolled her over so that she was now under him. "That's my intention."

"But it's so soon," Molly pointed out with an answering chuckle. "You…we just came."

"I know, but don't you feel him growing, even as I'm speaking?"

Molly merely sighed and placed her arms around him. For the longest time thereafter, the room was quiet except for their moans.

A short time later, they faced each other satisfied, but worn out from their marathon evening of lovemaking.

"So, Mrs. Cavanaugh, how was your day?" Worth asked in a husky tone, his eyes still a bit glazed over with passion.

"Good, Mr. Cavanaugh. How was yours?"

"Busy as hell."

"That's a good thing, right?"

"Right, my precious."

Molly was quiet for a moment, reveling in the glow of happiness that had surrounded them since that day they both learned the truth about their pasts. Although they had yet to tell Trent that Worth was his real father, it didn't matter, at least not now.

When they told him they were in love and were going to get married, Trent had asked if he could call Worth daddy.

Thinking back on that day still tugged at Molly's heart and would be forever imprinted there.

She had cooked a special dinner with all the trimmings—candlelight, flowers, pot roast, Italian cream cake—wine for them, a Shirley Temple for Trent. Once the meal was over, they had gone into the living room where Worth had reached for Trent's hand, drawing the child onto his lap.

"Your mom and I have something to tell you," Worth said in a none-too-steady voice.

"What?" Trent mumbled, eyeing his mother and sounding uncertain.

"It's okay, sweetie," she responded with a smile and a wink.

"How would you like to live here all the time?" Worth asked, also smiling.

"Wow!" Trent cut his gaze back to his mother.

Molly grinned. "That's what I think, too."

"Your mom and I are in love and want to get married."

Trent made a face. "Does that mean you'll be kissing Mommy all the time?"

Both adults laughed without restraint.

"I'm afraid so," Worth finally admitted, having regained his composure.

"I guess that'd be okay." Trent cocked his head to one side as if trying to figure out how best to communicate what was churning in his little mind. "Would you be my daddy?"

"You betcha."

Trent seemed to think on that for a moment during which Molly held her breath. She suspected Worth was doing likewise.

"Can I call you Daddy?"

Worth's mouth worked. "I'd like that a lot."

A smile broke across the child's face. "Man, now I'll be like all my friends. They all have daddies."

Molly looked on as Worth grabbed Trent and hugged him

tightly, all the while seeking her eyes that were filled with tears. Only after blinking them away did she see the ones in Worth's.

Several days later she and Worth exchanged vows. From that moment on, they had become a family.

During the year they had been married, her mother's back had completely mended. And though she had insisted on keeping her job as housekeeper, Worth had said no, that it was time for her to retire and enjoy life—mainly her grandson.

Maxine hadn't argued, and thus was having a ball.

As for Eva and Ted, they were another story altogether. Even though civility became the order of the day, a wedge remained between Worth and his parents. While Molly hated that, and felt responsible to some degree, there was nothing she could do. Worth had to work through his problems with his parents in his own way and in his own time.

Following that fierce altercation with Ted and Eva, Worth had decided not to run for office, vowing, instead, to concentrate on making her and Trent happy, along with building his horse breeding empire. He and Art had figured a way to make it work without Olivia's land.

"You're awfully quiet," Worth said, interrupting her thoughts, dropping a kiss on the tip of her nose.

"I was just thinking about this past year and everything that's happened."

"Such as?"

"Us. Trent. Your estrangement from your family."

Worth grimaced. "I've been thinking about that, too, but right now I still can't get past their mean-spiritedness."

"Maybe one day you can because of Trent. They are, after all, his grandparents, and I want him to know them."

"You're right, of course. I'm sure they're sorry and are suffering, but I can't completely forgive, nor can I forget." His grimace deepened. "They cost me almost five years of my son's life."

"I know how deeply that cuts, but—"

"You think I should try and make amends?"

Molly nodded her head. "I'd like that for the reason I just said, Trent. However, it's your call as to how you handle your folks."

"Well, Christmas is knocking on the door." He paused. "We'll see what that brings."

Molly smiled, then kissed him. "You're a good man, Worth Cavanaugh."

"And you're a liar, Molly Cavanaugh. I'm a son of a bitch and we both know it."

They giggled, then hugged.

"Do you miss your work?" he asked when their laughter subsided.

"A little," she said truthfully. "I miss Dr. Nutting, my old boss, but he certainly understands why I didn't return."

"Have you thought about working here full time? I want you to be happy at home, but if not, that's okay."

She heard the forlorn note in her husband's voice and laughed. "Are you sure about that?"

He grinned. "Well, I might be a tad jealous."

"Actually, I was thinking about doing some volunteer work at the local clinic a couple of days a week. That way I can keep my license current. I just hadn't gotten around to telling you."

"Hey, that's a great idea."

"I thought so, too." Molly stretched, and in doing so, exposed a nipple to his greedy eyes and lips. He latched on to it and sucked.

"You know our life is pretty much perfect," she whispered, "even if I am married to a badass."

He laughed again, then sobered. "I just wish we could have

another child. I'd like to be there for the whole meal deal, so to speak, watching your belly grow and feeling our child move."

"There's no time like the present to get started."

Worth gave her a perplexed look. "You know what the doctor said."

"Doctors don't walk on water. They make mistakes every day. I suggest we begin right now proving yours wrong. And the rest of our tomorrows, if that's what it takes."

"Oh, God, Molly," Worth whispered, tossing a leg over her hip, "I wouldn't want to live life without you."

"Nor I without you." She smiled at him with love. "So how about we get busy and make that baby."

* * * * *

Raintree: Inferno

by

Linda Howard

Dante Raintree stood with his arms crossed as he watched the woman on the monitor. The image was in black and white to better show details; color distracted the brain. He focused on her hands, watching every move she made, but what struck him most was how uncommonly *still* she was. She didn't fidget or play with her chips, or look around at the other players. She peeked once at her down card, then didn't touch it again, signaling for another hit by tapping a fingernail on the table. Just because she didn't seem to be paying attention to the other players, though, didn't mean she was as unaware as she seemed.

"What's her name?" Dante asked.

"Lorna Clay," replied his chief of security, Al Rayburn.

"At first I thought she was counting, but she doesn't pay enough attention."

"She's paying attention, all right," Dante murmured. "You just don't see her doing it." A card counter had to remember every card played. Supposedly counting cards was impossible with the number of decks used by the casinos, but there were those rare individuals who could calculate the odds even with multiple decks.

"I thought that, too," said Al. "But look at this piece of tape coming up. Someone she knows comes up to her and speaks, she looks around and starts chatting, completely misses the play of the people to her left—and doesn't look around even when the deal comes back to her, just taps that finger. And damn if she didn't win. Again."

Dante watched the tape, rewound it, watched it again. Then he watched it a third time. There had to be something he was missing, because he couldn't pick out a single giveaway.

"If she's cheating," Al said with something like respect, "she's the best I've ever seen."

"What does your gut say?"

Al scratched the side of his jaw, considering. Finally, he said, "If she isn't cheating, she's the luckiest person walking. She wins. Week in, week out, she wins. Never a huge amount, but I ran the numbers and she's into us for about five grand a week. Hell, boss, on her way out of the casino she'll stop by a slot machine, feed a dollar in and walk away with at least fifty. It's never the same machine, either. I've had her watched, I've had her followed, I've even looked for the same faces in the casino every time she's in here, and I can't find a common denominator."

"Is she here now?"

"She came in about half an hour ago. She's playing blackjack, as usual.

"Bring her to my office," Dante said, making a swift decision. "Don't make a scene."

"Got it," said Al, turning on his heel and leaving the security center.

Dante left, too, going up to his office. His face was calm. Normally he would leave it to Al to deal with a cheater, but he was curious. How was she doing it? There were a lot of bad cheaters, a few good ones, and every so often one would come along who was the stuff of which legends were made: the cheater who didn't get caught, even when people were alert and the camera was on him—or, in this case, her.

It was possible to simply be lucky, as most people understood luck. Chance could turn a habitual loser into a big-time winner. Casinos, in fact, thrived on that hope. But luck itself wasn't habitual, and he knew that what passed for luck was often something else: cheating. And there was the other kind of luck, the kind he himself possessed, but it depended not on chance but on who and what he was. He knew it was an innate power and not Dame Fortune's erratic smile. Since power like his was rare, the odds made it likely the woman he'd been watching was merely a very clever cheat.

Her skill could provide her with a very good living, he thought, doing some swift calculations in his head. Five grand a week equaled $260,000 a year, and that was just from his casino. She probably hit them all, careful to keep the numbers relatively low so she stayed under the radar.

He wondered how long she'd been taking him, how long she'd been winning a little here, a little there, before Al noticed.

The curtains were open on the wall-to-wall window in his office, giving the impression, when one first opened the door, of stepping out onto a covered balcony. The glazed window faced west, so he could catch the sunsets. The sun was low now, the sky painted in purple and gold. At his home in the mountains, most of the windows faced east, affording him views of the sunrise. Something in him needed both the greeting and the goodbye of the sun. He'd always been drawn to sunlight, maybe because fire was his element to call, to control.

He checked his internal time: four minutes until sundown. Without checking the sunrise tables every day, he knew exactly when the sun would slide behind the mountains. He didn't own an alarm clock. He didn't need one. He was so acutely attuned to the sun's position that he had only to check within himself to know the time. As for waking at a particular time, he was one of those people who could tell himself to wake at a certain time, and he did. That talent had nothing to do with being Raintree, so he didn't have to hide it; a lot of perfectly ordinary people had the same ability.

He had other talents and abilities, however, that did require careful shielding. The long days of summer instilled in him an almost sexual high, when he could feel contained power buzzing just beneath his skin. He had to be doubly careful not to cause candles to leap into flame just by his presence, or to start wildfires with a glance in the dry-as-tinder brush. He loved Reno; he didn't want to burn it down. He just felt so damn *alive* with all the sunshine pouring down that he wanted to let the energy pour through him instead of holding it inside.

This must be how his brother Gideon felt while pulling lightning, all that hot power searing through his muscles, his veins. They had this in common, the connection with raw power. All the members of the far-flung Raintree clan had some power, some heightened ability, but only members of the royal family could channel and control the earth's natural energies.

Dante wasn't just of the royal family, he was the Dranir, the leader of the entire clan. "Dranir" was synonymous with king, but the position he held wasn't ceremonial, it was one of sheer power. He was the oldest son of the previous Dranir, but he would have been passed over for the position if he hadn't also inherited the power to hold it.

Behind him came Al's distinctive knock on the door. The outer office was empty, Dante's secretary having gone home hours before. "Come in," he called, not turning from his view of the sunset.

The door opened, and Al said, "Mr. Raintree, this is Lorna Clay."

Dante turned and looked at the woman, all his senses on alert. The first thing he noticed was the vibrant color of her hair, a rich, dark red that encompassed a multitude of shades from copper to burgundy. The warm amber light danced along the iridescent strands, and he felt a hard tug of sheer lust in his gut. Looking at her hair was almost like looking at fire, and he had the same reaction.

The second thing he noticed was that she was spitting mad.

Celebrate 100 years of pure reading pleasure with Mills & Boon®

To mark our centenary, each month we're publishing a special 100th Birthday Edition. These celebratory editions are packed with extra features and include a FREE bonus story.

Now that's worth celebrating!

4th January 2008

The Vanishing Viscountess by Diane Gaston
With FREE story The Mysterious Miss M
This award-winning tale of the Regency Underworld launched Diane Gaston's writing career.

1st February 2008

Cattle Rancher, Secret Son by Margaret Way
With FREE story His Heiress Wife
Margaret Way excels at rugged Outback heroes…

15th February 2008

Raintree: Inferno by Linda Howard
With FREE story Loving Evangeline
A double dose of Linda Howard's heady mix of passion and adventure.

Don't miss out! From February you'll have the chance to enter our fabulous monthly prize draw. See special 100th Birthday Editions for details.

www.millsandboon.co.uk

FREE

2 BOOKS AND A SURPRISE GIFT!

We would like to take this opportunity to thank you for reading this Mills & Boon® book by offering you the chance to take TWO more specially selected 2-in-1 volumes from the Desire™ series absolutely FREE! We're also making this offer to introduce you to the benefits of the Mills & Boon® Reader Service™—

- ★ **FREE home delivery**
- ★ **FREE gifts and competitions**
- ★ **FREE monthly Newsletter**
- ★ **Books available before they're in the shops**
- ★ **Exclusive Reader Service offers**

Accepting these FREE books and gift places you under no obligation to buy; you may cancel at any time, even after receiving your free shipment. Simply complete your details below and return the entire page to the address below. You don't even need a stamp!

YES! Please send me 2 free Desire volumes and a surprise gift. I understand that unless you hear from me, I will receive 3 superb new volumes every month for just £4.99 each, postage and packing free. I am under no obligation to purchase any books and may cancel my subscription at any time. The free books and gift will be mine to keep in any case.

D8ZEE

Ms/Mrs/Miss/Mr..............................Initials ....
BLOCK CAPITALS PLEASE

Surname ....

Address ....

....

....Postcode ....

Send this whole page to:
The Reader Service, FREEPOST CN81, Croydon, CR9 3WZ